ROMMEL IS DEAD

ROMMEL IS DEAD

A WORLD WAR II ALTERNATIVE HISTORY

Merrill Hardy

© 2014 Merrill Hardy
All Rights Reserved.

No part of this publication may be reproduced, stored in a retrieval system, or transmitted, in any form or by any means, electronic, mechanical, photocopying, recording, or otherwise, without the written permission of the author.

First published by Dog Ear Publishing
4010 W. 86th Street, Ste H
Indianapolis, IN 46268
www.dogearpublishing.net

dog ear
PUBLISHING

ISBN: 978-1-4575-2678-7

This book is printed on acid-free paper.

This book is a work of fiction. Places, events, and situations in this book are purely fictional and any resemblance to actual persons, living or dead, is coincidental.

Printed in the United States of America

Table of Contents

Introduction viii

Foreword ix

PART I - A Day Remembered By All – November 18, 1941 1

Chapter 1 – Heinz Guderian 2

Chapter 2 – An Italian Prospective 8

Chapter 3 – Erwin Rommel 13

PART II – Operation Crusader Begins 17

Chapter 4 – First Blood 18

Chapter 5 – A Change of Fates 25

Chapter 6 – Layers of Chaos 32

Chapter 7 – Heinz's Alternate Plan 37

PART III - Dismantling Crusader 41

Chapter 8 – Crusader Peaks 42

Chapter 9 – At the Egyptian Border 54

Chapter 10 – Too Little, Too Late 59

Part IV – End of British Relief Efforts 63

Chapter 11 – No Where to Go 64

Chapter 12 - Tables Are Turned 75

Chapter 13 – Back to Russia 85

Part V – Hitler's New Enemies 95

Chapter 14 – Japan Strikes 96

Chapter 15 – Glory for All 101

Chapter 16 – Tobruk Dividend 107

Chapter 17 – Mussolini 114

Part VI - Russia 117

Chapter 18 – Von Ravenstein 118

Chapter 19 – Fortress of Malta and Black Sea Waters 129

Chapter 20 - Fulfilling Guderian's Dream 133

Chapter 21 – Admiral Lutizo 138

Chapter 22 - Under the Guns of Maxim Gorki 145

Part VII – The Tide Turns 151

Chapter 23 - Convoy Challenge 152

Chapter 24 - Skip-Bombing in Russia 164

Chapter 25 – A Life for a Life 169

Part VIII – Working Behind the Scenes 177

Chapter 26 - Desperate Men – Special Weapons 178

Chapter 27 - Lost Engine Found 183

Chapter 28 - Some Help for the Infantry 189

Part IX – Secrets and Setbacks 193

Chapter 29 - Alkett Saves the Day 194

Chapter 30 – The God Haters 197

Chapter 31 - Worn Down 202

Part X - Epilogue 205

INTRODUCTION

The Last Good War that Wasn't

Many myths concerning World War II (WWII) continue to be promulgated as facts. One predominate myth is that WW II was "The last good War." Nothing could be further from the truth. Before it was concluded, many millions died or had their lives changed forever. The real victors were Stalin and International Communism. The real loser was Western Civilization.

We still live under the negative consequences of this Great War. Research reveals few lasting positive gains from WW II and begs the question could these benefits not have been achieved with less loss of life, suffering, horror, destruction and generations of continued dissension? Even recently revealed information continues to confirm WW II as a catastrophic failure in world leadership.

Few world leaders receive high marks for their job performance and instead most jumped on the fiery train pulled by the engines of fear, revenge, egotistical pride, greed, racial and class hatred. They continued to disgorge self-seeking dictates as moral pronouncements while millions suffered and died. Sadly world leaders and leaders in general have failed to take note of these blunders of our ancestors that are so blatantly visible. These mistakes include, but are not limited to the following:

- Failure to realize the end result of unbridled selfish ambition
- Failure to properly interpret the motivations of one's enemies and instead propagandizing them into anathemas
- Failure to maintain an environment that promotes and nurtures talented and successful innovators
- Failure to align one's actions with Divine Guidance

Don't ever say, "I'll get you for that."
Wait for God ; he'll settle the score

The Message, Proverbs 20: 22

Foreword

What Really Happened?

It has been almost 70 years since Erwin Rommel was forced to committed suicide to save his family and to this day he remains one of the most well known and controversial figures of World War II (WWII). To question his military reputation, judgment and skill even today is frowned upon in certain circles. That he enjoyed the absolute support of Germany's psychopathic dictator Adolph Hitler up until almost the very end is an indisputable fact.

Rommel's most severe criticism came from his fellow German officers. The Chief of the Army General Staff, General Hadler, once described him as "that officer gone stark raving mad." Other criticism involving poor decisions, conflict with allies, unnecessarily high casualty rates and trumped up subordinate court marshals were not as well known, but no less damning.

Apparently none of this ever mattered to Hitler. Rommel was promoted ahead of all his peers, received Germany's highest decorations and his commands were lavished with resources unequaled in quantity and quality. Public records confirm Rommel's influence on Hitler, but there are historical hints Rommel's influence on Germany policies may have been far greater. During the progression of WWII Hitler's poor decision making spread from situations involving just Rommel to everything else.

After 1942 Nazi Germany had only two chances to avoid total destruction and possibly obtain a negotiated peace. The first chance was to fight the Soviet Union to a standstill. The second chance was to avoid losing the Battle of the Atlantic.

Stalingrad not only cost the Germans two of their Armies, but four of their allies Armies (two Romanian, one Hungarian, and one Italian). Although German armed forces where able to recover somewhat, the military contribution for the remainder of WWII from these three nations offensively was none and defensively minimal.

Winning the code war (breaking the German Enigma code) cost the Germans the Battle of the Atlantic. Also diversion of German U-boat assets at critical times to other Theaters, especially the Mediterranean was a contributing factor.

Rommel/Hitler Alliance Drain on the War in Russia

Rommel was sent to Africa in 1941 with orders to hold off British Commonwealth forces and keep Italy from being knocked out of the war. It did not take him long to violate these orders and attack British forces. This created an opportunity for Rommel's superiors they did not ask for and obligations they could ill afford with the Russian invasion staring them in the face. It also handed the German Army its first real defeat at the gates of the fortified port city of Tobruk.

One mark of a great military captain has always been his ability to get the best from his allies. No one gives Rommel high marks for his relationship with his Italian ally. From failure to inform them he was retreating in Crusader and leaving them to fend for themselves to open and implied insults regarding everything Italian. He even implied they were passing information to the British.

During the first half of 1942, the German Army rebuilt nine panzer and six motorized divisions in preparation for their summer Russian offensive. To do this they stripped their factories and other Russian front panzer divisions.

Post Crusader, from Dec 41 to Jun 42 approximately 330 German tanks were shipped to Rommel's forces in Africa, including those sank in route. During this same period in Russia the ratio of German to Soviet tank losses averaged 1:6. Therefore, if these same tanks were instead shipped to Russia and all lost in combat they could theoretically have accounted for some 2,000 Russian tanks.

A similar analogy can be made for troops, planes and guns shipped to Russia instead of Africa. Interestingly the ratio of German to British tank losses approached this ratio during the first part of Operation Crusader.

For the second half of 1942, prior to Stalingrad an additional six panzer and two motorized divisions were scheduled to be built or rebuilt. Instead, the tanks to rebuild two of these panzer divisions were shipped to Africa. These were used again to rebuild Rommel's destroyed two panzer divisions and save his command.

Moreover, in late 1942 one of the other four (Tenth Panzer) was sent to Tunisia. Additionally nearly one half of the new Tiger tanks manufactured in 1942 were sent to Tunisia. Still more tanks and technically advanced equipment was sent in early 1943 all in the middle of the catastrophic events following Stalingrad.

Added to the tanks were invaluable vehicles, personnel, guns and above all planes. The ground personnel and equipment was formed into an entire Panzer Army. This pattern continued throughout 1943 as another entire Panzer Army was formed in the Balkans. Hundreds and then thousands of planes were sent into the Mediterranean and lost in the Allied meat grounder.

A similar pattern occurred for Italian tanks, planes and war material. Not a single Italian medium tank served with their Eighth Army in Russia. Yet many hundreds were lost in Africa or in transit. Consequently, by the time of the invasion of Sicily, the Italian military was an empty shell.

History has many military mistakes to lay at Hitler's feet but buying into Rommel's strategy of taking the Middle East through Africa while fully engaged with Russia and with Malta sitting across his supply lines has to be considered as one of his top blunders.

Rommel/Hitler Alliance Impact on the Battle for the Atlantic

Much has been written about the monumental shipping losses to U-Boats off the American coast during the first half of 1942. Admiral Donitz had planned for the first installment of this destruction to consist of 12 long range U-Boats. Because of the dire straights Rommel's Army was in he was only able to send five. From 21 Sep 41 to 7 Dec 41 18 U-boats either entered or tried to enter the Mediterranean. From 9 Dec 41 to 15 Jan 42 an additional 17 U-Boats were sent.

This large number of U-boats was deemed necessary to save Rommel's forces. In less than one month Donitz's five U-Boat sent to America sank 25 ships. During all of 1942 numerous U-Boats in the Mediterranean sank a total of 81 ships with high losses to themselves. That the presence of 17 (or more) additional U-Boats off the American coast in early 1942 would have had a noticeable effect upon the war has to be without question.

Of even more consequence was the loss of U-559 in October 1942 in the eastern Mediterranean. Before she sank, British sailors captured U-559's code books. This allowed the Allies to drive the U-boats from the Atlantic by May 1943. This in turn set the stage for the necessary supplies and troops to be accumulated in England to assure a successful D-day operation.

But prior to this U-boat operations enjoyed their most successful month of WWII destruction in November of 1942. The Allied supply situation was so strained that English fuel stores were reduced to less than a three months supply.

Hitler's other Generals

Heinz Guderian (Heinz) and Erich von Manstein (von Manstein) – Two of the greatest German generals of WW II and perhaps of any war in history.

Both were Prussians, a political subdivision that no longer exists and veterans of WW I. Their joint efforts contributed to many great military achievements including defeat of France and bringing the German army to the gates of Moscow. Heinz's troops were stopped by advanced Soviet tanks (T34 medium and KV heavy tanks) and von Manstein by the Fortress of Sevastopol in the Crimea.

Both were dismissed from service after disagreements with Hitler. Both refused to make militarily stupid decisions that would result in unnecessary waste of soldier's lives and military resources. Both were masters in using military technology.

Both invented and fielded successful vehicle innovations in armored warfare. Both men had sons serving in the German Army. After the war von Manstein served four years of a 12 year sentence for "neglecting to protect civilian lives" and using scorched earth tactics. Heinz was never charged with war crimes. Following a successful career, von Manstein was finally dismissed by Hitler in 1944 after disagreements regarding military policy and tactics.

Heinz was the heart and soul of Germany's Panzer arm in addition to being an exceptional field General. After Heinz's dismissal in 1941 he struggled with medical issues. In 1943 he was reinstated as Inspector General of *Panzertroopen*; he inherited a convoluted mess from over a year of Hitler's meddling with Armored Vehicle Design overlaid with Nazi political infighting. This damage could not be undone.

Heinz did try to salvage and redirect the program. He proposed a new infantry assault-gun/ mobile anti-tank weapon which ended up as the Hetzer. Over a year later, large numbers of Hetzers began to roll out of the factory in April 1944. Simple and effective, it was too late to have much impact on the war.

PART I

A DAY REMEMBERED BY ALL

CHAPTER 1

Heinz Guderian

November 18, 1941 - Russian Front - a few miles from Moscow

As his radio operator took a break to relieve himself, German General Heinz Guderian treaded to the opposite side of his armored command vehicle to stand quietly in the snow and for a brief time to be alone with his thoughts. It seemed every hour of this so-called "Operation Barbarossa" brought news of fresh German disasters.

Their current military circumstances demanded all of one's energy; there was little time to think of anything else or to have any time alone to one's self. Now it was snowing again and very cold; this miserable Russian weather was getting worse every day. And yet most of his troops were still fighting in their original summer uniforms or what was left of them.

His troops had fought their way clear across western Russia and it was rumored one could see the spires of Moscow in the distance when the weather was clear. Yesterday, his brave troops had been stopped and even given ground to superior Russian tanks.

Even their few heavy German anti-aircraft guns turned into anti-tank guns in this emergency had trouble dealing with these tanks. Heinz wondered if this wall of tanks would decide today to move west and simply brush their defenses aside. What was left to stop them?

In final acts of desperation, only heavy divisional artillery pieces could effectively knock out these monsters at ranges greater than 1,000 meters. Unfortunately, there were very few of these large and difficult to maneuver guns available.

The shock of Soviets possessing such impressive tanks had still not worn off – the advance of whole divisions stopped by a single tank and its stubborn Russian crew. A German Infantry Division breaking and retreating. Heniz was a great promoter of "Tank Terror", but certainly not among his own Infantry. He remembered what in complete frustration he had confided to his staff:

"God help us if these Russians had possessed leadership, training, advanced tactics, and organization to go along with their superior tanks. Our troops do not warrant this setback with what they have endured and I fear many will not survive."

Of course, he mused, Germany had Stalin to thank for taking care of Russian leadership concerns. Russian Army officers had been specifically targeted in the Soviet dictator's bloody purges during the 1930s, with many capable ones of all ranks executed or sent to Siberia. This was how Stalin chose to deal with anyone he thought might eventually pose a threat to his reign of Communist terror.

Although disorganized in many ways, Heinz knew the sheer size of the Soviet Military machine paled only when compared in size to a country that possessed these massive military resources. These newer Russian tanks were more akin to ideal tanks of the future he had suggested in his book, *Achtung Panzer*, than tank types his *panzertruppen* (tank or armored troops) currently fielded.

He had already sounded the alarm and urgently requested rapid production of a heavy anti-tank gun to counter the threat these new tanks posed. Surprisingly, he had just learned that two of the very first of these guns coming straight off of the factory floor were shipped to Africa, not Russia.

Heinz's desperate troops had even resorted to using captured Russian field guns in an anti-tank role. Russian ammunition was of substandard quality, but many of their guns were excellent. Indeed, mountains of Russian war material had been captured, much of it undamaged. Unfortunately, they did not have the necessary manpower or resources available to collect, repair or transport these vast quantities of equipment.

Heniz had also recently spoken to a commission visiting the Russian front looking into requirements for a new German tank able to take on these Russian types. Actually, he had helped design some of Germany's existing tanks so that they could be upgraded over time to remain effective tank killers. But against heavy Russian tanks, in head to head combat Germany's current tank models were at a severe disadvantage.

Only by skillful maneuver, had his tank crews stood any chance at all. He was well aware how long it could take to perfect a new reliable tank design and the German economy had not yet even been put on a full war footing.

To top it all off, Hitler was not even releasing newly produced tanks as Russian Front replacements, but rather using them to form new divisions. Thus, there would be no help anytime soon for his overstretched panzer divisions.

Disaster was staring them in the face. Winter chill and this sense of foreboding made him suddenly shiver as some dry snow that had been resting on his coat again became airborne.

Everything now seemed to be working against them. General "mud" and General "winter" were now fighting for the Soviets. Transportation of their supplies was still hindered by lack of proper rail transport. All Russian train tracks (those that the Russians had not already destroyed during their retreat) had to be modified to fit German rolling stock. Even their supply trucks were more suited for transportation between European rail lines, not this seemingly endless country. Moreover, there was talk of embolden Russian partisans beginning to operate in their rear areas.

Many of "Ivan's" wonder tanks had been captured with no more damage than an empty fuel tank or half sunk in bogs and swamps with no visible damage at all. But it was difficult to immediately turn these on their former owners in sizably numbers, for newer Russian tanks were based on a diesel engine. Since nearly all German vehicles and even their aircraft engines were based upon a common gasoline grade, to fill even a few tanks with a different type of fuel would be difficult.

Supplying them fuel for active operations was completely out of the question. Not to mention being fired upon by your own anti-tank gunners who had been taught only too well a healthy fear of Russian tanks. Many of his *panzertroopen* he had talked to thought that Russian T-34 tanks should just be copied. He was anxious to see what findings and recommendations this tank commission he had requested would come up with.

It was common knowledge that he was not a patient man when faced with ineptitude and he had reached the end of his rope. Even his fertile mind could not conceive a way out of impending doom. If the drive for Moscow had been attempted earlier, as he had suggested, maybe the Russians would have broken and his troops might be sitting in warm Moscow houses at this very moment.

He had always said there were no desperate situations, there are only desperate people, but soon there would be no more options. It seemed the colder it got the more aggressive Russian troops became. Soon there would be only one course of action. He had already made the decision, if it came down to it he would save as many of his troops as he could, orders or no orders.

What would be the fate of his two sons? Both were *panzertruppen*, following in their father's footsteps. Wouldn't he want their commander to make a similar decision in their behalf?

You cannot fight a war if all your troops are dead and your armies are destroyed, he thought to himself. From everything he observed, it would not be long before he faced a fateful clash with his superiors over this impending crisis.

He knew he had enemies in Berlin secretly eager for his failure, especially the Army Chief of Staff, General Halder. Sadly, mercy and understanding from a pack of wild dogs might be easier to come by than from Hitler and some of these "associates."

Nevertheless, he determined that he would not burden his conscious with the hopeless and unnecessary deaths of his men. Besides, if Hitler would let them save their army then maybe they could rebuild and hit Stalin again next year. That is if they could somehow remedy their current severe tank gap.

He turned to see his radio operator and his driver staring down at him. He stepped back into the open topped armored half-track which was a little warmer than outside, but not by much and picked up the hand full of messages he had been sorting through.

Winston Churchill

London, November 18, 1941

Far away in his London war room bunker England's Prime Minister Winston Churchill was as usual chomping at the bit.

"What is the word on the commando raid from last night", as Churchill briefly laid aside his cigar and addressed General Sir Alan Brooke, Chief of the Imperial General Staff and a certain Colonel Bentley of the Intelligence Service.

"Not good, I am afraid, Prime Minister. Apparently bad weather took its toll on the mission. A few German supply troops dead, but no sign of Rommel. Also looks like we took a lot of casualties", replied Bentley.

"Well it was worth a shot. Perhaps we will get future intelligence to try it again. Has this blasted Mediterranean weather affected the timing on the rest of the offensive Bentley?"

"Unfortunately reports indicate it has, Prime Minister. But so far everything is still progressing forward, but I am afraid many of the RAF preemptive strikes are a no go at this point."

"Well I still expect us to catch them with their pants down. We know from our code breakers that Rommel has positioned his troops to strike Tobruk with his back toward us.

Including units in transit and tanks in the supply system, we now have more than 1,200 first line British and American supplied tanks available for Operation Crusader. Against this we know their combined tank strength stands at barely 400.

Moreover, we have successfully cut off their supplies and in addition greatly outnumber them in nearly every category on the land, at sea and in the air. We will drive them back down the road they came from and then push them out of Africa and I hope drown them in the Mediterranean."

"Prime Minister, isn't sending in a hit team to murder Rommel a little over the top," questioned Brooke?

"Nothing is considered over the top to save the Empire in this war - *or expand it, he thought to himself.* I have made a pact with that Devil himself – Stalin and our very future is being mortgaged away to the Americans to purchase their weapons.

If I had enough bombers I would burn to the ground every Hun City and destroy every house in Germany. So I would suggest if something makes you squeamish you find yourself a different war, Sir Alan."

Wilhelm Bach (1)

Halfaya Pass, North African Coast - November 18, 1941

Major Wilhelm Bach motioned with his hand for Sergeant Major Ziegler to approach him:

"Has the damage to our positions from last night's rain been repaired, Sergeant Major"?

"Jawohl, Herr Major, almost as good as new, except for some mines that were washed away or are still under water."

"Replace them from the reserve stock and borrow what you can from the Italians. I hear Tommy is knocking on the back door and may soon pay us a call. Unlike General Rommel, I believe Italian intelligence may be right in predicting an immediate attack. Tell the men to stay alert."

"But Herr Major, do you think they have so quickly forgotten what happened the last time they tested the defenses of what they now call 'Hellfire Pass'? They received a good dose of our 88s. Now it seems as if we have a gun behind every rock. Nothing can keep us from holding out for weeks, if necessary."

"I am sure they have not forgotten, but the coastal road and this pass are critical to supplying their further movement east. The British would love to lay some train tracks right along the coast road.

Yes Sergeant-Major, I believe they will come again with everything they have. We must be ready. We may yet become the German equivalent of Tobruk. Be sure to also check on all nearby Italian positions, including Major Pardi's artillery" replied Wilheim.

"Jawohl Herr Major, will there be a special Sunday service for *Todentag* (German war remembrance day)?

"Of course, if we don't have to spend Sunday in our foxholes. This crisis may bring a few more of our hard core holdouts into Church." Wilheim added as he turned to continue checking their defensive positions.

(1) Wilhelm Bach (Wilhelm) – "Pastor of Hellfire Pass" - Brilliant line officer and Lutheran Pastor whose position and troops were abandoned by Rommel following the "Crusader" battle. He surrendered together with his men on 17 Jan 42. He died before the end of 1942 of cancer while in captivity.

Chapter 2

An Italian Perspective

November 18, 1941 – Southeast of the British occupied port city of Tobruk, North Africa

After the evening mess, Italian Lieutenant Gian Bindy slowly walked back to his unit headquarters tent. With a bland taste in his mouth added to his lack of anything close to a full feeling in his stomach, he judged his evening meal lacking both in quality and quantity. A cigarette would help with both problems, but he was out.

His armored car platoon had been ordered to move their unit east to Bir el Gubi tomorrow morning closer to where Ariete Armored Division was dug in; maybe he could rankle his way into a better meal. However, the odds were probably against it. He felt sure that Ariete's mess personnel had heard the full litany of fairy-tales from troops trying to get extra food, but he would try anyway. Lately, their lack of fresh food and unchanging menus was going from bad to worse due to supply difficulties.

He finished making arrangements for tomorrow's move and now he had the rest of the evening to do as he pleased. So he decided to spend it relaxing and writing a letter home. Above all, he needed a little time alone to think things through, but time along was a luxury reserved for civilians.

As he watched the African sun going down, the temperature began to drop. The desert did not hold her heat for long once the sun set. He stopped, closed his eyes, breathed in and could almost imagine himself back home, but when he reopened his eyes the familiar snow capped Alps of northern Italy were of course not be visible. What would his life be like if this war had not come along? He had put his life on hold to attend University and now it was again on hold living out of a tent like some desert nomad with material comforts reduced to less than bare minimum.

Just one more trick of this dreadful never-ending desert to distract him and destroy his focus. He had to admit, he was homesick. Yet for a brief moment he did allow his mind to drift back to a happier time. But there was no lasting peace to be had, for thoughts of loss, apprehension and disgrace again overhauled him.

Certainly his youth had been pleasant enough. He had been born during World War I and fortunately he had little memory of the hard times his parents had endured during the war and in its aftermath. Some of his earliest and most vivid youthful memories occurred during the interlude of Italian Dictator Mussolini's rise to power.

Under Mussolini's early influence the Italian Empire had expanded and flourished. Italy seemed to be turning into a real country. Gian's home town, in the northern part of Italy grew somewhat prosperous under Italy's dictator, enough so that his family was able to help send him to a University. This was in contrast to what was happening across Italy's borders in Germany and Austria which experienced a post war nightmare that continued for years.

For a short time after graduation he had taken a job in industry. However, with the coming of war, he decided to volunteer for military reserve service and become an officer before he could be drafted as an enlisted soldier. His older brother was already in the Navy and eventually Gian quit his job and joined Mussolini's Army fulltime, despite his mother's objections.

Thus, he had witnessed the outbreak of WW II as a member of Italy's military. Italy maintained her neutrality in 1939 as Germany conquered Poland. She had also stood by in the early part of 1940 and watched as Germany's Army and Air Force (Luftwaffe) invaded Norway, Holland and Belgium and then finished off France and even threaten England.

However, the lure of French territory possibly up for grabs was too much for Mussolini. Thinking Italy might find herself on the wrong side of the conflict and miss out on the spoils of war, he declared war on France and Britain fourteen days before France surrendered. Even though Mussolini knew Italy was not prepared to go to war the temptation to increase the size of his Italian Empire was just too great.

After declaring war, Mussolini started on a binge of conquest which quickly turned sour. The year of 1940 ended on a terrible demoralizing note for Italy when English carrier based aircraft attacked the Italian harbor of Taranto. These carrier planes sank one Italian battleship, damaged two others and would provide Japan inspiration for their future attack on Pearl Harbor a year later.

By early 1941 Mussolini's Italian Empire was under siege on all sides, thousands of Italian and colonial troops would end up in captivity. Finally Hitler stepped in and stopped the hemorrhaging first in Africa, then in Greece.

Gian's unit was sent to Africa as part of ongoing reinforcement along with German troops formed into what was now *Deutsches Afrikakorps* (DAK). The most frightening part of his service to date had to be sailing across the Mediterranean Sea. During their passage he imagined his corpse rotting at the bottom of the Mediterranean in an unknown grave, yet another specter that haunted him.

He had greatly feared becoming one of the hundreds that were drown attempting to make the perilous journey. The British controlled island of Malta's planes and submarines claimed the life of many a soldier and sailor, first Italians and now Germans.

Death and Revenge

In the midst of Italy's military setbacks, Gian remembered how his entire family was devastated when his brother was killed March 28, 1941 in yet another Italian naval defeat. He had yet to make up his mind if his brother's death brought him closer to God or pulled him further away, but he knew he could not sit on the fence forever. He must decide one way or the other because soon he could be dead. He did return to confession - as if there was anything to confess in this God forsaken desert. Skirt chasing opportunities were indeed few and far between.

His brother's death had another unsettling effect on him and transformed his feelings toward the British from reluctant admiration into implicit hatred. For him war had morphed from youthful adventure to coldly executed vengeance. As a result, he swallowed his Italian pride and using his knowledge of German both openly and in secret he redoubled his efforts to learn as much as he could about German war craft. This knowledge might provide just the means to someday exact his revenge on the English and in the process perhaps survive this ordeal.

Once in Africa, instead of being given a combat command, Gian found himself slated to perform liaison duties at German Fifth Light Division headquarters. He had obtained a working knowledge of German at an early age from boyhood friends and their parents in his home town. These childhood friends belonged to a German enclave and were required to speak Italian in school, but German by their parents at home. It was this skill that landed Gian his assignment with Fifth Light Division.

One day he overheard a staff officer voice the opinion that Rommel's ill-planned actions resulted in excessive and unnecessary casualties. This officer then noticed the shocked expression on Gian's face and realized that his conversation had been overheard. Later he pulled Gian to the side. What the officer told him that day he now remembered word for word.

"Bindy, have you ever been in combat before?" Gian shook his head and replied that he had not.

"Well then listen very carefully; I may just save your life. Before your first combat you will feel fear and uncertainty. As a good soldier and officer you will overcome your fear and obey your orders; there is danger in this act, but it can not be avoided. But more importantly you must overcome your uncertainty. If you do not overcome your uncertainty there is a greater danger that you along with your men will not survive.

Using cold unemotional reckoning and every asset available to you decide before taking action the best way to accomplish the mission with minimum loss of life. Then execute with complete absolute confidence; focus all your energy on the action, hold nothing back. Our esteemed General Rommel has got the second part down pat. It is the first part that seems to be missing. Even when the mission is successful, the cost is too high in German and Italian lives. So learn this Bindy and maybe you will live through this war. That is if you are meant to."

Eventually Gian was promoted and given a combat command of a motivated group of very bright young men, some former University Students, as the Italian forces in Africa were once again being increased. He found himself in an elite armored car company as part of the most powerful Corps in the Italian Army. For his Twentieth (XX) Corps was well equipped, at least by Italian standards. Now he hoped to give his men every chance he could to succeed; so he conducted continual training both conventional and non-convention to the maximum extent he could keeping the German officer's advice in the back of his mind.

Pending Attack

Yesterday, he picked up rumors at his Regiment's headquarters of an imminent British attack predicted by Italian intelligence. He had also heard that Rommel when confronted with this intelligence information had refused to believe it or to alter his plan for an all out attack on Tobruk.

Well, enough idle thinking; it was late and time for bed. There was a full day laid on for tomorrow with a possibility for action and besides his letter home was finished. As he nodded off he worried that such a serious disagreement between Allies could be a recipe for yet another African disaster. His money was on Italian intelligence. If their intelligence information was correct, it could be Ariete Division that got hit first. How would he hold up under his first real action? Would Ariete survive or would they be fatally crushed by another powerful English onslaught?

Chapter 3

Erwin Rommel

November 18, 1941 – *Panzergruppe* **Africa Headquarters, North Africa**

As he stared down at the situation map in his mobile command vehicle German General Erwin Rommel could almost envision his tanks and troops slicing their way through the obstacles as they fought their way to the center of Tobruk. Meter by meter, it must be so. Victory was near, very near indeed.

For too long Tobruk had been a thorn in his side. He well remembered the first day he had set eyes on its fortified perimeter. It was April 13, 1941. On that fateful day he had thrown his troops against this mighty fortress without any advanced preparation or detailed knowledge of its skillfully conceived Italian built defenses.

Sitting almost right in the middle of the North African Mediterranean sun drenched coast, Tobruk sat defiantly still blocking his advance to the east. England's Prime Minister Winston Churchill boasted openly that Rommel's siege would fail and that Tobruk would never be retaken.

Churchill's troops had taken Tobruk from Italy earlier in 1941 on their way to successful annihilation of an entire Italian Army. At this stage of the war it had become a symbol of British resilience and he had heard that even English school children knew where Tobruk was.

He regretted that many German and Italian lives had been lost on repeated attacks. Clearly visible burned out shells of wrecked ships, planes and armored vehicles littering Tobruk's harbor and landscape testified to the struggle's intensity.

Unfortunately for him this failure to capture Tobruk on his watch was now becoming known as the first out and out failure of Nazi ground forces since the beginning of the war. Consequently he knew his fortune was now entangled with that of Tobruk. However, capturing Tobruk would get the demon off his back and put his military career back on track.

Many horrific and momentous battles were being fought and won by other German generals on the steppes of Russia - absent him. Moreover,

Adolf Hitler's attention was glued to events in Russia these days. Surely there would be more Field Marshall batons handed out after Russia fell, just like after the fall of France. Not to mention exceptional military decorations and "extras" doled out by Hitler for Russia's conquerors, especially to those judged to correctly fit the Nazi mold.

Rommel couldn't help but worry that hostilities in Russia might end soon and he would be left out of the limelight. However, even with the increasing desperate demands of Germany's Russian front, Hitler had gone out of his way to try and give him whatever he asked for in men and equipment. Some said that he exercised an almost hypnotic influence over Hitler.

Perhaps they were correct – what of it? After all, a lavish abundance of material and human talent had found its way to Africa. To do so, troops and equipment had actually been stripped from other German units. Even captured foreign weapons from past German victories found their way in quantity and were allocated to Africa, *but as far as he was concerned, this was all justified.*

Of course Hitler favored him. This time he would take Tobruk, whatever the cost. Three days and it would all be over. Losses would be high, but then he would personally lead those troops who survived into Egypt and perhaps beyond. For this assault even his supply staff seemed to be on board, though they always seemed to be hampering him with their limiting projections.

He grimaced as he remembered the scathing report the head Quartermaster of the entire German Army, stoic General Paulas, had given his African operation. Some of the harsh words still echoed in his mind.

"Given the fragile state of the supply system it is not possible to achieve anything of lasting military significant in North Africa."

Should a great General be limited by these technician's incessant calculations and warnings? Besides they were just too conservative. He pretended to listen, but he made the decisions.

Hadn't he shown them all? Besides, when it came to choosing between him and one of those pompous Prussian Generals, he knew which way Hitler would lean. After all, hadn't some accused Hitler of reckless behavior? Besides, Hitler understood how important intuition was and besides supplies could be gotten from many sources. Therefore, his logistical staff types just needed to show more ingenuity and backbone.

He pretended not to enjoy attention from propaganda that Goebbels had been spreading about his African victories in the German press.

However, Goebbels' publicity certainly had not hurt sales of *Infanterie Greift An*, his first book.

His second book about his exploits with Seventh Panzer Division during the conquest of France had still not received censorship approval for publication from that pompous Prussian, General Hadler, the German Army Chief of Staff. In fact, he knew that Hadler had once referred to him as that:

"General gone stark raving mad." Hadler had told him straight up:

"Stop worrying about Tobruk and prepare your troops for an English attack."

But he had about as much use for Hadler as Hadler had for him. Notes and letters he was sending home to his wife would provide a basis for a third, grander book about African victories. Good book sales and prestige at home could always be enhanced by more victories.

Moreover, unlike his previous Tobruk attacks, this time nothing was left to chance. He knew his detractors had accused him of conducting these previous Tobruk attacks with little to no planning, slim reconnaissance and in the face of direct confrontation by its defenders.

Once Tobruk fell, he intended to drive at the front of his panzers to Egypt. Just the other day Italian commanders had expressed concern and felt certain a major British attack would come soon, but they could be ignored and controlled. His recent meetings with *Commando Supremo* (the Italian High Command) had not been difficult at all. If he didn't like a set of orders, he would bypass the chain of command by going directly to Hitler. Hitler would then call Mussolini, the Italian dictator, and have the order reversed.

Still, *Commando Supremo* was forcing him to stick to a fifty-fifty Italian/German split of all supplies and for what. But there were ways of getting around this issue as well. He would just take a greater share of captured British material as he had done before. With his blessing, his men took whatever they needed or wanted from the abundance of Italian and British battle damaged equipment scattered all over the Desert. But enough thinking and talking it was time to act as he headed for the door of his command vehicle.

PART II

Operation Crusader Begins

Chapter 4

First Blood

November 19, 1941– Rommel's Headquarters

"I will hear no more of this old washer woman talk about delaying our assault on Tobruk. These activities are just British units engaged in reconnaissance and deception, that's all." Rommel stated as he lectured a concerned Lieutenant General Cruwell, commander of his Africa Korps.

Even Cruwell is getting nervous, thought Rommel. Finally giving in, he dispatched elements of 21st Panzer division (one of only two German Panzer Divisions in North Africa) to reinforce 33rd Reconnaissance Battalion.

Having already been strengthened once, 33rd Reconnaissance Battalion was responsible for blocking one of the main routes British troops must use to relieve the Tobruk garrison.

"We have this miserable rain to thank for an absence of air reconnaissance with our forward airfields almost unusable. Fate chooses a time like this to rain in the desert", asserted Rommel.

Tanks and More Tanks

Near Bir el Gubi in the North African Desert on November 19, 1941

When Gian arrived at the fortified positions of Ariete armored division shortly after 09:00 everything was a buzz; rumors were flying that action was eminent and that Twentieth Corps armored cars were already engaging the British to their south.

As the morning mist cleared off, he took some time to observe the defenses that Ariete's troops had prepared and the location of their guns. But what a muddy mess rain had made of the desert floor as he felt the extra weight sticking to his boots with every step.

Having studied engineering before the war, he was a studious observer of German tactics, training and equipment. He knew the men he commanded were able and capable soldiers, many from north Italy, like himself. They were the best Italy had to offer and they were receptive to learning German tactics. His unit was also fairly well equipped as Italian units went, but they were always on the lookout to become better, more effective soldiers.

But despite a war, these days his thoughts also wafted from his brother to Aldina, a young Italian colonist he had recently met in Benghazi. He needed to find an excuse to get back to see her.

This girl was intriguing, but not as much as a Luftwaffe Nurse he had tried to date at Derna three months ago. Even in this desolate place there was not a complete absence of women, but they were certainly rare and of course the competition was a lot stiffer. Suddenly, Gian was suddenly startled back into the reality of war.

"Enemy tanks approaching." Gian heard an observer shout some distance to his front.

He quickly grabbed his binoculars from their case and scanned the horizon. This lookout was dead on; slowly he made out more and more tanks. To their flanks were also numerous armored cars. Gian stopped counting tanks at 40; these tanks were headed straight for the dug in positions of Ariete. As the tank images grew larger in his binoculars, he identified only tanks mixed with a few infantry carriers and armored cars.

Where was the dreaded British artillery; why were only a few artillery shells falling on Ariete's positions? Even Italian tankers were respectful of British artillery and their 25-pounder guns. Twenty five pounder, it kind of rolled off your tongue. Gian had been quick to learn that the British characterized many of their guns by the weight of shell that it fired.

Also, where were their supporting units, especially infantry? He looked carefully again, there did not even seem to be accompanying engineers present to deal with Ariete's minefields. Had British contempt for Italians risen to an even new level? Still, facing down a tank attack was a very nerve wracking experience. It looked like they intended to simply crush the Italian division positions in their path as they raced across the desert.

"Highest state of readiness, prepare to repel tank assault", was the warning given by Ariete's Italian officers and NCOs.

Gian's stomach knotted up, there was no time left to return to his unit. His fellow soldiers would be envious; they had been itching for a fight to try out their equipment. He figured if Ariete's troops did not lose their nerve, these British tankers could be in for a rude shock.

From his earlier observations, Ariete's small 47mm anti-tank guns were in good fortified positions. These anti-tank guns were backed by supporting artillery including a battalion of 105mm artillery guns which could also be used as anti-tank guns in emergencies. Gian knew that Italian artillerymen were usually utterly dependable and would not give up their guns without a fight.

Gian knew that even Germans admired Italian skill in constructing effective fortifications in this tough environment. Although usually out classed by British tanks, the Ariete's division's tanks also seemed well positioned to counter this assault if their primary defenses faltered.

There was another surprise awaiting the British for in Gian's unit, the Giovanni Fascisti Reconnaissance Regiment or GF-RECAM, the last thing on anybody's mind was retreat. GF-RECAM had mounted many of their guns on captured British trucks. As if this wasn't enough, there were even a few large 102mm naval guns mounted on trucks.

Gian's keen eye missed nothing when it came to weapons of any kind. He was familiar with strengths and weaknesses of various Allied vehicles and had made a great effort during the summer to develop a working knowledge of these.

This British attack looked pretty major to Gian, there now appeared to be well over a hundred tanks plus armored cars headed straight for Ariete's positions. Italian command had information that a major British attack was expected, but was the entire weight of attack to fall on Ariete? This might be the day that Italians would earn some respect from the British and maybe even Rommel himself. But could they hold? To wait for a tank to roll over your position and grind you under its tracks is a fearful thing.

If these British tanks made it past mines, artillery, their few anti-tank guns and Italian tanks, the Italian Infantry would be powerless to stop them. From as far as Gian could see there were tanks, at least a whole armored brigade. He felt helpless in what was to be his first real combat; all he had brought with him was his service pistol. Therefore, he decided to help with manning one of the heavy 105-mm artillery pieces that could also be used in an anti-tank role.

As the tanks got closer, Gian quickly identified them as British Crusaders. He was familiar with this tank and had actually examined one last week. Some previously captured models were even being used to supplement Ariete's armored units.

He knew that British tanks frequently carried one or more "Tommy" guns. He dreamed of getting his hands on one of these prized "gangster" guns which was a real status symbol among Italian troops. Despite all his exploring of previous battlefields, someone had always beaten him to the punch and he had never been able to get his hands on one.

###

All afternoon Gian stayed with the gun crew as the fighting ebbed and flowed. When it was all over, Gian counted more than fifty British tanks disabled in and around Ariete's positions. From what he could see, a few appeared to have suffered no battle damage. They had simply broken down during the fight and then were abandoned. In some places Ariete's troops had given ground, but then their tanks had counter-attacked and now it was British tanks that were retreating. Gian was elated at their success.

Other British tanks had only land mine damage to their tracks and could probably easily be repaired. A great victory. Even older exhausted veterans of this long war were excited. They had stopped the British.

Moreover, this attack was definitive evidence confirming Italian intelligence information of a large British offensive. What these Ariete troops had experienced was certainly no "reconnaissance." Maybe Rommel would now listen and postpone his attack on Tobruk.

Sometime later, remaining British tanks that were able were observed rolling back the way they had come admitting that they were unable to force Ariete's defenses. Gian knew the British would not give up that easily, more would come. Italian causalities had not been severe for such an extended battle. Except for their damaged tanks and knocked out anti-tank guns, the British attack had done little to permanently diminish the combat ability or defensives of Ariete.

"Hey you, what are you doing here, you are not an Ariete officer?" A somewhat excited Bersaglieri Major yelled to Gian.

"I was just awaiting orders for my armored car platoon and got caught up in the fighting, sir." Gian quickly answered.

"Well then I expect you know how to drive. Get your head out of the clouds and into the game. You and the rest of this gun crew that is not wounded help us recover those British tanks before we are hit again. We need every tank in the line we can get and we are short tank crews. Most of our qualified tank crews are busy repairing their own tanks. There are even more British tanks beyond the minefields that appear to be just broken down. If we don't take care of them, the British will. Go now, it will be dark soon."

This was just what Gian wanted to hear. He would be able to do a lot of scavenging, which was becoming his favorite pastime, in the dark. Later Gian sent word back through a runner for his men to drive to Bir el Gubi and help repair some of the less damaged British tanks.

Unfortunately, Gian knew that Ariete's recovery efforts were limited by lack of suitable vehicles and prevailing ground conditions. Recent rains had made the desert difficult to navigate even for British and Italian tanks. Gian's armored car company had a few extra trained drivers and he hoped that they would be allowed to keep some of these British prizes. More likely, they would just be used to replace or add to Ariete's tank strength.

Gian had encouraged his men to learn how to drive a variety of vehicles and tanks. These men in GF-RECAM were quick learners. Captured tanks could add to their mobility, especially since the rain was making the open desert difficult for wheeled vehicles.

That night, Gian had helped himself to a few of the submachine guns and ammo taken from other abandoned Crusaders for himself and his men. Finally, he had an American "Tommy" gun. Sub-machine guns were always useful weapons and were sure to come in handy later on as he knew the British were sure to try their attack again.

Tobruk Forces Join Crusader

Morning of November 21, 1941 - *Panzergruppe* Africa Headquarters

"Herr General Rommel, we now have a full report. Tobruk's garrison troops, in particular their 70th Infantry Division, have broken out with tank support and have successfully stormed many of our defensive positions.

Their timing and direction of attack can only mean one thing. Their objective is to join British forces attacking from the south. I foresee a very serious battlefield situation developing." Colonel Westphal, Rommel's operation's officer, reported.

Armed with this information Rommel knew he could no longer ignore obvious British intentions and the immediate danger posed by their actions. A successful British attack from Tobruk could link up with what was now recognized as the entire British Eighth Army already on the move headed north. If these two forces joined together it would effectively divide the Axis Army in two.

Battlefield reality was now undeniable, a conclusion that Italians and his staff had come to some time before. German Third Reconnaissance Battalion, supported by a battery of feared 88-mm guns, was selected to put out the fire. Rommel's instincts led him to the most critical point on the battlefield.

"I will personally lead Third Reconnaissance Battalion's counterattack; these British will not break our siege." Thundered Rommel, as the hard charging General raced off to the sound of the guns in his armored half-track.

Rommel's Death

As Third Reconnaissance Battalion was halting 70th Division's advance a small piece of shrapnel from a 25-pounder high explosive round struck Rommel behind his right ear as he was standing upright in his command halftrack. This shell was fired by artillery supporting British 70th Infantry Division's attempt to pierce Tobruk's siege ring.

Death came almost instantaneous as Rommel's lifeless body collapsed on top of his radio operator. His terrified radio operator and Colonel Westphal moved quickly to place him flat in the cramped vehicle, but it was already too late to render any assistance.

Westphal with his uniform tunic and gloved hand still stained with Rommel's blood immediately sent a quickly written note to General Cruwell by motorcycle messenger. A returned message from Cruwell followed shortly. In it Cruwell instructed Westphal to take Rommel's body covered in the floor of the halftrack to a field hospital located in El Adem for official medical conformation of his death.

Due in part to Rommel's quick counter attack, the Axis siege ring was held, but just barely. It was now up to Cruwell to decide the fate of Axis forces.

With medical conformation of Rommel's death, Cruwell immediately fulfilled his duty and sent word directly to Berlin via a coded Luftwaffe message. Cruwell ordered all personnel with knowledge of Rommel's death to remain tight lipped. He wished to give no satisfaction to the British or cause for alarm to the Italians.

News of Rommel's death, which was immediately given to Hitler, sent shock waves through out the German high command. Cruwell was ordered to hold his defensive positions and counterattack to regain lost territory. He was told that a replacement for Rommel would be arriving as soon as one was appointed and could be transported to Africa. From now on, Cruwell would concern himself with survival of forces under his command and continue to keep the death of Rommel a closely guarded secret.

Chapter 5

A Change of Fates

November 21, 1941 – Russian front near Moscow

Heinz was surprised that his recall had come this quickly and no special action had occurred recently other than the worsening brutal clash in front of Moscow. He knew his conflict with General Halder had worsened and Halder had recently tried to discredit him in front of Hitler, but to be recalled in this almost frantic fashion was not what he expected. The emergency message in his hand ordered him to immediately relinquish his command and board a special plane bound directly for the Fuhrer's headquarters was unheard of short notice indeed.

Now he would plead his case directly to Hitler and maybe reason would prevail and his troops could be withdrawn to set up winter defensive positions before it was too late. As ordered, he lost no time in preparations; spending less than 20 minutes in transition with his staff while his bag was being packed. So here was perhaps one last chance to end this madness.

Heinz knew he had a reputation for being concise or blunt in his statements; perhaps he could put those skills to use now as an immediate meeting with Hitler loomed. He almost looked forward to a long plane ride west as a chance to rest and to free his mind from his intense anxiety. After a flight lasting several hours they touched down in Berlin with Heinz's mind a little more at rest.

"All one can do is one's duty", he whispered to himself.

Such momentous times, was it not all in God's hands? He had not thought this way in quite some time?

November 22, 1941 - Fuhrer's Headquarters, Berlin

Was he to be sacked in public, why was he ushered immediately from his plane in such secrecy? As he was directed into a large map room to meet with Hitler, Heinz observed all those present, some he expected but not Grand Admiral Raeder (Head of the German Navy) and there was even the fat man himself, Reich Marshal Goring (Head of the German Air Force).

Was it just Hitler or did every other dictator manage to surround himself with such pretentious bullies and never-do-wells with just a spotting here and there of an honorable man. Perhaps this unique type of personality was just attracted to the exercise of unrestrained power. Many old-line military men, especially among his fellow Prussians, shared a similar view and in fact held several in the Nazi Government in abject contempt.

Stressful conditions at the front, his fragile health, a cumulative lack of sleep combined with a long flight did nothing to enhance this group's image in his mind. Then he remembered that even Rommel, one of his former panzer generals, had once been part of Hitler's "street gang." Also, his precious panzer troops, what was left of them, owed their existence to this man. Maybe, just maybe, reason would prevail.

This whole group looked rather sober, then again what was there to be confident about? Only General Halder, Germany Army Chief of Staff had a slight smile on his face and Heinz knew this was not a good sign. He knew his star had fallen in Hadler's eyes, so much so that some officers expressing loyalty to him had recently been exiled to Africa. Hadler might even be the one directly behind his recall. Heinz felt his only chance was to present his case directly to Hitler.

Indeed, he figured Hadler was secretly delighted with the current situation. Perhaps this was the very chance he had hoped for to completely remove Heinz's influence with Hitler.

Hadler's face did indeed betray his feeling. Although Hadler regretted Rommel's very recent death and the current African crisis it seemed to be producing; he had come to have no use for Guderian or his entire "modus operandi." Now Heinz's most ardent followers were to be joined by their leader and exiled far away from real war.

To add insult to injury, Heinz was to be given a lesser command and would have to report to an Italian commander. Also, a Luftwaffe General was going to have overall command. *How fitting for the all knowing Guderian*, thought Hadler.

As Heinz was motioned toward Hitler, everyone in the room followed his progress, but no one said a word. The Fuhrer spoke first,

"General Guderian, please take a seat, I would normally speak with you in private, but a crisis has arisen that requires immediate action. This crisis requires your utmost efforts and indeed the attention of the entire German Reich."

"Yes, I know, my Fuhrer, I have seen it with my own eyes", snapped Heinz.

"You have not seen this with your own eyes, Herr General, I am referring to Africa not Russia. I will resolve any problems with the Russian front very shortly. This conversation will be confined to the African Conflict. Is that understood?

I know of the interest you expressed in our African front in the past, that knowledge will be useful in your new assignment. You are to fly immediately to North Africa and assume command of *Panzergruppe* Africa."

"Africa? But my Fuhrer, *Panzergruppe* Africa is General *de Panzertroopen* Rommel's command."

"Rommel is dead. I still can not believe it myself. Rommel started on the streets with me and would have become a great General for all German people. I tell you, it is a great loss to Germany and National Socialism. The Tobruk Rats have broken the Italian siege and are very close to linking up with their XXX Corps advancing from the southeast. A very significant British offensive appears to be occurring all along the front with their other Corps, XIII. I am concerned. Our coastal strong points have been attacked and are cut off.

Look at this British newspaper (slapping the paper down on a near by desk). Their press is reporting a smashing victory – they claim our entire tank force has been destroyed. They further state that a major battle has been going on for four days. I would not put it past the Italians to be retreating again. I do not believe any of the information I am getting. We cannot let our enemies run us out of Africa and possibly knock Italy out of the war.

General Rommel believed his plans for the capture of Tobruk were betrayed. Italian command appears near panic and claim their concerns were ignored. I believe that this British offensive is underway to distract us from finishing off Russia. This will not happen. You will leave immediately and stabilize the situation. Another fresh plane and crew is standing by for you.

"As you wish, Mein Fuhrer, however, for flexibility I would like to request command of the ground forces in the Balkans and Crete." Heniz decided to make the most of the situation and as a subtle hint to Hitler that he regarded Africa a lesser command.

"In time, all of Germany will mourn General Rommel's death; in fact, I have decided he will be buried as a Generaloberst. However, for now you will tell no one who does not have an explicit military reason to know of his death. I have determined to hide it from our enemies until you and General Cruwell have stabilized the front. Even our Italian allies are only being told that he is wounded and temporarily unable to command. I intend to even postdate his official death.

"What additional help can we count on, Mein Fuhrer?"

"I have instructed the Luftwaffe and Kriegsmarine (German Navy) to provide your ground forces with all support they will need to assure victory. We will soon flood the Mediterranean with our planes and submarines. Africa must not be lost. I will make sure you are sent some of our latest weapons just as I had promised Rommel.
Additional tanks, weapons, and replacements have already been allocated for your desert Army. I will ask, for the time being, you be given command of all Axis front-line troops in Africa. Field Marshall Kesselring, when he arrives in Theater with Second Air Fleet will assume overall command. You have your orders, report directly to me personally after you have accessed the situation."

Hitler paused briefly to gather his thoughts before he answered fully answered Heinz's question.

"I will give you temporary command of Crete forces, but not our Balkan forces. Also, you will clear any major troop movements from Crete directly through me." As Hitler's nod meant that their conversation was at an end.

Heinz had never expected this and as he left the room even Russian Front problems seemed suddenly distant. It looked like Hadler had finally done his worst. He was to be exiled to Africa along with other officers that supported his ideas. Consequently, Hadler would be rid of all of them for good. It was an independent command, but he was placed under command of a Luftwaffe officer.

###

As Hitler mentioned, in the past, Heinz had suggested that Panzer Divisions be sent to Africa as early as June of 1940 and he was familiar with some of the specific problems being faced at the Desert front. He wondered how bad it really was. Was Cruewell dead as well? How much of Africa Korps was lost?

He told the adjutant sitting at the desk outside the map room that he wished to speak in private to Admiral Raeder. Would Raeder speak to him? A meeting in a private room was arranged. He knew that reasoning with Goring was next to pointless, but Kesselring could handle Goring. However, Raeder was known as a very honorable and reasonable man. The Grand Admiral would be thinking about the overall Mediterranean tactical situation so he determined to make use of this opportunity and pick his brain in private.

###

As Heniz left to begin the next leg of his journey to Africa he felt the seed had been planted. Admiral Raeder had been cordial and receptive, but he had his own ideas and concerns. Raeder echoed Hitler's concern about the looming oil crisis and drain the Mediterranean front was having on these scarce resources, especially the Italian Navy's appetite. However, even with recent loss of a British Carrier in fierce Mediterranean naval conflicts, the British still had a considerable naval presence, including several Battleships.

If and when the current crisis was solved, Heniz was determined to contact General Student. Raeder told him that Student had already devoted some planning time to "Operation Hercules", the invasion of Malta. He also needed to discuss Mediterranean strategy with Kesselring. He hoped Kesselring would be receptive; dealing with Kesselring's boss Goring was worse in some respects than even dealing with Hitler.

Already Lost?

From additional briefings received in transient to Africa, Heinz learned the situation might be even worse than expected. He found it hard to believe Rommel had delayed repositioning his units and continued to hold on to the idea of taking Tobruk ignoring explicit warnings of a major British offensive. However, because of his relationship to Hitler, Rommel had managed to amass considerable important equipment of all sorts in North Africa despite the recent collapse of his Mediterranean supply line.

Still his overall strategic aims did not take into account massive current German commitments and more recently, impending doom looming over all of the Eastern Front. As far as Heinz could determine, German commitment in Africa could never be more than a holding action until the Russian question was resolved.

Unfortunately, because of his obsession, it looked like Rommel had managed to place both Axis partners in an almost untenable position. He knew most certainly both egotistical Axis leaders needed no help in biting off more than they could chew. Apparently, Heinz surmised, blockade of Tobruk had also been a costly failure. Perhaps German submarines (U-boats) being sent to the Mediterranean could help change this.

Moreover, betrayal of Rommel's Tobruk assault plan timing was also a distinct possibility. Heinz had determined from briefings, which both a Naval and an Army officer gave him; that recent heavy loses in German and Italian shipping may have already decided Africa's fate. It was developing into a dark time for Axis forces in the Mediterranean and so once again he found himself being thrown into the middle of a very desperate military situation.

##

Heniz was aware that General Paulas, another personal favorite of Hitler, had concluded that Rommel had lost sight of the significance of the African Theater. First and foremost, German involvement had been to preserve the Italian flank while the bulk of German resources were occupied with invasion of Russia.

Exposing valuable German Panzer units to British naval and RAF destruction was incredibly short-sided. Heinz knew these well-trained units (his creation) were the main advantage that Germany possessed when it came to ground warfare. Yet he didn't fully appreciate that Rommel's African campaign provided another sinister benefit.

Minister Goebbels had been using Rommel's romantic tropical adventures to distract the German populous from the huge losses currently being experienced on the Eastern Front. Now these mounting losses in the African Theater were to be kept secret from the general public. Rommel's death thus suddenly became a political as well as a military problem for the Nazis master of spin.

Also, yet another severe defeat would place Italian dictator Mussolini in a very bad position. Hitler was also worried about not only his allies, but also the impression of other currently neutral nations. Many of the world's neutral nations were simply sitting on the fence waiting to pick a winning side. Quickly finding a well-known replacement that had the confidence of the German and Italian public at large to fill the void left by Rommel's demise was important.

He saw why his detractors probably didn't object to this assignment; even Hadler used him when the task was urgent enough. With a looming Russian crisis, the Mediterranean Theater had of late been only an afterthought to Hitler. Now he was concerned about potential loss of his Italian ally.

Heinz had learned from his briefings that from June to October, 1941 over 40 Axis supply ships had been sunk. Projected losses for November, as reported by German Navy sources, were that three out of every four ships sailing from Italy would be sunk. So, British planes, ships and submarines were sinking virtually every ship sent from Italy to Africa. Even a new alternate route to Benghazi, giving a wide berth to Malta, was at risk from a cruiser force newly stationed at Malta.

Many lives and valuable material had been lost. Conditions did appear desperate; these heavy shipping losses had prompted current extreme German reaction to British acts. Small wonder Admiral Raeder had been so receptive to his plans, but still insisted on his own take on the most important priorities to defeat the British.

Yes, everyone had his own idea for the Mediterranean Theater. How could current Axis troops even be evacuated from Africa with such high rates of sinking? The plan he had quickly discussed with Raeder called for very bold far-reaching actions, was there even a chance it could be pulled off? First the fighting force in Africa must be saved.

CHAPTER 6

Layers of Chaos

Afternoon of November 23, 1941 - North Africa Crusader Battlefield

Heinz's flight plan had called for them to land at an airfield near Gambut, located just southeast of Tobruk. From there it was a short drive south to German Africa Korps (DAK) Headquarters. Once there, he planned on reviewing the latest battlefield status with General Cruwell. However, when the radio operator of Heinz's plane was unable to raise DAK Headquarters by radio, he began to worry.

As his aircraft approached Gambut's airfield, Heinz could clearly see from out of his window supplies for their forces stacked neatly in rows or under protective tents. He knew that these were perhaps the last supplies they would see for a while. This was at first comforting to Heinz, for at least these supplies looked to be safe and sound.

As his plane made a wide turn south to land he again looked out the window, but this time with horror. For below them coming from the southeast were massive British formations of vehicles complete with tanks. All of a sudden anti-aircraft fire from these columns streaked toward Heinz's plane forcing its pilot to quickly try and gain more height. Plane damage appeared minimal from this hostile fire, but they dare not try and over fly this area again.

As Heinz was thrown back in his seat he instantly knew why they could not raise DAK headquarters, the area near the last known location looked to be completely overrun by enemy forces. From the air it looked like the only thing keeping these British away from their supplies at Gambut were some weak forces. Another commanding General need not be killed or captured so Heinz ordered the pilot to divert to the west and land at near by El Adem.

After safely landing and a brief exchange of information, Guderian addressed a group of some what excited and surprised officers.

"Yes, I will want to look at these purportedly authentic captured British battle plans, but I need to know our unit dispositions, supply situation and losses. You are telling me our tank losses have been light until today, but the British are pressing their Infantry attacks like all of our tanks have been destroyed. Now you tell me we have lost our entire DAK headquarters and I saw with my own eyes that the British are trying to cut us off from our supplies in Gambut and Bardia.

If we lose our supplies, how can we hope to save our frontier units? Also, at current usage rates how many days of fuel and ammunition do we have left? Without such information and with the loss of our headquarters how will we be able to determine how much longer we can resist? I must talk directly with General Cruwell. Where is he?

"Herr General Oberst, he has assembled all our tanks to the south for an all out attack," reported an artillery officer.

"Also, I require a detailed assessment of tank strength and losses of British 32nd Armored Tank Brigade during their Tobruk breakout attempt. The British may have committed their infantry tank reserves too early. We may have an opportunity to give the Tobruk garrison a little shock if we can clear up the rest of the front.

I am ordering up what Italian reserves that can be spared to try and protect our supplies around Gambut. Like General Cruwell, I do not want the British to concentrate in the south. However, we must make every effort to preserve our forces here in the Tobruk corridor and our valuable supplies." With this Heinz ended his conversation and started moving back toward a small airplane that had been waiting to take him to find Cruwell.

"Jawohl Herr Generaloberst", replied a major as he made a snappy salute and followed Heinz to the plane whose engine was already turning over.

Despite their Gambut near miss, Heinz was glad he had insisted upon flying near Tobruk and then directly into El Adem airfield. With this first hand aerial view, the briefings he had been getting and assorted maps he would be able to make sounder judgments. He must confess, from these first impressions, the British seemed to be following their recently captured plans to the letter.

Heinz again took to the air this time in a small Storch single engine plane. Glued to his window as they flew south Heinz observed the battlefield from the previous days fighting.

Seeing many damaged British and German tanks, displayed on a battlefield of death and destruction that seemed to stretch for miles, he inquired as to the status of tank recovery and repair. He wanted these tanks. He also was concerned that by allowing British troops to make in some cases simple repairs, it could mean having to fight the same tanks again.

Tobruk Still a Possibility?

Heinz thought, perhaps the Tobruk Garrison's forces had been weakened at a time when Axis divisions still packed a punch. In the midst of all this battlefield confusion was Tobruk ripe for a *coup de main*? No one would expect this. It would be like a medieval dream come true where castle defenders under siege were tricked into leaving their castle and then destroyed in the open.

Moreover, they may never get another opportunity like this again. A future follow up attack on Tobruk might not be possible for several months, if ever at all. If the bulk of British forces could be contained by strong defensive action, then destruction of Tobruk through this open door might be possible.

"Send our captured British heavy Matilda tanks to assist Italian Pavia division defenses and be ready to counter attack if the Tobruk foray threatens our artillery at El Adem. Tomorrow is another day for maximum effort." Heinz ordered the two officers that had accompanied him in the small Italian plane and were now serving as his temporary staff.

###

Heinz knew that British Matilda Infantry tanks had been nicknamed the "Queens of the Desert", slow and armed with a small 2-pounder gun their thick armor could be penetrated at long range by few guns. Even more attuned to concerns about heavy enemy tanks by his recent experiences in Russia; he realized concentrated attacks by Matildas could prove almost impossible to resist.

Using these tanks, one British armored division had destroyed an entire Italian Army. Even the presence of a few Matildas during the invasion of France had caused the German problems. Heinz therefore decided to take even more radical measures.

"Send immediate word to General Böttcher. I want his ten-centimeter artillery pieces used in field direct fire role to defend against those British Matildas that are heading our way from the east of coming from Tobruk. Matildas may again decide the battle if they cannot be stopped. Our 10-centimeter heavy guns have saved us many times in Russia when we were faced with heavy Russian tanks. My intent is to use any weapon we can to stop Matildas and these guns are even more effective than our 88s, if handled correctly.

Their employment as anti-tank weapons might make the difference over the next few days. Our tank guns and a lot of our anti-tank guns are near useless against these beasts. Obviously they are the most effective way the British have of overcoming our prepared defenses. Witness the rift in our lines that their breakout from Tobruk accomplished. What reliable reserve troops are available to send to defend our supplies at Gambut? Artillery and anti-tank guns alone cannot hold Gambut."

"Herr Generaloberst, there is a battalion of Italian paratroopers that could be moved very quickly. With air transport they could be in Gambut before nightfall," the other staff officer chimed in.

"Send them," Heinz ordered.

But before Heinz had gotten far in his quest to find General Cruwell, he was urgently called back to El Adem. For an attack launched against 361st Infantry Regiment was growing in intensity. After Heinz landed, he was told by an excited Lieutenant that a new type of heavy British Infantry tank was being used in this attack. Also the Tobruk breakout force was on the march again with newly repaired Matilda tanks.

So not only did the British seem to have countless light tanks, but a new heavy tank in addition to Matildas. No wonder the British seemed so unconcerned about the heavy tank losses they had endured. What other surprises did these British have in store for them?

Earlier in the day, General Cruwell had ordered the bulk of Axis heavy artillery to prepare to fire south in preparation for his impending attack. Heinz's first major decision on African soil was to countermand this order. Instead, because of 361st Regiment's urgent request for assistance, he ordered this heavy artillery to fire in defense of escarpment point 175.

General Boettcher also complied with Heinz's earlier order and his 12 ten-centimeter guns were distributed as follows: one battery each to the

Tobruk front, 361st Regiment and the mixed Italian German forces defending Gambut.

###

After reading Heinz's message, General Cruwell's scowl betrayed to his aid that he was not pleased that his attack had been halted. Moreover Cruwell had already clashed with some of his officers over his movement decisions this morning. To be perfectly honest; Cruwell was tired. He felt that it was better to quickly attack and finish his faction of British XXX Corps off.

Back in his Storch aircraft late that afternoon, with little daylight left, Heinz finally located Cruwell. Before Ludwig Cruwell had received Guderian's order to hold he was just about to attack. For this purpose he had taken the time to assemble 15th Panzer Division, 21st Panzer Division tanks and the armored spearhead of Italian Ariete Armored Division. This was essentially the entire Axis armored force.

Heinz told Cruwell that he was concerned that Axis plans and troop dispositions possibly fell into British hands when the Africa Korps Headquarters had been captured.

"Ludwig what other possible explanation can there be for XXX Corps' current behavior? While Tobruk force and XIII Corps was attacking us in the north XXX Corps was preparing their defenses. Could they have captured our plans and thus known of your intention to join with Ariete and then attack. Perhaps I was wrong, but I sensed a trap.

Tomorrow we must again strike these British where they do not expect it and return to defend the critical area to our north before our meager forces are defeated. Tomorrow I expect XXX Corps to wait again for an attack that will not come."

CHAPTER 7

Heinz's Alternate Plan

Taking note of Italian General Gambarra's body language during their discussion it became clear to Heinz that Gambarra did not like being placed under German command. He realized that he must work on this relationship less the Italian General's attitude impact the battle's outcome.

"All Axis armor will attack south to destroy most of First South African Brigade before they can join the balance of British XXX Corps. Motorized troops, artillery and anti-tank guns will shield our tanks from northern intervention as this attack is progressed. Take note to maneuver your tanks around this marshy terrain", as he pointed out its location on their table map.

"Next, we will again swing our armor northeast and spread out across Eighth Army's supply tail. In the process we will collect or destroy all damaged tanks we run across. Later in the day we will again concentrate out armor to cut off and divide Second New Zealand Division which is in the process of advancing up the road to Sidi Rezegh, here," as he again pointed to the table map.

" At the end of the day we will reassemble at Gambut to rearm and refuel. Subsequently we will leave the bulk of Axis reconnaissance forces, some light tanks and remaining German Africa Korps artillery in the south. Their goal is to try and keep XXX Corp isolated and .make them think the entire Africa Korps is still in the south.

Finally, all our remaining mobile forces, joined by Italian infantry will attack and destroy the 70th Infantry Division sortie from Tobruk on the morning of the 25th. Relocate and align your tank Regiments in battle formation facing south after dark. Ariete (132nd) in the center, Fifth on the left flank, and Eighth on the right. You are dismissed."

Brandenbergers Turned Loose

"Herr General *Oberst*, you requested my presence?"

"And you are *Oberlieutnant?*"

"Von Koenen, Herr General, commander of your African *Brandenberger* half-company. May I say what an honor it is to serve under your command."

"You may change your mind when I tell you what I have in mind for your detachment. First, Von Koenen, if all goes well, on the morning of the 25th you and your men in British trucks and uniforms will take and hold the main British egress through their minefields into Tobruk for our follow on troops. Second, after you are relieved, you will make preparations to lead a major raid behind the main enemy line as soon as possible."

"We will require more trucks, especially if we are to conduct a lengthy foray behind enemy lines, Herr General. However, if I may speak freely, I don't think a raid with my small force will have much of an impact on the battle currently underway."

"What would you suggest?"

"If we can get hold of enough vehicles, why not take the opportunity to infiltrate a much larger force into the British rear. Using this force we could cause real damage to British airfields and supplies. Furthermore, our 361st Regiment contains former French Legionaries; they are perfect for a mission such as this. We could conduct the raid you speak of with a significant force and then when the British react and think they have us cut off, we head south. After traveling some 100 miles to the south we capture the desert outpost and southern flanking position of Oasis Siwa.

Herr Generaloberst what I am proposing is not just my thinking, but in many ways represents the thoughts voiced by many of our desert experts. They feel the British are using our open desert flanks to defeat us in Africa as proved by their incursion into the desert far to the south of us. They are positioning themselves to raid our rear areas; we should turn the tables on them and destroy their bases of operation."

"*Oberlieutenant* von Koenen, what you are proposing is an ambitious and insightful plan, especially in light of our current circumstances. I don't think British vehicles are going to be a problem, I am sure we can get you all the equipment you need for your expanded plan. Troops may be the major issue. First of all, we will see how many of your men are left after you gain us access to Tobruk. Bounce your raiding idea off 361st commander; tell him I will approve the operation if he is in agreement.

What you propose needs to be studied, but is just outrageous enough to be workable. Pick some Italians if you think you can use them, but for God's sake don't let them take you for British and shoot you. We must think and move faster than our enemies, but that is what we do, are we *clear*.

"*Clear*, Herr Generaloberst"

After leaving, Von Koenen thought to himself about what Guderian had said. Koenen's *Brandenbergers* spoke many languages, but they were short those who spoke Italian. What von Koenen needed was to quickly recruit Italians who also spoke German and if possible passable English. As far as he was concerned he had just been given Guderian's permission to begin this recruiting.

###

As he stepped outside in the night air, Heinz was glad that he had brought his greatcoat from Russia. He had not expected the desert to be so cold and there was mud everywhere - if you could call it mud - from the recent rain. Rain had given the finely divided sand a consistency of modeling clay.

All Axis troops were adequately prepared for these cold desert nights, not like his poor troops in Russia. Having at least this level of protection could save many a life and ease needless suffering in Russia. Each day from now on in Russia, it would grow colder and their suffering would increase.

Here, in Africa, he had his hands full, but still felt guilty for what his troops were going through in Russia – without him. However, he must focus all his energies on the here and now. There was a lot to learn and many difficult decisions to be made. If defeat could be avoided in Africa, he determined to send what aid he could spare to help out German soldiers in Russia.

Somehow, it did not seem right as he stepped up into Rommel's Mammoth Moritz command vehicle, but after all Rommel had probably acquired it from some dead British General. So now a different General is taking up residence in this vehicle. In fact, Heinz noticed that some of Rommel's personal effects had still not been removed for shipment back to his wife in Germany.

Generals come and go and still this war goes on. Tonight the men, most of them, should be able to get some sleep. They would need it. Cruwell had done his job; he had reassembled most of their armor in a central location, kept anti-tank guns in excellent defensive positions and thrown the British out of Sidi Rezegh airfield. And perhaps Heinz had kept him from leading their remaining armor into a British trap.

Much of Africa Korps' tank force was still undamaged, especially 15th PD. Many times these troops required no commander, only to be left alone to do their job. Most would do their duty, remembering their training. Many fine young men would not leave Africa or Russia alive. Others would suffer debilitating wounds and illnesses. Heinz felt these men required protection from those who would use them up for their personal gain. For these people and especially the stupid ones, he had no sympathy.

PART III

Dismantling Crusader

CHAPTER 8

Crusader Peaks

November 24, 1941– Day of Battle

As predicted, in the morning a heavy mist again clothed the desert. With this mist, neither side would be able to determine exact status of the other except at short distances.

Moving south in three parallel waves, the first line of Axis tanks was to literally drive through and over the South Africans. Contained in this first wave would be all captured British tanks that were currently being used by Ariete Division.

As these attack waves moved south they were to never lose sight of the tank to the right and left of them. Gradually as visibility improved they could move further apart.

This morning mist should also adversely affect the accuracy of respected British artillery and even their anti-tank guns. Twenty First Panzer Division tanks would be on the right flank, 15th PD on the left in battalion echelon. In the center the slower Italian tanks would control the pace of movement. Mines were not expected during the attack south as it was unlikely South African engineers would not have laid mines in their expected avenue of advance.

Heinz planed a strict timetable. His tanks were to halt this skirmish after exactly two hours or less if they first fired off one half of their remaining ammunition. He hoped German fighters could somehow keep RAF planes away from his troops as they commenced their day's movements. For their vehicles would soon be exposed to air attack after the mist cleared. Heinz's before dawn briefing outlined the day's major objects to his staff.

"We must keep these South Africans from joining their brothers in arms south of Sidi Rezegh and thus immediately reopening their lines of communication. First South African Brigade must be quickly destroyed and so must as much of the New Zealanders as we can catch in the open later in the day."

Other issues quickly discussed were the disposition of captured and damaged British equipment, in particular tanks and artillery. It would take more time, but they must try to sweep the battlefield as they headed back toward Gambut. Since it would be hard to transport the damaged tanks with them, he intended to collect as many as possible at Bir El Gubi. What's more, abandoned British trucks and personnel carriers were also being collected at Bir El Gubi for a possible future raid into British rear areas.

In the north, all remaining mobile forces were put on alert for a possible attack on Tobruk. Leading the attack into the fortress itself would be captured Matilda tanks, followed by small Italian and German flame throwing tanks.

Heinz explained to his staff as their meeting was concluded:

"We pay dearly for our equipment with the currency of the lives of brave Italian and German sailors who now face an extreme high probability of death crossing the Mediterranean. The British have a less risky journey, but a much longer one around Africa. Coming from Russia, I can tell you I doubt that there will be much equipment made available to replace our combat loses.

Consequently, we must make every effort to be sure that damaged British tanks and other equipment do not make it to British rear areas to be repaired. Units that surrender will be left with a guard, but the attack must continue. Keep account of your losses and report locations of damaged tanks."

###

Heinz's morning attack was preceded by a low intensity artillery bombardment just to hide noise from Axis tank engines. However, this attack did not go according to plan, but it was not directly the Italians fault. Their tanks could simply not keep up and there had also been breakdowns.

Thus some South Africans escaped their grasp and fled south absent their equipment. They had been mauled, but not destroyed; however, the attack had resulted in a morning of confusion and much consternation for the British. He was concerned about ammunition and fuel for his tanks and so he wished to quickly redirect his forces toward Gambut and his supplies.

At this point Heinz determined to leave Ariete's tanks at Bir El Gubi and advance northeast with his German forces alone. Maintaining firm control of Bir El Gubi, which the Italians had demonstrated they could do with their tank support, was very important. Bir El Gubi could provide a good jumping off point for further action to the south.

Elements of Ariete were already collecting British equipment and supplies from the battlefield, which would render the defenses at Bir El Gubi even stronger. Heinz noted how pleased his Italian Allies were to put the South Africans to flight and to "trade up" for captured British materiel.

Later in the morning as the German Panzer Divisions advanced to the northeast, their attack on a spread out Fourth New Zealand Brigade had gone better. They had hit these New Zealanders in the flank and pretty well eliminated or scattered their entire Brigade, with few losses to themselves. Thus they had managed to effectively split the tough New Zealand Division in two.

In the process, a significant portion of XIII Corps' Infantry tanks had been destroyed or captured. During their sweep northeast they had even managed to recapture some Africa Korps Headquarters Staff Officers and undamaged communications equipment to the welcomed relief of all.

Also, Axis losses to RAF planes had been minimal in transit due to difficulty in distinguishing friend from foe on the extended battlefield. More importantly, they had secured most of their endangered supplies and their airfield at Gambut could be quickly put back in service.

Two German reconnaissance Battalions together with Italian GF-RECAM were to give an impression that German Panzer Divisions were still holding blocking positions southeast of Sidi Rezegh. This force was reinforced with many of Africa Korps' light tanks, which were primarily used for reconnaissance in the individual Panzer battalions.

To carry out the rest of his plans, Heinz decided to pull all reserve tanks and mobile anti-tank guns from his remaining units, including some self-propelled 20-mm AA guns. He again emphasized how important it was to quickly return damaged tanks to service. Especially needed were his repaired medium tanks.

###

At precisely 19:00 hours, Otto Heymer, commander of the Luftwaffe in Africa, reported to Heinz. He had not looked forward to this meeting primarily because he was used to Rommel's routine "fits" about breakdowns of Luftwaffe support for his ground troops. One listened to

Rommel; he did not listen to you. Heymer had been made to feel that in Rommel's eyes the Luftwaffe was on a par with worthless Italians.

It was a terrible blow for morale to have constantly "never done enough", especially when command decisions required troops and equipment to be used in inefficient, inappropriate and dangerous ways. It was a depressing state of affairs to report to such a man. The result of such discussions was usually excessive casualties among his aircrews, especially Stuka pilots.

"Is there any way you can provide adequate fighter cover over our forces to the south in two days, I must know for sure? If we can stabilize the front, we are going to try and rescue our garrisons to the south." questioned Heinz.

"Not all of the advanced fields are usable, the weather is still not good and as you know the supply situation with regards to fuel is limited. However, we are receiving some fuel by air and some Italian fighter reinforcements have arrived.

These new Italian fighters have more range than our Luftwaffe counterparts and may better meet your needs to the south. In fact, our best option may be to try and destroy some of these British fighters on the ground. This is really the best use of our limited forces, if we were given a free hand. However, we would need help from Italians fighters together with our longer range Messerschmitt 110 fighters to conduct such attacks. The remaining Messerschmitt 109 fighters will hold the rear areas while these raids take place."

"Agreed, concentrate your fighters over Tobruk tomorrow. I like your idea of using these new Italian fighters for raids on one or more of the British airfields to take some of this pressure off? This plan meshes nicely with other proposed raids behind the British lines. Push the Italians to get more of their new fighters here as soon as possible. With Kesselring coming into the picture, all of us now have the same boss, even the Italian air force.

Also whatever you do, don't bomb our own people. Our communications are in a pitiful state. It is a confusing battle; your pilots must make sure they are attacking the enemy. I noticed Italians especially have a lot of captured British equipment in service. In fact, our whole Army appears to be turning more and more British everyday. Your pilots must be careful, this battlefield is very confusing."

"Jawohl, Herr General Oberst, we will begin the planning at once. Italians are still sending some of their older models, but they also promised almost three groups of new Macchi 202 fighters, similar to our Messerschmitt 109 fighters. I hope they arrive in time. We will certainly need more fuel. Also, for our part it would help if we were not shot at by our own people"

"Agreed, Heymer, it appears a lot more communication needs to take place on both sides."

Another long night, Heinz thought as the Heymer left the command vehicle, but tomorrow may spell an end to Churchill's offensive.

Battlefield Fate

Gian's unit, GF-RECAM, was now integrated with two German reconnaissance elements that had been trying to hold onto roads linking Bardia and Tobruk. Much of the artillery possessed by Gian's unit was mounted on trucks and they stood a better chance defending these roads than trying to maneuver in the soggy desert.

Even tanks were having a hard time with the mud like sand. However, German tracked vehicles seemed to be fairing better with the wet sand. Moreover, traveling in these conditions consumed more fuel, which was in short supply. They even began to look forward to the unrelenting desert sun drying this mess out.

GF-RECAM personnel quickly learned from Italian paratroopers about the usefulness of German ten-cm artillery pieces. These artillery pieces were used as heavy anti-tank guns to deal with Matildas and Valentines remaining to British XIII Corp. GF-RECAM's truck mounted guns would prove useful as both as artillery and anti-tank guns. Most of the effective truck mounted 102-mm guns remained with Ariete Armored Division to the southwest, but GF-RECAM had managed to borrow two of them.

It was at this point that Gian came face to face with battlefield fate. Because of his language skills, he and his men were selected to command a platoon of recently captured Matilda tanks. In turn, they were to turn their light tanks over to other tank crews who had recently lost their own tanks in the chaotic fighting to the south. Moreover Gian was told that these very same captured Matilda tanks, still with their British markings, were to lead an attack into Tobruk tomorrow morning.

Accompanying Gian's Matilda platoon were some very fit looking elite German infantry also riding in captured carriers, some dressed as British troops. Their job was to capture British bridges over the tank ditches for following Infantry, light tanks, self-propelled guns and engineers. Gian's Matildas were then to try and break into Tobruk's second belt of defenses. It all sounded so very simple and sane. Tomorrow morning they were to capture Tobruk.

German armor was to cut off Tobruk Garrison troops that were fighting outside Tobruk and/or prevent their interference with German and Italian troops making the main attack. This plan could turn tables on the British or it could backfire and result in trapping of a large fraction of existing Axis forces.

So, Gian thought, he would get his wish with this crazy plan; he would die as bravely as his brother had. He tried to present the mission in the best light possible to his men as they witnessed their comrades headed in a different direction toward Bardia. To be honest he did not see how they would make it up the road in these unfamiliar tanks, much less through the muddy morass into Tobruk. Gian's heart was racing in his chest, but he tried not to show his concern to the German officer who was to command their mixed battle group.

Unbelievably, all but one of Gian's Matildas made it to the jumping off point and the last one arrived later that night. They felt especially lucky since this had been done without running out of fuel. Fortunately, very detailed maps of Tobruk perimeter defenses were available for them to study.

They were allowed some sleep that night, but part of the night also had to be spent with additional instructions on operating their Matilda tanks. Germans who had more experience in handling the slow tanks gave Gian's crews further driving instructions, with Gian having to translate for his men.

Other Germans and Italians would be attacking from the other side of the breakout corridor; they also had a few earlier captured Matildas. Germans and Italians were working hard to get as many Matildas running to take part in the attack as possible.

One of the biggest concerns was, of course, not getting the Matildas stuck in the muddy sand and shell cratered battlefield. Gian and his men spent part of the night practicing towing operations. He must admit he felt safe when he crawled inside his thickly armored tank. Thankfully they were lucky and had no dead British troops to remove or blood to clean up inside their tank. Still there was a strong smell of sweat, British sweat that seemed to have permeated into the Matilda's metal.

Their attack was supported by dozens of Italian and German mortars pooled from the surrounding units. Heavier artillery was not used on proposed paths the attack force was to take to avoid tearing up the desert surface even more. Also repositioning a lot of artillery might alert the British as to their intentions, which could easily be detected from the air. For the skies seemed to always be full of British planes.

During early morning they were disturbed from their remaining two hours of sleep by the sounds of German tanks moving into attack position behind them. Gian had not felt the need to pray in quite some time, but this morning he did. So in the heat of this struggle his decision was made, God would accompany him from now on. Surely it was only right that his parents had one son survive this war.

Gian could not believe considering the size of the operation that it had been organized so quickly. Germans had literally planned this well coordinated attack overnight modifying parts of a preexisting plan.

On the morning of November 25th, as the attack began, on either side of the path that led into Tobruk German and Italian troops were isolated by blasts of artillery shells and exploding bombs. Never had Gian experienced such battlefield noise so close at hand. It was exciting and yet it was intensely uncomfortable. Massed mortars decimated infantry positions in front of them and British troops were powerless to stop Gian's Matildas as they rolled forward over the shattered positions and then veered right.

On their left filed by scores of German tanks. Already some of these tanks had started unleashing a hail of fire on British artillery positions barely visible in the morning light.

After a brief time, which seemed like forever in their slow tank, Gian located one of the four bridges British engineers had constructed over their anti-tank ditch. They followed a clearly worn trail over this bridge. Next his Matildas would try and locate marked gaps in Tobruk's second and final mine belt. Once they were through this minefield, they were to hold this gap open for follow on troops.

###

Gian's crews kept their tanks moving as they continued to follow a well worn trail. Coaching his driver, Gian's tanks concentrated on trying to keep moving at a steady pace that would prevent their Matildas from getting bogged down.

No one they passed seemed concerned or even bothered to challenge them; in fact most of the few British troops they saw seemed content to seek protection from the bombs and artillery in their bunkers and trenches. Considerable movement of British forces was occurring as troops were being shifted from the fortress to and from the breakout positions.

Contrary to the original plan, and failing to find a marked minefield, Gian kept his tanks moving further than was intended. It was the job of those that followed behind to secure these crossings, he felt it was his job not to stop and immobilize his tanks in the torn up sand.

After what seemed a short distance, they turned left and soon came in contact with a section of field guns. His tanks machine-gunned the crews and drove over the gun trails. Gian began to feel that they would actually take Tobruk all by themselves, but the last of the field guns began to turn their way. What had they gotten themselves into? Also, of all things, captured Italian 20 mm anti-aircraft guns began firing at them as well. Once discovered, there seemed to be no choice but to keep going.

The din from a 25-pounder shell hitting their Matilda was deafening, but they had survived. What a tank; apparently striking at an angle this deadly projectile had failed to penetrate their Matilda's thick turret armor. However after this narrow escape but less than a minute later a terrific explosion took place outside their tank.

Apparently a large artillery shell had hit very close to them. From the lack of response to their driver's gearshift and steerage controls it appeared that the Matilda was done for with track and possible engine damage. Quickly grabbing a signal pistol Gian opened his top turret hatch but he exited into a hell of smoke, noise and an indiscernible mixture of noxious smells. Collecting himself he raised his hand over his head and fired the prearranged green German flare, but he was already too late.

They were smack in the middle of Axis counter-battery artillery fire. Looking behind him Gian could barely make out his two remaining Matildas in the distance. He had to get them out of this. There had not been time to become familiar with their tank's British radios, so next he fired off a white flare. This was the agreed upon signal for retreat. His men did not want to leave him, but there simply was no choice. If they did not leave, they would be destroyed as well. They were helpless in their Matilda and could do nothing but wait it out.

"Must be what it feels like in a submarine under depth charge attack", muttered one of Gian's crew members.

Giuseppe Cenni

Giuseppe Cenni (2) was very familiar with the interior of Tobruk and its anti-aircraft positions. But he simply could not believe what he was seeing, but there it was clear as day, the correct color recognition flare coming from a British tank sitting square in the middle of British artillery.

He pulled his Stuka up and began circling to radio this information. He had taken a chance attacking through the artillery fire, but he had hoped to catch the vicious Tobruk anti-aircraft gunners with their heads down.

Now he requested a halt to shelling in the immediate vicinity of this tank that had fired off the correct recognition flare. No Axis troops were yet supposed to be this far inside the fortress, but recognition signals must be responded to. It took only a short while for the artillery to completely stop.

Well, it served him right, now they wanted him to fly down and check out this tank. At least he did not have to expose himself or his gunner to another dangerous high altitude bombing run.

Not only did it appear that the tank in question was firing on the British, but British anti-aircraft guns in the area were firing at the tank instead of at Giuseppe's Stuka. Thinking out loud, Giuseppe spoke to his rear gunner.

"This tank appears to be one of ours; I can see our flag draped over the engine compartment. It is inside the second defensive line and even taking on the British artillery. All the British guns in the area appear to be trying to destroy it and the tank is returning their fire. I think I will try and take out one of the anti-aircraft guns while they are occupied with our friend there."

Giuseppe returned for another pass to rake the area with machine gun fire, which resulted in knocking out the remaining 20 mm gun by killing the crew. As they headed back he again spoke to his rear gunner.

"If it is one of ours, someone had better get some help up there before they run out of ammo and the British infantry get them."

Giuseppe then radioed this important information back to his airfield. He had doubts as to what the results of his requests would be with everyone as fully engaged as they were, but one just did one's duty.

Giuseppe's squadron had only recently been ordered to the front from Benghazi and he was not sure that even his entire unit had even been fully accounted for in the confusion. As he left the area, he wondered what would become of this brave tank crew. He wondered if he would ever meet this brave tank crew, would they even know who had saved them?

###

Finally the counter battery artillery fire lifted and moved on. Luckily, their Matilda's turret could still turn. Using their turret machine gun and a few rounds of 2-pounder ammo, they managed to take care of most British gun crews around their tank that had survived the pounding. They were aided in their efforts by a friendly Stuka who helped them finish off gun crew survivors plus a few odd infantry that were in the area.

"Lieutenant, I am familiar with Tobruk, maybe while it is clear we should leave the tank and find a place to hide until reinforcements arrive; the British will not leave these guns unmanned for long. Maybe we can make a contribution to capturing Tobruk on foot?" Gian's driver suggested.

"So ordered, if we stay here immobilized we will surely end up captured or dead, lead the way", Gian replied to his driver.

So the four of them set off, figuring at any minute to be shot or captured. Their chances of carrying off the ruse were improved by their uniforms together with the prized captured Tommy guns they each carried. Many of Tobruk's defenders had taken to wearing comfortable Italian uniforms that were theirs for the taking along with other spoils when Tobruk fell to the English. It was hard for Commonwealth troops to resist using Italian equipment they found abandoned in and around Tobruk, even artillery, which was so readily available.

Gian could speak a little English but with a very heavy accent, so they needed to find a suitable hiding place soon. With his driver in the lead they headed away from their tank deeper into the fortress toward the caves that were dug into the side of the closest escarpment. By passing many obviously well used caves they came upon a well-hidden cave off by itself.

This seemed their best chance as Axis shelling was commencing again and getting closer. A posted guard at the cave entrance immediately challenged Gian and his men. A short burst of Gian's Tommy gun solved this problem.

Now there was now no choice and into the cave they charged. Inside the cave shocked operators immediately raised their hands when confronted with the four heavily armed men. On top of tables and in cabinets along the wall there was all matter of electronic equipment. Gian was curious, but that would have to wait. They could go no further or they would have to shoot their captives. This Gian was not willing to do, especially since the cave guard was the first man he had actually killed face to face. So here they would stay as long as they could.

"What is this equipment?" Gian asked one of the British captives in his broken English. He received no answer and even pointing the Tommy gun at him still produced only silence. But these men were clearly disturbed beyond what might be expected from simply being captured, especially the two officers.

Two of Gian's men dragged the dead guard inside and with some rope they stumbled across they tied the rest of their captives up. Gian figured their only chance was to try and get a message out about their condition when it turned dark, if they were still alive. The crew member familiar with Tobruk was chosen for the job of returning to their lines and bringing help.

It began to dawn on Gian that they had found their way into a very important Military installation. Even though they had turned off the lights, there was still an eerie glow from the equipment in the cave. They waited all day; at about 20:00 hours they heard voices and two torches began to shine off the cave walls. One of the tied up British officers began to stir.

##

Expecting an attack at any moment and not fully realizing what had transpired to their south; British XXX Corps troops waited in vain on the 24th for supplies and reinforcements. Only one brigade of Second New Zealand Infantry Division arrived on their right flank and most of this brigade's attached Valentine tanks had already been put out of action.

Also, one of this brigade's infantry battalions had been wiped out in an attack on positions held by German 361st Regiment on the escarpment. Then the rest of this brigade was shelled by heavy Axis artillery specifically ordered by Heinz when they tried to renew their attack. To further complicate matters this New Zealand Brigade like the northern half of XXX Corps was also running short of supplies. So, in some respects they were a liability to the South Africans and other surviving troops south of Sidi Rezegh they were sent to aid.

(2) Giuseppe Cenni (Giuseppe) – Promising Italian fighter ace, dive-bomber and fighter bomber pilot who was the original inventor of the naval "skip bombing" technique. Using his technique, a Stuka or any plane for that matter approached an enemy vessel low over the water similar to what a torpedo bomber would do.

The plane's bomb was released at some distance from the ship and allowed to skip along the water surface hitting the side of a targeted ship. Resulting damage was often at or near the water line similar to damage caused by a torpedo hit. In fact, vessels bombed in such a fashion typically thought they had been struck by a torpedo. He was killed in action on September, 1943.

Chapter 9

At the Egyptian Border

November 25, 1941 - Halfaya Pass, Axis position, African coast east of Tobruk

"What was that", questioned Major Wilhelm Bach as he emerged from his bunker. They could sense that this explosion was not close at hand and that it had been massive. It was a sound that produced a feeling in the pit of your stomach that let you know something significant had happened.

Staring out to sea, they could see smoke rising from far out in the Mediterranean. They had been under almost continuous attack for several days, but this was different. Whatever it was, it had been massive and the sound had been reflected across the water back to them.

"Inform Africa Korps Headquarters", as Wilhelm nodded toward Lt. Mann.

"Herr Major, we have been unable to make contact with Africa Korps Headquarters since the 23rd", replied his signal Lieutenant.

"Then relay the message through Bardia, maybe they will be able to reach them. Also see if they know how the rest of the battle is going", instructed Wilhelm.

Wilhelm hoped this latest event indicated that something had gone wrong for the British. Their position, Halfaya Pass, was located on the Egyptian border and was part of the Axis first line of defense. Since November 21st, their position had been out flanked, bypassed and under siege. Some of their border strong points had fallen, but these had made the British pay dearly for every foxhole.

Halfaya, Bardia, Sollum, and all Axis positions to their West held by Italian 55th Savona Infantry Division were now surrounded and cut off. An attack on their positions from the sea was certainly not out of the question.

Could the explosion have been somehow related to a new British attack on their position? No Axis planes had over flown their position since the 21st, so obtaining aerial reconnaissance to identify the source of the explosion was not possible.

Their present condition was not totally unexpected and consequently his troops had stockpiled enough supplies to be able to hold out for three weeks, but Wilhelm always planned for the worst. Even though he was on good terms with Rommel, he knew both the British and Rommel could be unpredictable. Therefore, shortly after the first British attacks he had instructed his men to use their supplies sparingly so if need be they could hold out even longer.

Churchill Releases Critical Information

It had been a temptation Churchill could not resist. He figured that revealing the knowledge of Rommel's death was just the thing the Eighth Army needed for final victory. So he violated his own rule about prematurely revealing information from the Ultra code breaking effort.

He waited one extra day and then revealed the information in a general message to all of Eighth Army. Surely by now Rommel's death was common knowledge in the Axis camp? Commando action to kill Rommel outright had failed, but now he was dead on the field of battle.

They had already taken Sidi Rezegh once. Couldn't they take it again, especially with Rommel now dead? The British were still unaware that Heinz Guderian, the father of German Blitzkrieg, was now leading Axis forces. Churchill even told Auchinleck to make use of this latest information to inspire the troops in their renewed attack.

The Royal Navy and RAF needed to pull out all stops. It would be a disaster to lose this battle and Tobruk as well. They must use the advantages the RAF and Royal Navy gave them to crush the Germans and Italians.

The fresh British 22nd Guards Brigade was ordered to advance together with the remainder of Second New Zealand, South Africans and a portion of an Indian division. Efforts were set in motion to send even more troops forward. With Germans now focusing on Tobruk, Axis forces in the field should be insufficient to prevent the complete joining of the two British Corps in the south.

They might even trap the last of the German tanks inside Tobruk. However, adding the Indian and New Zealanders troops to the attack would mean giving up on finishing off the Axis forces in coastal areas.

The British reasoned that there were no Axis troops available to take advantage of this vacuum. Threat of a renewed combined force heading for the Sidi Rezegh gap should be sufficient to halt the Axis attack on Tobruk and refocus Axis attention on a renewed threat from the south.

###

Continuing Commonwealth setbacks began to mount as better information from the confusing battlefield found its way to Eighth Army headquarters. These dismal results weighted heavily on Cunningham, the commanding British General. He began to feel powerless as the initiative was flowing to the Axis. He felt another attempt by remnants of XXX Corps to save the trapped 70th ID troops were doomed to failure.

Thirtieth Corp was not receiving all their supplies and remained almost completely surrounded, but disengaging from the enemy was not without risk. The optimistic appraisal of the battle given by the British newspapers after the first days was definitely out of date.

Thirteenth Corps' advance up the Bardia road was making little progress against stiff opposition and most of the Axis frontier strong points remained unconquered. New Zealanders were also beginning to be short supplies as the Axis continued to try and disrupt their lines of communications.

Indeed, Cunningham began to be concerned that both his right and left flanks might suffer the same fate as XXX Corps and 70th ID were experiencing. He still had reserve tanks to return XXX Corps to a respectable fighting unit if they could be safely gotten to the front.

When Cunningham was able to confirm that Axis forces had established a firm footing inside Tobruk and 70th ID was near collapse, he felt it was time to call the relief effort off. He had few resources left to counter this latest move and was having trouble just supplying remnants of his three armored brigades. He decided to abandon the Sidi Rezegh link up. He ordered Commonwealth troops in the Sidi Rezegh pocket to wait until the night of the 26th and breakout.

However, General Auchinleck, his immediate superior, cancelled this order. Auchinleck instead ordered all units to concentrate and try to retake the Sidi Rezegh corridor. He told them that supplies would be pushed to them and to fight with what they had.

After all, he had been told Rommel was dead and Africa Korps Headquarters had been captured. He figured that Axis losses had to also be high in tanks and men after several days of continuous fighting and if anyone had supply difficulties it should be the Germans and Italians. A battle of attrition was theirs to win.

One more push might do the job and they must save the brave men of 70th ID. Consequences of losing this battle were simply too great, what about the Indian Brigade that had fought its way into the western desert and had used all their fuel doing it? What would be their fate if the British offensive failed and the British retreated and what of Malta?

Auchinleck ordered what reserve units he could put his hands on to make all haste to join battle. If worse came to worse, he still had two divisions in the rear areas that he could throw into the battle. In order to hedge his bets, Auchinleck did decide to begin to strengthen his defenses along the Egyptian border.

During all of Crusader, Cunningham had been concerned about his flanks. Now Auchinleck was ordering an all out attack with the XX Italian Motorized Corp still sitting on the British western flank. Indeed this whole Italian armored Corp was still in fairly decent fighting shape. However, Auchinleck intended, with Churchill breathing down his neck, on calling the bluff on the Axis attack on Tobruk.

The original premise of Operation Crusader was now in play; that is to attack Axis forces in the rear while they were attacking Tobruk. For Auchinleck's latest attack to work his remaining Infantry divisions must concentrate. Their slow speed and the poor condition of the desert surface added to their supply situation meant this movement would take precious time. Additionally, aggressive Italian units that had been defending the coastal Bardia road were pursuing the remaining New Zealand troops as they attempted to comply with Auchinleck's orders. Fending off these Italian thrusts caused their supply situation to grow worse by the hour.

###

Churchill received more bad news on the 26th. For the explosion heard by Wilhelm Bach and his men on the 25th had been the catastrophic destruction of British Battleship *Barum* by German submarine U-331. *Barum* had been in route to search for Axis convoys to North Africa as support to Operation Crusader. Also *Barum's* presence in the immediate area was to help put additional pressure on the Sollum front defenders.

Churchill's thinking was that Royal Navy warship assistance had caused Italian defenders to surrender Bardia before; maybe their presence could affect the outcome of a battle again. An accidental and record breaking dive to over 800 feet (one of the U-331's depth gauges was broken) saved U-331 from suffering any consequences in the aftermath of this successful attack.

With the loss *Barum* , the Royal Navy was reduced to two battleships in the eastern Mediterranean. Since the escorting destroyers for these two remaining battleships failed to locate any trace of U-331 their mission was immediately cancelled. Shocked and puzzled by this heavy loss of life, the whole fleet turned around and headed back to Alexandria.

CHAPTER 10

Too Little, Too Late

Working their way through the lines some Italian Bersaglieri (motorized troops), with Gian's Matilda driver's guidance, located Gian and his remaining two crewmen still guarding the radar control installation they had captured. With Gian in command and their experienced guide, this group of Bersaglieri quickly secured much of Tobruk's Headquarters complex; temporarily severing Tobruk's communication with the outside world.

Moving with lighting speed, they next targeted Tobruk's POW cages. Gian's driver commandeered a British truck and crashed the compound's main gate while the accompanying Bersaglieri took care of the guards.

These now freed Italian and German POWs had been the very troops who before their capture had been preparing to lead the initial attack into Tobruk. If they could be rearmed, they would be the freshest troops on the battlefield having spent the last few days with nothing to do but stare at barbed wire. Within an hour additional cave to cave searches successfully discovered sufficient arms for these former POWs.

Now these freed troops leveraged the training they received the past months to further dismantle Tobruk's undermanned defenses. Any risks of death from British mines, fortifications, artillery and tanks were now substantially reduced for these troops as Tobruk's interior installations began to fall into their hands.

Now tables were turned, it was fortress defenders who were short necessary infantry to defend numerous forts and strong points. Their fortifications were facing the wrong way from this new threat. This was especially true in central and eastern parts of Tobruk.

Inside the Fortress

After taking a pioneer Captain's report Heinz spoke to him as directly as he could.

"We can not offer you much artillery or Luftwaffe support, unfortunately it can not be spared from the major effort. Matildas, small flame throwing tanks and self-propelled guns will provide what assistance they can, but we may soon run short of ammunition.

I will also try and send you some more captured British tanks, if we can get crews. Execute your remaining work very carefully. It would appear that time is now on our side. Make sure there are no unnecessary casualties."

"Jawohl Herr Generaloberst, it will be dark soon and we now know these fortifications by heart. We discovered a very valuable fact. Our troops are able to achieve far more with their flame throwers after dark. This should help convince Tommy that his situation is hopeless." The pioneer Captain asserted.

Heinz was starting to feel that they had reached the turning point in the fight for Tobruk. If so, then their next order of business would be to reestablish a firm link with their surrounded troops of the Sollum front. But first he would briefly rest his tank crews, reorganize and appraise the supply situation.

He also figured that they would need some type of Italian naval aid to help secure the port of Tobruk. There was still a possibility that the British would attack from the sea or at least try to rescue the remaining Tobruk defenders.

Back on the front southeast of Tobruk, the fighting was still intense. Heinz had deliberately given a fairly dismal report to Hitler, telling him the Tobruk breakout was being contained and that many British tanks had been destroyed.

In order to keep the pressure up, he inquired into when the new Second Air Fleet commander would enter the Theater. He reported limited supplies, Luftwaffe resources and difficult weather conditions were currently the greatest problems in attempting to shut down the British offensive.

Moreover, he specifically requested that Second Air Fleet's Chief of Staff meet with him as soon as possible. At this point Hitler cut him off and suggested he personally pass this request on to the Luftwaffe. He was busy with Eastern Front concerns and in the future General Guderian should make his report through the new overall commander.

With the situation on the ground looking better, Hitler told Heinz that he was prepared to release the information regarding Rommel's death. Hitler set the date of Rommel's death as November 26, 1941. This would be the date officially communicated to Italian and German troops. Only

Hitler's inter circle, those soldiers with Rommel when he died, medical personnel and a few select Afrika Korps staff officers knew the actual date. With existing paranoid over Rommel's suspected Italian traitor all of these individuals were sworn never to reveal the actual date.

So, Heinz was on his own until the new commander showed up. However, Hitler did express interest in the possibility that Tobruk might soon fall. Secretly, he was very impressed that Heinz seemed to have straightened out a serious British threat situation rather quickly.

Heinz's report to Italians was more positive and he praised performance of Italian divisions, something they were not used to. He suggested, because of the immense burden that Malta was imposing on their fragile supply system that they both should keep their supply requests to a minimum. He wanted no more Italian and German shipping sunk, every effort must be made to make supply lanes secure.

Night had not stopped the fighting inside Tobruk. Many Italians were now fighting inside the fortress perimeter. Loss of central communications from Tobruk stunned even Churchill. Also shocking were reports of ships in Tobruk harbor being fired on from the town and heights above the harbor.

Auchinleck's order for Tobruk's garrison to retreat back into the fortress had come at a very bad time, adding to the confusion in British ranks. Tobruk's garrison commander was starting to appreciate the hopelessness of his situation.

Italian XX Corps was absorbing causalities as a result of British units attempting to assemble south of the Sidi Rezegh airfield. Heinz requested an all out effort from Luftwaffe assets on Crete and anywhere else that planes could be spared. Both Italian Corps commanders were now willing to launch an all out attack to finish the action inside Tobruk. Remaining British fortress artillery could not provide support to all sections; therefore, in many fortified installations Tobruk defenders could respond with small arms fire only.

By midmorning of November 26th more gaps in the first and second defensive lines were cleared. Additional bridges were thrown across the anti-tank ditch and more Italian engineers and infantry moved into the fortress. By midnight of the 26th, Axis forces were firmly entrenched inside Tobruk controlling almost one half of the Fortress.

Heinz felt it was important to consolidate their Tobruk gains and give his exhausted troops some rest. However, with threats to the south, this might not be possible. He also kept in tune with the flow of Luftwaffe reinforcements and supplies. An accurate assessment was made of Axis logistics; both German and Italian staff officer's opinions were that supplies and equipment on hand would be sufficient for ground troops for the short term. Most ammunition hadn't reached emergency stock levels, but they were getting close.

Axis losses were significant, but less than British. Much of Tobruk's equipment and facilities were being captured without damage, thanks to the fast pace of the assault.

A well planned raid by some newly arrived Italian fighters and a German bomber raid on Sidi Barini airfield had gone well. This resulted in some reductions in British air activity. Several bothersome British bombers were destroyed on the ground, especially at Sidi Barini. These airfield raids were, for the most part, conducted by Italians with few losses. Valuable reconnaissance information on British troops was beginning to come in, but overall the communications situation was still poor.

General Auchinleck still had tanks but he was missing a large percentage of troops that had made up XXX Corps and most of the units remained too fragmented for coordinated offensive action. Thirteenth Corps had also lost significant numbers of troops to various causes and nearly all their tank strength mostly due to their vigorous offensive actions. Also Italian XX Corps was still firmly entrenched on XXX Corps' western flank.

Moreover, Axis Reconnaissance and anti-tank units were harassing Commonwealth troops on their right flank and their lines of communication. If they tried to move their troops close to Sidi Rezegh they were pounded by combined Axis heavy artillery, which could now almost give them their undivided attention.

Part IV

End of British Relief Efforts

CHAPTER 11

No Where to Go

November 27, 1941

It was becoming intoxicating, could they actually pull it off. How many months had they waited in front of this accursed fortress? How many had died, been wounded, hospitalized because of the harsh desert climate, or been captured?

Taking Tobruk provided every motivation that drove a soldier: patriotism, pride, revenge, honor, success, booty, a chance to rest, but most of all, a chance to go home. Every potential hiding place was searched again for fuel, emergency airlift requests were made again; this task must be completed.

Somehow, the Italians needed to find a way to get more supplies across the Mediterranean past Malta. The attack must continue - one bunker at a time. They fought on. Anti-tank guns were manhandled forward.

A lot of smoke had been used to obscure their positions and hide their attack. Special requests were received from outlying units to join in the attack. Never had such enthusiasm been generated during this long desert war.

Axis troops had been inside the Fortress before, but had been thrown out by counter attacks. Now, Tobruk defenders had few if any reserves left. During their breakout attempt and subsequent brutal fighting to cut through Axis lines British troop and tank reserves had been used up. Many felt that this worthless piece of desert had definitely soaked up more than its fair share of blood.

November 28, 1941

Churchill called up Auchinleck and demanded action. Tobruk must not fall, but the all important relief corridor was simply too well defended. Too many heavy tanks had been lost, these slow moving heavy tanks that had accomplished so much in the past were actually being hunted down and destroyed. Garrison troops should have been ordered back inside Tobruk before they could be cut off by the very Axis armor that should have been destroyed earlier.

Now, all help must be given to the valiant defenders. Churchill ordered the Royal Navy to come to the aid of the garrison defenders, but Tobruk harbor was already in Axis hands.

The Royal Navy had just lost one of their Battleships on November 25 to newly arrived U-boats. For once, Admiral Cunningham sought to be cautious and argued to save his last two Battleships. The much sought after Axis airfield complexes west of Tobruk were still operational. Admiral Cunningham feared it would be a repeat of Crete, except this time his ships would face U-boats in addition to skies filled with Axis aircraft.

Auchinleck realized too late that the Tobruk defenders should have already been ordered to begin the destruction of supplies, sensitive equipment and important documents contained in Tobruk. Nothing should be allowed to fall into the Axis hands.

All available Desert Air Force planes were ordered to attack Axis troops trying to break into Tobruk. But by this time, the defenders and attackers were so intertwined that Allied air attacks could be nowhere near 100 percent effective. Also, with the newly arriving Italian fighters, Axis fighter strength was increasing rather than decreasing.

Auchinleck began moving forward his reserve infantry division and a newly arrived armored division. He asked Churchill to release additional RAF and ground units from Syria. He knew one more try was about all his troops had in them, he hoped it would be enough. However, he could not afford to leave Egypt uncovered and it would take time to organize an effective defense.

Fresh attacks by Italian troops were just too much for Tobruk's defenders; they knew they were doomed in their trenches and bunkers. Selected heavy Axis artillery pieces pounded hold out forts and individual positions as very accurate fire could now be brought down on centers of organized resistance. Much of Tobruk garrison's artillery had been captured and was being used against their former owners.

Italians took control of most of the interior part of Tobruk, including the harbor and town. Little organized effort had been made to destroy supplies or other sensitive equipment. This would prove a most disastrous mistake for British interests. No one, not even Axis troops were prepared for how quickly Tobruk fell. Heinz's calculated gamble had paid off handsomely.

Churchill now began to worry about Malta. It would be more difficult if Tobruk fell to keep the island supplied. However, if combined with the destruction of Cunningham's ships it would be next to impossible. Also, what if the Italian battlefleet decided to put in an appearance? So Churchill relented on the proposed Tobruk naval relief effort.

The island of Malta had been transformed into a powerful British base, home to a large contingent of troops, some 200 anti-aircraft guns, planes, submarines and even a cruiser force. Malta very effectively blocked the way between Italy and North Africa. However, all these men and equipment, not to mention the island's civilian population, required continual supply of basic and military necessities.

A loss of significant number of Cunningham's ships would not only jeopardize Egypt, but also ability to supply Malta's needs. They might save Tobruk and lose Malta, or both could be lost.

This was a sad day for the British Empire. New Zealander and Indian division troops broke through the weakly held ring around XXX Corps, but now they found themselves about to be surrounded too. Remaining Africa Korps armor and Axis reconnaissance forces were quickly filling the gap that movement of XIII Corps had left on their right flank. Even the RAF was struggling to maintain control. Could the fate of Egypt be in the balance?

Churchill finally agreed to a general retreat but he was infuriated with Auchinleck. He informed Auchinleck that:

"All your forces should reassemble at Sidi Omar and attack again."

There simply was no excuse - overwhelming strength, a weak enemy with no supplies and Rommel dead. Could he even politically survive this disaster and what about the impact to Malta? He would not even speculate what his enemies and that pig Stalin would say. After things calmed down, Churchill was determined to replace Auchinleck.

Off Again

This raid had been billed as a suicide mission to keep the British off balance, thought up by some crazy German officer. Gian and his crews had been tracked down for this new adventure and given almost no time to rest. Why had he made the mistake of letting the Germans know he could speak some English?

He was already beginning to regret his decision to volunteer for yet another mission. Not because of the danger, but because he would be missing the final stages of the capture of Tobruk. For it was a great moment in recent Italian history. At last, perhaps a first real step in a long journey to defeating the British.

Their raiding combat group was scheduled to leave right before dusk. Gian was not quite sure his crews had completely mastered their British armored cars. This was to be the third type of British armored vehicle they had operated in the last few days.

Because of his English speaking ability, Gian was placed in charge of a company composed of captured armored cars. *Brandenbergers* had as much as adopted this young Italian Lieutenant and his brash comrades who could be counted on to pull their own weight. Already, stories were starting to circulate about him and as a result he had to turn down Italian volunteers for this new adventure. Enjoying the attention, he did nothing to discourage the continuation of these stories.

Altogether, their combat raiding group was able to scrape together some 20 odd captured British armored cars to be joined by other armored cars of German origin. Twentieth Corps personnel had been accumulating captured English vehicles for just this purpose.

They were headed south to the domain of numerous British scout cars and the feared Long Range Desert Group. So, this new German General was now making it clear that he intended to challenge the British on their open desert flank thought Gian. Rounding out the raiding group were numerous British trucks and Bren carriers filled with men and equipment of German 361st Infantry Regiment.

That evening, Gian's armored cars' primary mission was one of reconnaissance and escort for the mostly truck mounted infantry as they attempted to slip around the far southwestern British flank. In the morning, Gian's armored cars were to split up and head for British fighter airfields. When they arrived at the airfields, this location information would be transmitted to waiting Italian and German planes for an immediate attack. After Axis planes finished attacking these Eighth Army fighter airfields, if possible they were to attack and finish off any planes that had not been destroyed by these attacks from the air.

At any rate, they were to cause as much confusion as possible riding in British trucks and armored cars and shooting up everything in sight. Once this action was finished, most of his captured British armored cars were to head back to the Axis lines.

In parallel, 361st Infantry troops, assisted by *Brandenbergers*, were to attack one of the British supply bases. Their mission was to abscond with all the supplies they possibly could and destroy what remained.

Gian knew members of 361st Regiment, two battalions strong, were all former members of the French Foreign Legion and had a well-earned reputation for scavenging anything that was not tied down. In addition to their infantry weapons, they were armed with small squeeze bore 20/28 mm AT guns, some artillery and anti-aircraft guns, including two 88mm guns.

These former Legionnaires were glad to be riding for a change as they, like the majority of the entire German Army, normally walked everywhere. After their raid on the British supply base 361st troops were to head south into deep desert.

Their ultimate target was the southern desert oasis of Siwa. Heinz's intent was to create problems for the British by capturing this remote, but very important desert outpost. The Axis would then hold a position from which they could outflank Eighth Army and threaten Egypt. This remote outpost offered a lot of potential and was not within easy reach of RAF fighters.

It was from another southern oasis, Garabub, near Siwa that the British had launched a flanking attack on the Axis with an Indian Brigade. This Indian Brigade had successfully captured another deep desert oasis, Jalo, some 200 miles to the west. But in the process, this brigade had suffered casualties in clashes with Italian Trieste division and from air attacks.

Moreover, they had not even carried enough fuel for the return trip, feeling a return trip would not be necessary. This would turn out to be a serious mistake. For Heinz wanted to isolate and destroy this brigade before the British could exploit this dangerous threat.

British Supply Dumps – The British Retreat Again

British depot supply troops were quite shocked when a group of British armored cars opened fire on them. Gian could not believe his eyes, for almost a square mile supplies of all manner of things stretched into the distance - an incredible treasure. For the Axis, this was truly a poor man's war.

These raiders had been given instructions as to types of supply items to concentrate on trying to acquire. Gian was concerned that their troops would become distracted with obtaining items for personal use, but this turned out not to be the case. After about four hours, they were able to regroup and in their captured British armored cars they headed for one of the targeted British fighter airfields.

At the same time 361st troops headed for the second supply dump. Unfortunately, even elaborate attempts at deception by *Brandenbergers* had no effect on the second supply depot; sufficient alarm had by then gone out. Tanks were driven from repair facilities and any item that could be used for defense was put to use by the now forewarned British.

Soon the whole RAF and Eighth Army would be down on their necks. One important task remained and that was the last of the British fighter airfields. Raiding British airfields would keep RAF planes occupied and prevent their interference with movement of 361st to Siwa.

Afterwards Gian wanted only to sleep, never had he felt himself so exhausted; he had enough of fighting for a lifetime. However, he still had to get his men back to their own lines. From the looks of it Italy had her lost territory returned and on that note they would like to see a quiet finish to 1941. They had their raid. It was now time to return to their lines and get some sleep.

Their journey back was not uneventful, for their highest losses occurred from their own troops as they approached Axis lines. Gian did not imagine that his exploits would soon be a topic of conversations all over Italy by a nation hungry for heroes.

##

Siwa easily fell to 361st Regiment as their arrival in British vehicles and a little help from von Koenen's English speaking *Brandenbergers* took the huge Oasis community by surprise. Three Hundred Sixty First Regiment began to set up permanent residence in one of the most beautiful and exotic places in the North African desert.

Their captured British supplies and trucks would make them self sufficient for quite some time to come. British armored cars and mounted troops sent to dislodge them would find the attempt to recapture Siwa difficult going.

Meanwhile, the rest of the raiding force had made their way in ones and twos back toward the main Axis positions, attempting to spread more confusion in the process. The whole operation had been very risky, but results had far exceeded expectations.

This group of desert raiders even managed to disrupt some very ambitious raiding plans the British themselves were hatching from their new base at Jalo. However, perhaps the most significant achievement was damage to the British fighter force.

Italian Macchi 200 and 202 fighters and German Messerschmitt 110 fighters had been very successful in strafing attacks on two British airfields. Additionally, a small group of Italian Reggiane 2000 fighters had dropped small fragmentation bombs on parked rows of planes. All together, more than 80 British planes were put out of commission by these air raids in combination with the raids by Axis armored cars. This loss of fighter support would make it possible for Axis forces to hold their own in the skies and thus possibly save their frontier fortifications.

These raids focused a lot of attention on the successful intervention of Italian fighters. At a time when the air battle was still very much in doubt, they had helped shift the initiative to the Axis. After all was said and done and the range of the little Reggiane 2000 plane was known, other missions were planned and executed.

These missions, together with successful reconnaissance efforts prompted Heinz's request for more of these excellent little fighters. But instead, a complete Group of the upgraded version, Reggiane 2001 fighters, with a German engine, were sent to Africa.

November 29, 1941

Although Auchinleck was able to quickly assemble a force around XIII Corps, remnants of other units and spare tanks, it would not be enough. It had now become clear that estimated Axis tank losses had been overstated at the same time that Commonwealth tanks losses had been understated. Even Auchinleck knew he would be sending what amounted to an armored Brigade against three armored divisions and the balance of three Axis Corps.

If this force was destroyed, the way lay open to attack Egypt. He called Churchill to inform him of his decision. Loss of Tobruk would be a major blow felt all over the Empire. Without Tobruk as a base and the entire Axis army left undestroyed, the march to Tripoli could not be continued. For Auchinleck, one very upsetting turn of events was the damaging attacks on his forward fighter airfields and supply bases by Axis raiders from the air and ground.

Reports indicated attacks on these airfields had contained a number of Axis fighters. It now seemed possible that the Axis were receiving considerable aircraft reinforcements.

Auchinleck knew a potential challenge of allied air superiority could spell the doom of a battle of attrition and also could be a disaster for any proposed naval intervention. If this were true, ground forces would need to be pulled back while they could still be protected and not destroyed from the air.

###

Heinz could not help but be impressed with the Royal Air Force, they were a real threat, they were far more numerous, skilled and dangerous than their Russian counterparts. For not only were the British receiving American tanks and trucks but also numerous America planes.

At times, the sky seemed to be filled with enemy planes. If Axis forces wanted to advance further east, something must be done about the RAF. Keeping lines of communication open with the British superiority in the air would be difficult. Earlier in 1941 Rommel had suffered heavy losses from the RAF when he had led 21st PD across the Egyptian border.

However, there were limited airfields and facilities to support the large numbers of Axis planes that were arriving in North Africa. Heinz was informed that new Italian fighters performed extremely well during raids on British airfields. Some of these planes had even been rushed to the desert without the proper sand filter modifications, as the Italians had struggled to meet the crisis.

Engines of any type did not last long in the desert without proper filtration. Italians had learned this the hard way and even some German equipment had adopted specially developed Italian air filters. Therefore, they must retrofit these new Italian planes as soon as possible.

###

No one was physiologically prepared for Tobruk's loss after the fortress had been successfully held for so long. Even Churchill conceded that their remaining forces were not strong enough. Auchinleck's aids noticed that he was visibly shaken to learn the famous Panzer General Guderian had replaced Rommel as early as November 23. Here was the very German General who had run them out of France.

Additional Commonwealth units began receiving orders to move from the Middle East for defensive duties in Egypt. Churchill demanded a strong defense line be created at the Egyptian border all the way south to Fort Maddalena and planning should immediately begin for yet another new offensive. He also wanted Commonwealth troops to force the Axis to fight for every inch of ground as they retreated.

Auchinleck considered Churchill's request, but also insisted that Mersa Maruth, about 100 miles to the east be strengthened as a final defensive point to protect Egypt. Auchinleck did not inform Churchill that he had ordered additional defensive positions prepared even further east. Churchill began to consider if it was time again to change commanders. To preserve his political career, he now required a suitable scapegoat. He also figured it was an opportune time to ask for more American aid.

One More Hurdle

This was exactly the type of response Heinz wanted. The Axis had taken one day to reorganize, concentrate and rest before starting their dedicated Sollum front relief effort. Once they received verification that critical sections of Tobruk were firmly in Axis hands, armored forces would be free for more mobile action to the south. The road to Bardia was now open and Axis tanks began their trek down this road toward Sollum.

With less emphasis on Tobruk, much of Axis artillery was free to concentrate on the combined British force in the south. If the British had attempted this combined attack from the very first, it would have been successful. Now there was not a single British unit in the field that had not seen heavy action.

Many of their units had suffered severe losses and had been fighting continuously for many days. Soon, they would be facing the entire Axis army, less mostly Italian units and German engineers that were becoming firmly entrenched around Tobruk's holdouts in the western section of the fortress.

Eighth Army that had once been composed of two Corps with several brigades of armor was now three under-strength infantry divisions left with barely a full brigade of armor. Throughout the whole battle, the Axis had managed to fight and defeat one isolated Armor or Infantry Brigade after another.

Now British forces were faced by the better part of two German divisions, one Italian Infantry Corp, and a steadily increasingly strong concentration of heavy siege artillery that Heinz was now moving south. On their west flank was the balance of Italian XX Corps and moving toward their rear on their east flank was what was left of German armor.

With their lines of communication in doubt and their supply dumps raided, their current position seemed clearly untenable. Catching sight of the still existing Panzers bearing down on them was simply too much for

British rank and file. They had their own take on how their battle plans were working out.

One New Zealand private's take on the situation captured the feeling of many.

"Where had these tanks come from? We were told that they had all been destroyed over four days ago. Where are all our tanks? Our tanker chaps are useless; we are going to get smacked again by these bloody Jerrys. I will never trust those tankers to take care of my skin again. Bloody incompetence. Just look at all those Jerry tanks; well I guess we will at least go out fighting."

Heinz knew if he committed his remaining tanks to block a British retreat, his loses could be very high. At present he didn't have sufficient fuel to chase them back to Egypt in force and RAF planes would probably destroy most of his vehicles in the first 50 km even if he tried.

Moreover, reports of strong resistance at Sidi Omar were coming in. His troops were exhausted and even if he managed to capture additional British supplies, shortages would still hamper combat effectiveness. Heinz could sense that neither his German nor his Italian units had much fight left in them.

Nevertheless, every effort must be made to separate the British from their heavy weapons and supplies. Of special importance were damaged and broken down tanks, which appeared to be everywhere. By doing this, it would interfere with British ability to quickly mount another major offensive. For Heinz knew his units would require much time to replace their supplies used in the extended and heavy fighting. Consequently, the British were to be gently nudged down the road with German and Italian armor nipping at their flanks.

However, Auchinleck's decision to hold Sidi Omar put a stop to this plan. Their Indian division had been reinforced and was putting returning stragglers facing forward again, attempting to form a solid line from the coast to Sidi Omar.

Sidi Omar

Heinz did not really want to invest Sidi Omar. However, if he was to save the brave defenders of Sidi Omar, there was no choice. They had defeated Eighth Army, but would not be able to destroy it. If Axis forces could reclaim Sidi Omar, their previously strong defensive line facing the British could be reestablished.

Heinz was having difficulty concentrating the forces under his control. Their dreadful communications situation after loss of Africa Korps Headquarters was still having a telling effect on coordination of any kind of offensive operations. Also, captured Tobruk supplies would at most provide only a temporary respite from the overall supply drought and then only in certain categories.

From a quick analysis, Heinz's forces now possessed an abundance of artillery. They had started the battle with over 1140 serviceable guns of various sorts; most of these guns had survived and were still usable. The British had initially brought over 1000 guns and 900 mortars to the battle; however, many of their guns were now destroyed or in Axis hands. If the skies could be made safe from RAF planes, a lot of this artillery could be moved to the Egyptian Libyan border. Then, if enough ammunition could be located and transported for the long-range artillery, they could pound Sidi Omar to dust.

At the very least, if the British continued to hold Sidi Omar they would succeed in saving the rump of Eighth Army. An all out attack on Sidi Omar might simply give the British a rallying point. However, with confusion reining on the battlefield perhaps other softer targets could be attacked to keep the British from becoming too comfortable.

A heavy Axis attack from the air was totally out of the question. Therefore, a quick direct assault could probably only be accomplished by again relying on captured Matildas. Once again, if they could get enough of these tanks running, they might just pull it off, but time was running out. Scarcely more than a company of German and Italian soldiers survived at Sidi Omar, but it was a tough group committed to following orders. So far, this brave company had managed to hold out against almost a whole British division with armor support.

Chapter 12

The Tables Are Turned

Remaining German tanks were putting up a good fight on the far southeast flank, avoiding any serious attempt to completely surround the enemy which might destroy their remaining armor. Also, if his armor moved from their present position there was a chance the British could again move to cut off Axis coastal positions or further envelop Sidi Omar.

Heinz hoped they could produce panic without risking further significant losses, but regardless they must maintain possession of the battlefield. The British were retreating with enough troops. If they were able to gain access to a large portion of their battlefield damaged tanks, vehicles and supplies they could once again pose an offensive threat in the very near future.

Crete Swap

When Heinz had asked Hitler for control of Crete forces, it had not been for the purpose of having a place to ship some of his excess infantry and prisoners. For now, Heinz felt comfortable considering immediately moving at least one Italian Infantry division to Crete, although he intended to keep most of their artillery regiment in Africa.

Officially, two German divisions were responsible for occupying Crete. They were 164th, an Infantry Division and Fifth Mountain Division, which was still being rebuilt after losses suffered during capture of this same island in May. Heinz had no use for Fifth Mountain in Africa, but he did not want to lose control of this well respected elite unit.

Heinz decided to loan this unit to General von Manstein, who was desperate for addition troops for his attack on Sevastopol. A huge manpower drain that was the eastern front was beginning to become a problem that would reach catastrophic proportions. As an additional benefit, he would supply Fifth Mountain with some spare specialized equipment and troops that would aid Manstein's assault on Sevastopol. In return, he would try and convince von Manstein to trade him 22nd Division, which had been trained for air landing assaults.

Africa Strategy

Clearly, Germany's strategic direction was lacking in outlying areas like the Mediterranean. Waiting until the situation became critical and then overreacting played right into your enemy's hands. With the massive territory the Germans had conquered, all the British had to do was raid the edges to cause shifting of precious resources.

It was worse than a two front war. Overreaction in Africa drew resources away from the major effort, which was now Russia. Well, two could play that game, the British also had interests scattered throughout the Mediterranean and Africa. For the time being they must remain on the defensive, but they could not afford to let the British control the initiative.

Although fuel and trucks were always critical, they were not the immediate need. Fuel stores and transportation were adequate for a stagnant defense of North Africa. Ammunition and artillery were currently the issue. Axis artillery ammunition had never been abundant in Africa and it was certainly no better after the recent fighting.

Therefore, priority was given to recovering from the battlefield and Tobruk all British 25-pounder ammunition. They would attempt to exclusively use these captured guns on their former owners. If Heinz's staff could find an alternate supply route for a few critical items, they could keep Italian naval ships in port and give Malta defenders no nighttime activity.

Right now, the Mediterranean was full of British planes, ships and submarines. Soon Sicily would be full of German planes. A major Luftwaffe and Kriegsmarine effort would be directed at this hornet's nest. It would be desirable to turn their Island Fortress into a trap. With their bases and naval capability, the British could always threaten an amphibious assault anywhere in the Mediterranean.

Change of Fortunes

Ober lieutenant Erbo Graf von Kageneck(3) had been inspecting his fighter Group's auxiliary fuel tanks on their brand new Messerschmitt-109F fighters went he got word that they would not be going to Africa after all. Instead, their place in Africa was to be taken by an influx of new Italian fighters. Since some of these Italian fighters would have to be removed from Sicily, von Kageneck's *Gruppe* would stay in Sicily to replace them.

Instead, von Kageneck's *Gruppe* together with Headquarters of JG 27(Fighter Wing 27) were ordered to start their own personal war against the Fortress of Malta. With capture of Tobruk intense pressure due to possible loss of the Axis African Army had lessened.

However, this Army could still be lost if a reliable stream of supplies could not be maintained. For this reason, it was considered more critical that von Kageneck's unit remain on Sicily until the bulk of Second Air fleet arrived.

Almost all of Luftflotte II had been slated for Mediterranean service and Kesselring had Malta in his sights. Unfortunately, they would not be anywhere near full strength until later in December. That's where Erbo's unit came in. The battle hardened III./JG 27 (Third Group of Fighter Wing 27) had an excellent record in Russia, claiming the destruction of no less than 224 Russian aircraft in four months of fighting.

Wearing Oak Leaves to the Knight's Cross around his neck, Erbo's own personal career score was 65. His Third Group had left the Russian front in mid October for re-equipping with the latest Model of Messerschmitt109, the F series. Messerschmitt-109F was Messerschmitt's latest attempt to breathe new life into an aging airframe. British fighter pilots on Malta were going to be in for a shock.

Erbo was glad his Group was not returning to Russian. To him, despite his success and increasing fame, there was something disconcerting about the nature of fighting taking place in Russia. It seemed the deeper they traveled into Russia the worse he felt about the whole situation.

He could not see the brutality isolated high above the battlefields in his Messerschmitt, but he had heard the rumors about what occurred on the front lines and in the rear areas. Now they were being diverted to Sicily instead of Africa. He had been stationed on Sicily before earlier in the year. He could abide Italians and maybe look up some old friends. Here everyone was chivalrous, even the enemy. Yes, this new assignment was definitely more to his liking; he would try and make the most of it.

(3) Erbo Graf von Kageneck (Erbo) – Exceptional fighter "*Experten*" pilot transferred to Africa from Russia with 65 confirmed Russian "kills" in a vain effort to stem the tide of the "Crusader" battle. Von Kageneck was one of the first Russian Front *Experten* hastily transferred from Russia who was killed in combat shortly after he arrived in Africa, but he was not the last as the pattern repeated itself numerous times. He died 12 Jan

42 from wounds received in combat on 24 Dec 41 during "Operation Crusader."

###

Some Luftwaffe attacks had occurred on the Sollum front; but were restricted by heavy British fighter aircraft presence. As the major fighting slowly moved south, some enterprising Luftwaffe pilots were using the hard surfaced Bardia road as a temporary airfield. Remaining German Messerschmitt 109 fighters were taking a heavy toll, cutting Commonwealth fighters and bombers to pieces but the contest was far from decided. Although word was leaking out about the successful capture of Tobruk, Guderian continued to send urgent pleas for fuel and additional fighter support.

It seemed to Heinz as though the situation on the ground here was very similar to Russia. Here, in Africa, it was heavy Matilda and Valentine tanks, in Russia it was the heavy KV and fast T-34 tanks. At least here his German tanks, anti-tank guns, and even Italian M13/40 tanks had a chance against most of the lighter British and American tanks in the open desert.

November 30, 1941 – Halafaya Pass

Heinz wanted to personally meet the famous Pastor of Halafaya who had won the Knight's Cross by capturing the pass and then defended it successfully twice against British attacks. This man was a mere major, an older Reserve Officer, yet he was the nominal commander of the entire border area.

"Well Major Bach, or should I call you Pastor? It seems you and your troops eluded British capture one more time and now except for Sidi Omar we are about to send them back to their starting point. Therefore, we must first run them out of Sidi Omar and rescue our brave lads who are holding on by their fingernails. I hear you are becoming somewhat of a legend to the British. Sorry, we had to leave you on your own for a few days."

"Herr Generaloberst, Major is fine or if you prefer, Wilheim. Here at the pass there was little danger, we have enough effective guns and defenses to hold against just about anything the British could throw against us, except perhaps battleships. Still, our boys and Italian troops had it pretty rough, especially at Sidi Omar and Sollum. As you know the British Indian Division managed to swing around and hit the Omars from the backside. Here, we could have held longer, if need be. As you say currently the only serious issue left is Sidi Omar. We made them pay dearly for what they captured and now with some help we intend to take that back.

We have established contact with 12th Oasis Company and they are directing some of our heavy artillery fire against the Indian positions, but I don't know how much longer they can hold out.

If we had more heavy guns we just might be able to convince the Indian troops to leave without a costly assault. However, these Indian troops have quite a lot of artillery themselves. I understand a very successful raid was just conducted on the British southern flank to help with their decision process."

"Yes, you are correct Wilheim, very pleasing results and quite a shock to the Tommies. Those crazy *Brandenbergers* with 361st Regiment have really turned the tables on the British. We are trying every trick we can to make it difficult for the British to hold on to Sidi Omar. From what I have been told they still have our minefields and obstacles to their back and that will make it difficult to supply and reinforce their position. However, if we give them more time they will solve these problems,

By the way, we are still checking your report we received concerning a large explosion on the 25th; our Kriegsmarine gentlemen are warming to the idea that the English Navy may have lost a major vessel to one of our U-boats. That is possibly why we have not recently seen their battleships put in an appearance. I would have thought our attack on Tobruk would have brought them out of port.

We may know more if we can get some reconnaissance aircraft back over Alexandria, but our U-boats have been put on high alert for any attempts to rescue those defenders of Tobruk who have not surrendered. When those battleships leave Alexandria, we should worry. At this point, I am not sure what is left of our aircraft or the Italian Battlefleet could rescue us. We are still not in a very good position sitting across the Mediterranean on this piece of sand.

On another subject, I am most impressed by your defenses here. Everywhere I look I see German, Italian, French and British equipment all put to brilliant use. Initiatives such as these have really been on my mind. Your fortifications here are very impressive and what you have accomplished with mixed German and Italian troops continues to be impressive. I certainly would not want to try and take this pass from you. Are the British as well dug-in on the coast road down below you?"

"Herr Generaloberst, with help from Italians and using their equipment, we have learned how to make the best use of what the good Lord has provided. Our supplies always seem to be meager, but we have received some help from the British from time to time. On the British side, they do not have the excellent ground we have to work with here.

Down below us (sweeping with his right hand) the coast road is located on a narrow stretch of land but significant reinforcements and their major airfields at Sidi Barrani are only a short distance away by air. One would first have to get through mines British sappers (combat engineers) have planted and their defenses. Furthermore, we know their airfields at Sidi Barrani are important to supplying Malta; the British would commit all they have to prevent their capture.

I wouldn't doubt that they would even send their battleships to take care of any advances we would try on the coastal road; it could be a nasty business indeed if not executed perfectly. Also, the last time General Rommel crossed the border above the escarpment (again sweeping with his hand in the direction of the open desert) my unit, 21st PD suffered a lot of losses from RAF ground attack aircraft. Even here at the pass we still have casualties from numerous British planes, despite a good stock of anti-aircraft guns. We were overjoyed to again see even a few German fighters in the skies above us again."

"Believe it or not, Wilheim, those are mostly new Italian fighters that made it out this far. So, now we have a battlefield full of all kinds of equipment and a need to have an even tougher defense to stop Tommies the next time they try and take Tobruk back. I have decided your next job, *Oberst* Bach (Heinz had wanted to size up the man before making the promotion official), is to make a Halafaya Pass out of our front facing the British and help with the defense of our open desert flank.

I want you to explore any new weapons that would help us in our next fight with the British. Berlin is in overdrive, but it seems like no one is talking to each other to come up with new widely applicable practical technical solutions.

Moreover, your unique use of Italian and British equipment to enhance this position's defensive and anti-tank capability should become standard practice by both us and the Italians. Incidentally, your new promotion comes with a Regimental command, but one that you will have to build from scratch. You being a man of faith, I have a vision for the Mediterranean and our Italian allies and I believe it can be accomplished with your help and guidance."

"That is all well and good Herr Generaloberst. However, if we want to hang onto Tobruk, we had better do something about the Royal Navy and the RAF."

"Well said, we of course will need some help with that one. In fact I would consider trying to ship supplies to us more dangerous business than kicking each other around in this desert. We held our own on the ground, but the British planes and ships may kill us yet. I think we can eventually do some good in the air, but with Malta and the Royal Navy we still have our hands full.

I worry about the intelligence in this theater. The British are good, but not that good. We are obtaining a lot of good intelligence ourselves, but it seems the "Tommies" know our actions almost before we do. We must try and stay one step ahead of them. One thing is for sure; we cannot hope to survive on Kesselring's air transports alone and now we have British prisoners to feed."

"Herr Generaloberst, there is a possible alternative for some of our food needs, if we can keep the Arabs and British out of Italian colonialist's gardens and orchards. I hear the French are willing to provide some food and other technical non-military material. Moreover, I would say our first need is to drop our troop levels to reduce our overall supply needs. If we play our cards right, we could almost live off the land on this side of the Mediterranean.

However, if you want someone skilled at building permanent defenses, I am afraid you are not looking to the right individual. Although we cannot afford to give up this pass, I believe as you do that we Germans hold our greatest advantage on a mobile battlefield. I am a *Panzertruppen* first."

"Naturally I agree Wilhelm, but I believe that the fate of our country will be decided in Russia, not here. Few if any new offensive weapons will be forthcoming from Germany for us. This is only right, especially with Tobruk now almost under our control. We will become an afterthought to the real struggle while the British will continue to rebuild their forces to protect Malta and Egypt.

Thus their efforts will probably intensify to try and get us to draw down our forces from Russia and elsewhere. However, we may be able to obtain some Russian and more French equipment to make out chance of survival greater."

"Herr Generaloberst, regardless of how we do it, I do not think we will survive here long taking a strictly defensive approach and letting the initiative pass to the British."

"Well Wilhelm, you are probably right, but I still believe you are the man for the job and suggest you begin your plan as soon as we conclude this business with Sidi Omar. I just know I will be impressed by what you can scrape off of the desert floor. The British will have left a few treasures among all the refuse, after all they left us quite a lot of usable equipment in France."

December 2, 1941– Sidi Omar

Once again Gian and his crews were asked to crawl into captured Matildas. German and Italian defenders of Sidi Omar could simply hold out no longer. Some supplies and a few reinforcements had made it to the holdouts, but this was barely enough to cover daily usage and losses.

Auchinleck knew they would have to make major shifts in their defensive line if the two Omar strong points could not be held. However, by now, his Indian troops were almost as bad off as 12th Oasis Company and the few remaining Italian survivors. A full attack could not be avoided, as the British might soon succeed in breaking into the Omars from the eastern side.

Accurate Axis counter-battery fire knocked out many of the defender's artillery pieces, but they had been well supplied with a good portion of Eighth Army's medium batteries. Also they were supported by artillery fire from other commonwealth units firing from the east.

All Matildas that could be gotten in running order would lead the Axis relief effort. These lead tanks were backed up by all Panzer IV tanks and flame throwing small tanks that could be scraped to together. Panzer IV tanks were to destroy identified Commonwealth anti-tank guns as these Matilda tanks charged forward.

This plan worked well. As the Matildas plowed forward, both Omars were taken. But losses in attacking Axis infantry were high as desperate Commonwealth artillery doing its deadly work tore bodies apart. It was the highest daily total of Axis killed and wounded for all of Crusader and as always with artillery; many of the wounded were horribly maimed.

Enough mines were still present to limit the speed with which attackers could enter the strong points. This increased the time Axis infantry spent under intense shelling. Many attacking tanks were damaged and would take considerable time to repair.

Heinz's German guns could ill afford another heavy expenditure of artillery ammunition; therefore, much of the final effort was executed using Italian artillery. Still, it was a victory and took away the last and only real significant gain Commonwealth forces had achieved during Operation Crusader.

It was a bitter pill to swallow for the British and of course someone must answer for this final defeat in a succession of failures. With surrender of the Omars, guns on both sides fell nearly silent as it was left to medical personnel to try and help relieve the suffering.

###

For the first time Gian experienced crushing human beings underneath his tank treads. With no other tanks to target, his Matilda 2-pounder tank gun proved almost useless in the desperate struggle. They ran out of ammunition for the single turret machine gun the Matilda contained. In desperation they exhausted their internal supply of grenades. Consequently, they then resorted to shooting at Commonwealth Infantry and Artillery with solid armored piercing rounds. If the 2-pounder had been able to shoot an effective high explosive (HE) rounds, fighting for the interior of the Omars would have gone much quicker. The exterior of their Matilda was a disaster, but somehow Gian and his crew had survived.

It appeared that some Indian Division soldiers were able to make their escape to their own lines with little to fear from the Matilda's useless main gun. Indian soldiers had acquitted themselves well, but their two brigades were no more. With their lives, they had bought time for their comrades to establish new defensive positions.

By controlling the Omars, they prevented an Axis pursuit of any kind as Commonwealth forces executed Operation Crusader in reverse. Up until this point, this Indian Division had been the only Commonwealth division involved in Crusader that had not experienced significant losses at the hands of Axis forces. Not only had this Division experienced personnel losses, but they also left on the battlefield equipment of all kinds, including heavy guns and tanks.

###

So this is what real victory felt like, the British kicked back into Egypt. Gian did not want his men to see him shaking, so he jumped out of the Matilda and immediately headed for the Italian and German survivors of the Sidi Omar siege. He felt doubly fortunate that these German defenders had not shot at his Matilda with their 88s and other heavy guns. Relief clearly visible on the faces of these Germans and Italians that the nightmare was over brought a welcome smile to all involved in the liberation of the two Omars.

Showing the strain of recent days, rescued Germans still expressed surprise when they discovered that it was Italians operating British tanks that had saved them. An opportune picture of this incident would provide Italians with a little propaganda of their own. Looking back, Gian felt they had accomplished quite a bit with these captured Matildas.

Standing beside his tank amid at all the death and destruction, he happily noted that neither he nor any of his crews had a scratch on them. He wondered, could these Matildas be modified to provide a better main gun? He had still not gotten his full quota of revenge on the British Empire.

##

In Heinz's mind the Omar assault justified his future plans. If he could get some decent armor and equipment into the hands of the better Italian troops they could hold their own against the British. Ultimately this must happen, for Germany was not in a good position to continue to pour more and more extensive resources into saving the Italian Empire. Yet survive it must. His African troops needed to come up with tactical and technical changes to keep the British off balance and if possible hold on to the initiative.

These Italian successes continued as promises of Italian captivity with a quick prisoner exchange lured exhausted Tobruk Czech, Polish and Commonwealth troops to surrender. Thus, hands were raised in Tobruk and then in the far desert to the southwest as lack of reinforcements and supplies also convinced the isolated third and last Indian Brigade troops not to fight to the death.

Chapter 13

Back to Russia

December 4, 1941 - Panzergroup Africa Headquarters

Heinz wasted no time in setting his agenda for the African Theater of war. He opened his first staff meeting after recapture of the Omars by saying.

"Because of our defeat of a large portion of British Eighth Army and the fall of Tobruk we find ourselves with an abundance of equipment in certain regards. There is also the matter of our comrades in Russia who are suffering from a lack of everything. I have a preliminary agreement with General Manstein for exchanges that I believe are of mutual benefit. I have received approval from Headquarters to immediately begin this program.

Von Manstein's Eleventh Army will help us recover Russian tanks from their battlefields and in return they will receive replacement tanks that had been promised to us. Eleventh Army currently has no tanks. I need you to cooperate in every way possible with these efforts which should substantially aid both our forces.

For the time being, many panzer tank crews whose tanks are currently undergoing repairs will be rotated out of Africa and flown to the Crimea to familiarize themselves with their new equipment. My intent is to move the flag of 21st PD to the Crimea from Africa. Some of our experienced African P*anzertroopen* will provide foundational staff for this division. It turns out our Africa Korps was allocated enough tanks, vehicles and artillery, including 88 mm guns, to equip this division in Russia.

We will be reforming and outfitting our remaining troops. I want to integrate battle-experienced troops into our remaining Italian and German divisions to the greatest extent possible. We will need to train new crews from among existing troops already in Africa on captured tanks, both those currently in Africa and on those we may soon receive from Russia. Training will be difficult with limited fuel, but we will do our best. I hate to interfere with unit integrity, but our countries have been placed in unique and demanding circumstances. We must all rise to the occasion."

Heinz paused briefly as he surveyed the room and examined the expressions on the faces of his staff.

"Both Italian and German Intelligence sources indicate that they doubt the British will not have sufficient resources to launch another major offensive again until some of their losses are made good. For the short term, we will be able to field more tanks and perhaps more artillery than they can. Sooner or later they will come again or we will be forced to attack them. I personally give us four to five months to prepare for the next engagement.

I want to procure heavy Russian tanks for shipment to Africa. There is simply no German manpower available in Russia to collect and repair all the Russian equipment that is available. The very poor effectiveness of Italian armor will be my major argument. By the same token, if something is not done quickly to collect these massive amounts of equipment in Russia; then their partisans in our rear areas will procure it for their own means or even render it unusable.

I know this may come as a surprise to all of you. Perhaps our German technology and production will catch up, but should we stake the lives of our troops on it? Not only will this be difficult, it will further dilute our experience level. We will also face transportation concerns and many training issues.

Supporting this large army requires significant resources. With Tobruk and Sidi Omar recaptured and our excellent border defenses, we no longer need a large investing army. I am recommending that most non-motorized troops be moved out of Africa, absent most of their artillery regiments.

With Italian help, phase one of this exchange can begin immediately using air transport alone on normally empty supply return flights. Use of our equipment and spare troops may help free Eleventh Army troops to quickly capture Sevastopol. The Panzer troops can train on new equipment and provide reserves until Eleventh Army receives its newly created Panzer Division in March."

##

This was only part of Heinz's plans to take a systematic and strategic approach to eliminating the British from the Mediterranean. His first step was to secure air space over his forces and their supply routes. For the time being he could do without one Group of German Stukas pilots. Italian pilots would temporarily take over their planes.

This Group of Stuka pilots would train with troops in the Crimea and could assist in the capture of Sevastopol. They were to be given the latest type of aircraft. Italian Stuka forces were to be expanded using trained Italian pilots. All these Stuka forces would eventually be needed for the invasion of Malta, but for now they needed to be divided between Africa, Sicily, and the Crimea.

Because of the success of Italian torpedo planes, he requested that more of these be stationed in North Africa together with as many of the new Italian fighter planes as could be freed from attacks on Malta. He wanted to build a very mobile, but very fuel-efficient force. Currently, the main goals of the aviation assets stationed in North Africa were continued attrition of the RAF and preventing supply convoys reaching Malta. Heinz further stipulated:

"I propose our German Divisions began to adopt captured British 25-pounders for general artillery use. We should also reuse British 2-pounder anti-tank guns which would normally be discarded. However, the British 2-pounder still has some use in this Theater, especially if we can give it a facelift.

Our operations to clear the south desert continue to go well. For the time being, captured British equipment is providing good service in ridding our right flank of the ubiquitous British scout cars. As you are aware, because of significant issues with Russian tanks, our own panzers are being upgraded.

I challenge all of you to suggest possible alternatives to making our stock of captured British tanks more reliable and combat usable. Especially since our homeland is now shipping anti-tank guns intended for Africa to our hard pressed comrades facing the Russians. You are dismissed. Colonel Bach, please remain."

"Well Wilheim I believe we have a good plan in place, but because of the terrible situation in Russia we must make do with Italian equipment and captured cast-offs. That is why I need you here and will not allow you to accompany your comrades to Russia."

"I am, of course, prepared to do what is deemed best for us to survive this war, Herr Generaloberst."

"Still, I would assume that you would rather be fighting Communist Atheists than these Christian British?"

"Generaloberst, I am not so sure that Atheist is the right term to describe the Communists we face in Russia. Did you know Stalin was once a Seminary student?"

"Yes Wilheim, I have heard that – hard to believe. If not Atheist, what term would you use to describe how these Communists view God?"

"Herr Generaloberst, Perhaps the more correct Biblical term was used by the Apostle Paul. I believe the Communist leadership is composed of *God Haters*. From my own experiences the most fervently declared Atheists are really not neutral in their feelings about God.
For various reasons they are angry with God and refuse to accept his judgments and the condition of the world he has created. They fail to realize that the evil present in this world is the result of actions of sinful men, not God. Even some of our esteemed leaders might fit into this category. They seem to want to reengineer the world based upon race."

"Well Wilheim, I did not intend to get you all tied up in a religious discussion. However, the awful reality of where this war is taking us would just about bring anyone to look beyond themselves to make sense of it all. Perhaps we will have extended time in the future for such conversations or should we call them confessions."

"Generaloberst, I hope I do not say anything that I could be arrested for and embarrass Africa Korps, but perhaps it would be the most honorable course of action. There are men in my civilian profession that are openly defiant of our leadership and are suffering serious consequences for their outspoken behavior. A number do not equate love of Germany with love of Hitler's policies."

"There should be no fear of that; private conversations among my staff officers stay that way. Your life is in my hands and mine is in yours. Surely we should travel the road to the abyss as brothers my dear Wilheim? Besides, I would never doubt the patriotism of a holder of the Knight's Cross."

Heinz stepped even closer to Wilheim and lowered his voice somewhat.

"Believe it or not I have heard a lot worse from many who would like a change of leadership. All of it is just talk. Our esteemed leader covers his tracks well; power could not be easily taken from him. He does not possess your religious conscious when dealing with his enemies or those he chooses to hate.

God only knows what all he has done. However, I have yet to hear any viable plan that allows us to exit this war with our honor as soldiers or provides suitable justification for radical action justifiable to the Germany people. Maybe God will eventually open a door for us so that a change can be made, but for now we just do our duty as best we can."

New Technology

December 6, 1941 – Rome, Italy – High level secret discussion among several Senior Italian Staff Naval Officers

"Preliminary investigations into the mysterious electronic equipment found at Tobruk lead us to believe it is a powerful British radar device. It is able to identify ships and planes on the open water for quite some distance." One Italian Commander reported.

"This could explain the destruction of our MAS units during their raid on Malta and our continued disappointing naval losses during night actions in the Mediterranean"; retorted another senior officer.

"Shocking - most shocking", chimed in another Italian Naval Commander.

"Yes, I mentioned this discovery to my German Liaison Officer counterpart and he immediately requested permission to be allowed to examine the equipment."

"A workable device based on this technology explains our terrible loss and humiliation at the Battle of Cape Matapan and possibly many other naval losses. We must investigate this further. To go to sea at night with the British possessing such a working weapon would be suicide. We must form a group of experts to examine and to see how quickly we can copy this technology."

"Indeed, in its current location we can study it and use it to forewarn Tobruk of impending British attacks." ....As their discussion moved around the table of officers.

"Absolutely, if we can keep it running? However, it must be copied immediately and countermeasures developed. Everyone who is aware of this discovery must be sworn to secrecy. Perhaps an immediate transfer of all knowledgeable Army individuals out of Africa is in order."

December 7, 1941 - Shock for Malta

Third Group's commander, Erbo Graf von Kageneck was unsure this was worth the effort. Bomb carrying fighters must fly low and maintain their speed in order to avoid detection by Malta's radar and have a chance of surviving the island's intensive anti-aircraft fire. Attacking from the west with a setting sun, barely 45 minutes was allocated for the first raid from start to finish. Moreover, prior to dropping their bombs, all fighters were to split up and strafe Malta's airfields.

Third Group of 27th Fighter Wing (III./JG 27) was an experienced fighter group. They had been in the process of moving to Africa; instead they were given orders to divert to Sicily. Just after arrival in Sicily their accompanying Wing headquarters section had been issued a tall order; devise a plan to shut down Malta. With less than 40 serviceable planes, few ground services and fewer supplies; it seemed an impossible task.

Once their arrival was noticed, Erbo knew their airfields would have the undivided attention of all British planes stationed on the island. Their only hope was to strike hard and keep striking to minimize their own chance of destruction. They were to work in concert with German Third Motor Torpedo Boat Flotilla who was to begin nightly mining operations against Malta's harbor at Valetta. Destruction of a cruiser and destroyer force stationed in Malta was deemed first priority. This force threatened Axis ships traveling on a newly established supply route to Benghazi in North Africa.

Instead of attacking immediately, Twenty Seventh Wing Headquarters instead began to plan for a lengthy campaign to bring Malta to its knees. They would first obtain all information they could from the Italians about the island itself and its defenders' habits. Normally, they would first gain and keep air superiority. Then, they would target naval activity.

An emergency shipment of bombs suitable for their fighters was requested so that naval vessels and other selected targets could be attacked.

However, they soon were made aware that all necessary bombs, fuel and equipment they needed were sitting in either ships or Italian warehouses near at hand awaiting transport to Africa. Although this material, especially the fuel, was desperately needed in Africa, it seemed the whole Mediterranean was full of British planes, ships and submarines through which no ship could safely pass.

Consequently, they quickly obtained approval to have some of this material shipped straight to Sicily. Although it would take some time to be able to fully utilize this material, it would provide an excellent base of aviation resources for a renewed campaign against Malta.

Third Group of 27th Fighter Wing's new Messerschmitt-109F fighters had been fitted to carry an external fuel tank for the trip across the Mediterranean. This same attachment point could be used alternately to carry a large single bomb. Low flying fighter-bomber raids were proving somewhat successful against England even in the face of extensive anti-aircraft defensive measures. Accordingly, these tactics were to be duplicated against Malta. When using these tactics Third Group would be joined by elements of JG 53's Jabo or fighter-bomber section, an additional recent arrival to Sicily.

Soon portions of other Luftwaffe elements began to arrive, especially more fighters belonging to JG 53. All told, they could now count on parts of five Groups of fighters scattered around Sicilian airfields. If all fighter Groups had been at full strength they should have had over 150 Messerschmitt fighters. If properly handled, just these fighters attacking by themselves might deal a telling blow to Malta. Even with the short range of their Messerschmitt fighters, being located only 60 miles from Sicily made a damaging fighter raid against Malta very feasible. Of course absolute and complete surprise for the first attack was paramount.

Most of JG 27 and JG 53's fighter pilots had not had much training dropping bombs. For inspiration, they were reminded of very successful efforts by Me-109 pilots during the invasion of Crete. These fighter pilots had even managed to sink a British cruiser and damage other vessels, including a British Battleship. A suitable bay with a "volunteer" Italian torpedo boat was found for practice attack flights and JG 53's fighter bombers took the lead role in instructing the rest of the pilots in proper bombing techniques. More promising pilots demonstrating some aptitude for bombing were identified from these training trials to be the ones designated to target the British ships.

Timing was extremely important; the last rays of the winter sun would be used to guide these planes back to their scattered airfields in Sicily. On landing, planes were to be quickly camouflaged and prepped for the next day's fight. There was immediate danger from Malta nightfighters bent on revenge as well as daylight raids the following morning. Every subsequent day was expected to produce a new set of tasks.

##

After all the planning and training, it seemed to Erbo that their bombing efforts had been a waste of time and resources. Out of all the bombs dropped, their Messerschmitt 109 fighters had not scored a single hit on any British warship. Even though their strafing runs had successfully damaged several aircraft on the ground, they appeared to have done no damage to the targeted cruisers, destroyers, and submarines.

But Erbo was mistaken; a near miss underwater could cause serious damage to naval vessels, especially to thinly armored cruisers and destroyers. With several wounded sailors, the cruiser *Neptune* began taking on water so badly she had to be beached to avoid sinking completely.

Another cruiser and destroyer would require repairs and could not make full speed. Furthermore a couple of "stray" bombs also caused damage to the important dock facilities, including the very important fuel transfer lines and their pumps. Secondary fires caused further damage and fuel loss. Thus overall damage temporarily put a halt to the very successful Malta cruiser raids.

Moreover, their fighter raid's shock effect prevented any immediate response; only one Messerschmitt 109 fighter failed to return and that pilot was later plucked from the sea by an Italian rescue aircraft. With the last rays of the sun fading in the west they touched down in Sicily. Erbo was the last to land, but they did not appear to have been followed. That night, no one in Malta took notice of additional mines laid by Third German MTB Flotilla.

Next day, the real fight began. All day long German fighters took turns over Malta, returning to Sicily only to rearm and refuel. Any British fighters that made it into the air where quickly dealt with; for the day, Erbo accounted for three of them. Following their routine, at the end of the day German planes dispersed to their selected airfields on Sicily. They waited for night bombers from Malta, who were expected to return the favor. This night several planes did come, but none of their fighters were located.

Repeated high speed strafing runs had left their mark on the three main airfields. Soon even more German planes would be filling up Sicilian airfields as the rested and refurbished fighter and bomber units made their way from Germany. However, Mediterranean weather did not always cooperate with either side's plans and few days were actually suitable for additional raids as December came to a close.

Part V

HITLER'S NEW ENEMIES

Chapter 14

Japan Strikes

U-Boat Commitment

After Tobruk's fall and Germany's Russian invasion turning into a nightmare of snow and blood; Hitler began to lose some interest in the Mediterranean. As all eyes were turned to Russia, he began considering a reduction of his promised Luftwaffe commitment to the Mediterranean Theater.

Furthermore, Admiral Raeder began to question Hitler's proposed large Mediterranean U-boat commitment which did not now seem appropriate. With the change in the tactical situation, lack of suitable facilities and other concerns expressed by his Admiral Donitz, pressure was mounting to reduce the number of boats preparing to make passage into the Mediterranean.

Moreover even Heniz himself recognized the significance of the British western Mediterranean fortress port of Gibraltar as a supply conduit to Malta and a potential base to invade French North Africa. Indeed, this scenario was a recognized threat to any Army operating in North Africa, especially in conjunction with strong support from Malta. The British had no problem whatsoever killing Frenchmen if it suited their needs.

Therefore, Heinz also began to feel that Donitz's U-boats might more effectively be used to blockade naval traffic from the Atlantic side of Gibraltar. And he was even more concerned with British reinforcements entering the eastern Mediterranean by way of the Suez Canal. He would soon learn that the British were even receiving supplies by way of a road that transversed all of central Africa from west to east.

Rommel had originally talked Hitler into agreeing to divert a significant number of U-boats to block British supply traffic into Tobruk; now this was no longer necessary. Another shared concern was a possible British invasion of French North Africa to trap Axis forces and regain complete control of the Mediterranean. Recently, U-boats sent to the Mediterranean had already made their presence felt by sinking a British Carrier and more recently a Battleship along with some other vessels.

Moreover, Admiral Raeder expressed his opinion that his Third MTB (Motor Torpedo Boat) Flotilla, together with the Luftwaffe and Italians, could accomplish the immediate mining of Malta. Raeder was never one to pass up an opportunity to mine anything. These mines would provide a final obstacle to isolate Malta if British supply ships were able to make it past other Axis forces.

Italians felt that emergency supplies and removal of POWs could be taken care of with their fast cruisers and air transport, avoiding some of the risk due to British submarines and aircraft. After discovery of a British radar installation in Tobruk, Italians realized the grave danger they faced in night naval actions. Appropriate responses to this discovery were now being considered by *Commando Supremo*.

By prior agreement, Italians retained custody of all POWs. Larger convoys would soon be necessary to supply Africa, but it was hoped that they would stand a better chance during the historically bad weather month of January. Also, by that time the Axis expected to have made some progress in elimination of the significant threat that Malta's resident forces posed to supply of Africa.

For the time being, some U-boats already in the Mediterranean would be stationed to defend Tobruk and other Axis North African ports from British Navy surface vessels. They would thus maintain approximately the same stations on the North African coast. This would protect the Axis Desert Army's exposed Mediterranean flank. Additionally, there was to be more frequent communication between the Luftwaffe and U-boats to include sharing of reconnaissance information.

This adjustment to U-boats dispositions also addressed the difficulty U-Boats were experiencing during passage through the Strait of Gibraltar. Since Gibraltar was such a problem, Heinz requested U-Boats and Italian submarines maintain a commitment to blockade this British Naval Base. This was to be done on both the Atlantic side in the west and Mediterranean side to the east. This arrangement, both the Italians, who already had an intense interest in Gibraltar and Admiral Raeder agreed to do.

Thus the Axis partners were in agreement that supply traffic from Gibraltar and Alexandria must be completely halted before Malta could be put out of commission. Heinz requested the Luftwaffe look into the feasibility of conducting bombing missions against Gibraltar. Attacks against the eastern Mediterranean port of Alexandria were already being planned, but they must first counter the advantage the RAF enjoyed in the air. Axis long-term strategy was to one day control the Mediterranean at the two major entrances, Gibraltar in the west and the Suez Canal in the east.

Heinz next obtained commitments from Italians to expand airfields on Mediterranean islands like Rhodes and even as far west as the Italian controlled island of Casteirosso. Captured British airfields in the desert area near Ft Maddalena also presented excellent staging areas from which to launch bombing raids or provide fighter cover for bombers coming from other airfields. These desert airfields became the basis for some of Wilhelm's desert strong points.

These strong points were to be protected by mines, barbed wire, artillery, anti-aircraft and anti-tank guns. They were designed to hold out for a month, longer if re-supplied. If by-passed, the attacker would find his supply lines harassed by tank and armored car raiding parties. At night, these strong points presented any would be intruder, or raider a complete 360-degree defense. By the same token, Italians had already proved they had no equal when it came to preparation of desert defensive positions. An Italian Engineering Officer recently remarked to Heinz:

"You Germans should do the fighting and let us build the defenses."

December 8, 1941 – Africa Korps Headquarters

As he read the dispatch in his hand Heinz's mind went in a million directions. This could change everything. A third major Axis partner had now made their move and what a move it was. As traveled as he was, he was unsure about these people, what new directions would the war take? He knew Hitler would be looking for Japanese assistance against Russia, could the Japanese even be trusted? Would this in any way affect their plans? If the British were also attacked, then some of the British naval assets may be shifted to the Pacific Theater.

However, a problem requiring immediate attention had just arisen. Admiral Donitz had just addressed an urgent plea to him concerning U-boat deployments to the Mediterranean. Donitz had requested an immediate halting of all U-boat deployments through Gibraltar to the Mediterranean. Two separate U-boats making their passage one on the first and the other on the second of December had been so severely damaged that they had to return to France for repairs. Now U-208, which should have made the passage on December 7 had not reported in and was feared lost.

With damage inflicted on two U-boats and possible destruction of a third in just a week, Donitz was very concerned. He suggested an immediate halt in deployment, until a better plan could be put in place. Rommel had requested U-boats to blockade Tobruk. Hadn't Tobruk been captured more than a week ago? Admiral Donitz also argued that Mediterranean facilities were currently inadequate to sustain a large U-boat fleet.

Additionally, the original premise had been to only send experienced U-boat commanders to the Mediterranean and Donitz was running out of these. At the very least, Gibraltar transits should only be attempted during nights when there was little or no moonlight.

He when so far as to suggest that some Italian submarines serving in the Atlantic might be used in the Mediterranean if additional submarines were really needed. Earlier in the year, ten of these Italian boats had already made the return trip to the Mediterranean. Why not send the rest of these boats back as well, before any more U-boats are sent?

Heinz was still concerned that the British would invade somewhere in the eastern part of the Mediterranean. Therefore it was agreed that U-boats preparing for Mediterranean service would instead temporarily join U-boats patrolling west of Gibraltar. Admiral Donitz, for the moment, won his argument.

A whole string of U-boat sailings were redirected. However, attacking heavily defended convoys west of Gibraltar was almost equally dangerous. Large Type IX U-boats currently on Gibraltar patrol, which Donitz never had cared for, were to be replaced by the smaller more mobile Type VII U-boats that had been slated for the Mediterranean.

December 10, 1941 – Africa Korps Headquarters

Heinz thought it was absolutely incomprehensible that Hitler had declared War on the United States. First, the Russian nightmare and now here was another powerful enemy to fight. How could Germany possibly overcome such odds? Now war was being waged against three great powers at once. Taking all three together, they controlled most of the world's resources.

As upset as Heinz was, he would soon be headed back to Germany to a promotion and a short rest. His wife planned to meet him in Italy and then they would travel back to Germany together. The North African front on the ground at least was somewhat stable, but the upcoming battle for control of the central Mediterranean shipping lanes was expected to continue to be most vicious. Much more would be asked of the Italian fighting man and his German ally.

December 12th – U-Boat Command

Long having to contend with what was really an undeclared war waged by the United States Admiral Donitz was actually somewhat relieved. In fact, seeing an opportunity he wanted to get an early strike against United States shipping before they could tighten up their defenses. Added to recent U-boat losses in the Mediterranean, the last two months had been very hard on his U-boat fleet. There had been some successes, but the most important effort to destroy the British merchant fleet was not going well.

Added to these difficulties were problems with manufacture of new U-boats and unreasonable demands of support to other theaters. There was even talk that many of his boats would be ordered to yet another operational area to interdict convoys bound for Russia. Moreover, many new U-boats now entering the struggle were longer range larger Type IX boats which Donitz did not consider suitable for important convoy attacks.

Therefore Donitz devised his strategy to utilize at least twelve of these long range U-Boats to strike the US. In light of the new circumstances, this of course was the right answer. He felt that the requested blockade of Gibraltar could better be accomplished with the existing type VII boats that were making their appearance in greater numbers. He should even be able to send a substantial number of his smaller type VII boats to Canadian waters including some of his most experienced commanders.

CHAPTER 15

Glory for All

It is hard to imagine the excitement that capture of Tobruk together with newspaper pictures of columns of British POWs generated in Italy. Mussolini finally had something to strut about again and at least part of Italy's empire that so much effort had been spent on was recovered. Reading Italian newspapers you would hardly know any Germans had taken part in this desert victory. Medals and congratulations abounded on the Axis side. Mussolini decided to award the Italian Gold Medal to his Corps commanders. Both Italians and Germans highlighted efforts of Ariete Division, Bersaglieri Regiments, GF-RECAM, paratroopers and Italian troops in general.

Heinz gave ample credit to tough Italian fighting. His credibility in Italian eyes rose to a very high level. No one could deny that his defeat of the English had been masterful. Even General Gambarra was in a good mood and became more receptive to Heinz's suggestions.

When Heinz visited Rome he laid out his proposals for increasing the effectiveness of the Italian Army and Italian war production. In this almost euphoric atmosphere, even Commando Supremo was favorably disposed to his suggestions.

Mussolini was even ready to capture Malta and he made the statement that with a source of oil (Russia?) there was nothing the Italian military could not accomplish. With troops released from North Africa, he was even amenable to increasing the number of Italian divisions being sent to Russia up to and including even armored divisions.

General Halder was not all that pleased with all the attention lavished over what he considered a minor African victory, but he was not about to suggest refusing the additional Italian resources. This was not what he had in mind when he had suggested Guderian be sent to replace the dead Rommel. Halder had been trying to exile all hardcore Guderian supporters to Africa and had jumped at the chance to get rid of the ringleader himself. He played down the capture of Tobruk and said except for his untimely death; Rommel would have been able to do the same thing.

A most curious statement, since the conflicted Halder had as much as called Rommel insane behind Hitler's back.

"After all, wasn't the plan for capture of Tobruk Rommel's to begin with?"

Promotion to the ultimate rank of Field Marshall and he was not even consulted. All for a few days of backfill command work, now that was certainly setting a precedent. Now Guderian was even trying to get involved in Russia again, working out troop swaps with Italians. He was even finding time to meddle in weapons selection and production priorities.

"As if Guderian knows better than anyone else how to solve all problems facing Axis troops in Russia", Hadler again confided to his aid.

To Germany at the close of 1941 North Africa was a minor theater. Hitler agreed but realized Mussolini would not be satisfied with such comparisons. Hitler needed to stroke his major ally; overall 1941 had been a very difficult year for Italy. Italian heroes were needed and so was more Italian cannon fodder for Russia. Also Moscow, Leningrad, and Sevastopol had not been captured and the situation in Russia was worsening by the day. Incentives must be provided for taking these difficult fortified areas and the German public distracted from developing problems in Russia.

Moreover, Hitler would not be outdone and overshadowed by Italians taking the lion's share of the credit for an African victory. Since Heinz had received practically every other award, Hitler made him a Field Marshall. Also, due to the overall fuel situation, Italian monthly allocation of fuel oil would soon have to be cut again. The fortunes and future of the Axis were beginning to look worse with each passing day in Russia. The great German Reich would require more help from their Allies to contend with this stubborn Russian problem.

Heinz was not aware of the decision Hitler had made in his regard. He was not sure he really liked being known as an expert in the reduction of well-defended fortresses. He did not believe engaging in this costly activity was the best road to victory if there was any way to avoid it. He had done what needed to be done, taking advantage of British mistakes. It would soon be time to discuss his plans with Field Marshal Kesselring. Surely this new commander would give his view on some of the more questionable parts of his long range plans.

Field Marshall or not, Hitler still gave Kesselring, who was himself a Field Marshall, overall command in the Mediterranean. Hitler had committed to Mussolini to send more planes, yet he was considering backing out on sending any additional U-boats. There were needs elsewhere and he had a short attention span.

Mediterranean Plans

The meeting had gone better than Heinz had expected. Kesselring needed to touch base with Grand Admiral Reader and together they would discuss strategy. Kesselring had at first been taken back, but joked that he had heard worse from Student and he knew "flexibility" was the Paratrooper General's middle name.

This could be a first, German Army, Air Force, and Navy working on a common goal. Heinz would still have an uphill struggle getting the Italian Navy to agree to the plan, but putting together these types of coalitions was the mark of a great General. Time was short, before long more Luftwaffe resources would be needed back in Russia.

Major modifications must be made to current Kriegsmarine plans if Hither would even agree to the new directions he was proposing. Also timing was good; things had started to go much worse in Russia. The Axis would be making a major redistribution of naval resources. It was tempting to send all U-boats that Hitler had allocated into the Mediterranean, but most realized that getting past Gibraltar represented a significant risk.

Results from U-boats already operating in the Mediterranean had been good, but losses were mounting. Some small Italian naval assets had already moved into Tobruk. Additional Italian naval raids were being planned. One such plan that was already underway was a raid into the very bastion of the English fleet, the harbor at Alexandra.

Heinz had requested extensive mining efforts around Malta and the Suez Canal. The head of German Naval Forces, Admiral Raeder, always seemed agreeable to the use of mines. Italians conducted reappraisals of past naval failures in light of the discovery at Tobruk. They now began to realize the grave danger that British Radar posed.

Naval engagements at night gave the British a distinct advantage. New plans and operational guidelines would have to be developed to both avoid British radar and develop an Italian version. While Italian industry could not soon hope to close the gap with new tanks and artillery, radar could make the existing Italian Navy more effective. The basic number and design of Italian ships was adequate, but they were up against the

British Navy with their radar and Aircraft Carriers. Italians and Germans were building carriers, but their construction would take time.

###

Initial Italian reaction to discovery of the Tobruk Radar installation was at first mixed. Some were still denying that such an advanced device was even possible. Those that realized the implications were in panic mode. Many suggested that all Italian ships should remain in port until counter measures could be developed, especially major Capital ships. How could any operations be conducted at night? When mentioned to the Germans, it was obvious that they did not appear to be overly concerned. Such devices they said could, of course, be neutralized by equipment Germans were developing. There was no reason to over react; the Germans had their own radar and it was really not a matter of grave concern.

"And just when were you going to share this information with us? Many Italian seamen and ships lie on the bottom of the sea floor as a result of this device."

One senior Italian Naval official had pointedly asked his German Liaison Officer. There was no answer, but there would be a request from Mussolini himself to obtain access to German radar sets especially for the major Italian Capital ships.

Italians began to realize they were involved in a death struggle with a technologically advanced enemy and in partnership with an ally equally advanced who was not prone to share. With advent of more German influence in the Mediterranean and arrival of Kesselring they would need to struggle to maintain their own identity. On the land, sea and in the air Italy was becoming more dependent on Germany for support.

Even the bulk of the coal that kept the country running on a daily basis came across the border from Germany. If Italy lost this war they knew what they could expect from the British and if the Axis won they might receive the same from the Germans. They needed to demonstrate to both that they could be a military force to be reckoned with, but how could this be done?

Stagnation

Knowledge of British radar continued to have a very chilling effect on the Italian Navy. A careful review of recent naval actions left no doubt to the prior existence of radar on British ships. Now being extremely paranoid, no radio messages were transmitted warning active Italian naval patrols and missions currently underway to the added danger.

This knowledge was not widely disseminated but all naval nighttime procedures were radically changed. Even though North Africa was critically short of needed supplies, a careful plan must be developed before additional convoy attempts were made. Italy's five operational battleships were restricted to port and an increased burden was placed on air transport. The burden to supply emergency needs would fall on fast warships, various shallow draft vessels and submarines.

Oddly enough, the British found themselves in roughly the same fix. Recent losses of a much-needed aircraft carrier and a battleship to U-boats had influenced the decision not to involve larger warships in any attempt to save Tobruk's survivors. Risks from the sea and air were simply too great and could jeopardize the safety of Egypt. Added to this were recent far eastern losses of a battleship and a battle-cruiser to Japanese air attacks.

The two remaining British Mediterranean based battleships would stay in Alexandria and that is where Italian human torpedoes (MAS) went after them. Three MAS torpedo teams penetrated Alexandria harbor looking for three battleships, they found two battleships and a large tanker. Both Battleships were holed by explosive charges Italian teams placed under their hulls and settled to the bottom of the harbor. As of December 19, the British Mediterranean battle fleet ceased to exist in a significant naval historical footnote.

An information battle was now fought between the Axis and British. Italians were desperate to know the fate and degree of success of the brave MAS teams; Churchill was just as desperate to hide that information. All six crewmen had in fact survived, but were British captives. British planes filled the skies over Alexandria with fighters and monitored all air traffic coming and going. Any plane that penetrated this umbrella would then face heavy anti-aircraft defenses.

To obtain this reconnaissance, Italians moved their single Reggiane 2001 Fighter Group to Africa. These single-engine fighter planes had the range to fly to Alexandria from current desert airfields and were no longer needed on the Italian mainland due to the reduced threat from Malta bombers. Thanks to their German engines, these Reggiane fighters also possessed the ability to fly at high altitudes where British fighters could not reach them. Two 2001 fighters with cameras and an escort of four more returned from their first trip with no losses. Therefore, a decision was made to return with bombs, once these 2001 fighters could be adapted.

What their pictures revealed simply floored Italians and later Germans. First there were only two battleships present in the harbor; this confirmed the sinking of one by U-331 earlier. Second both of these battleships were sitting on the harbor bottom. The Axis realized an opportunity like this must not be wasted. The small number of 2001 fighters suddenly assumed an importance out of proportion to their numbers and orders for anything that had the name of Reggiane in front of it was looked upon with favor. Their share of the precious German engines increased dramatically. It was not hard to convince anyone of the sudden importance of this plane.

CHAPTER 16

Tobruk Dividend

Heinz sought to follow in the footsteps of Rommel when it came to underreporting his tank strength. No mention was made of previously wrecked German tanks they had discovered inside Tobruk left behind from Rommel's unsuccessful previous attempts to gain access into the fortress. Heinz would not have Hitler short his divisions as he had done in Russia. Two can play this game of "holding back the tanks."

Speaking to his staff Logical Officers, Guderian stated:

"I want to make it clear that I, alone, am responsible for reporting operating tank strengths to Berlin. I will review all numbers before they are transmitted. Even when reporting on captured and damaged equipment, I do not want any misinterpretation of our capabilities."

Including severely damaged vehicles, Germans could put their hands on over 300 German tanks. Many German and Italian battle damaged tanks could be made functional again without a great deal of effort. First priority of repair shops would be to get as many Axis tanks operational again as soon as possible.

Second priority would be to get as many British and American tanks working as possible. Those Axis tanks that could not be made to run or required upgrading that could not be done in the desert would be shipped back to Germany and Italy, or be stripped and used in defensive positions.

Wilheim had proven especially good with constructing effective defenses with weapons and equipment remaining on a battlefield. Soon they would have more tanks working than qualified crews to man them.

With lower tank availability numbers he was reporting to Berlin and capture of Tobruk, Guderian proposed that his remaining tanks be combined into only one Panzer Division. He recommended a more balanced force combining ground, air and naval assets be deployed in this part of North Africa.

It was his view that it would probably take some time before British ground forces could set out on a massive offensive again. However, the closer Axis forces got to Alexandra, the shorter would be British supply lines and greater the danger of a massive British counterattack.

Surrounded by staff officers of more than passing ability, Heinz challenged them to examine all possible scenarios for actions in the Mediterranean. There was no clear majority opinion, but some very interesting ideas and thoughts were discussed. Unfortunately, several severe and limiting restrictions regarding this Theater became even more apparent.

One overriding and uncontrollable consideration was Russia. Respected German military practitioners had historically warned of the dangers of a two front war. They were currently faced with not only a two front war, but the North African Theater was a multi-front war in and of itself. Facing up to the reality of British in the Eastern Mediterranean was bad enough, but then you had to deal with Malta and Gibraltar.

Clearly, no more Italian defeats could be allowed to occur. In the past, Mussolini had bitten off more than he could chew. Many divisions of Italian soldiers were currently behind barbed wire in British POW camps. In fact, there was no room for any more mistakes in the Mediterranean Theater.

The Tobruk victory had taken some of the edge off, but Italians needed to become more efficient. Italian soldiers needed more justification for why they were fighting this War. Heinz thought to himself, indeed, more justification for why all of us are fighting this war would be appropriate.

Conversely, the crippling losses being suffered by Germans in Russia would not help the mystic of the infallible Fuhrer. However, Hitler would prove more adept at successful "scape-goating" than Mussolini. In fact, Hitler would convince himself that he had saved the German Army by forbidding them to retreat. In consequence, thousands of German troops would fall victim to disease and frostbite. The Russian winter, poor planning and even worse intelligence would do what the Soviet military machine could not.

The sheer size of the Soviet military had been a shock to the Germans. However, a greater shock was the amount and quality of Soviet equipment. Goring even had his staff officers travel to Soviet airfields to count the number of claimed destroyed Soviet aircraft. This count revealed the hundreds of claimed destroyed Soviet aircraft, if anything, to be too low.

Stalin had been simply waiting for the right time to unleash this destructive might on the world. Whole Soviet Armies had been eliminated, but many more remained. A population pool that Germany could not match would be used to create even more complete Armies. For the time being, Stalin would have to put his plans of world domination on hold while he attempted to destroy the hated invader.

###

Axis future in North Africa had been made more secure by acquisition of Siwa Oasis, located in the southern Egyptian desert. This deep desert Oasis now anchored the Axis right flanking position. Using Siwa as a jumping off point offered several attractive possibilities for causing the British trouble in eastern Africa.

A Move to the Crimea

Heinz wanted to reconstruct Panzer Divisions as he had originally intended, not the watered down versions that had been created prior to Barbarossa filled with diminutive Panzer I and II tanks. Fifteenth PD was to remain in Africa and would assimilate many tanks of 21st PD.

Major General Hans von Ravenstein (4) was sent to the Crimea in early December to take command of the first four companies of replacement tanks and artillery batteries that had been slated for Panzer Group Africa units. Using equipment allocated to German Africa Korps, Hans would reform 21st PD in the Crimea.

Four more companies of replacement tanks and more artillery was added by the end of 1941, including a whole battalion of powerful ten-centimeter guns. This provided a strong base to rebuild 21st PD in Russia. Additional replacement artillery was also allocated to von Ravenstein's group, as well as much of the equipment previously scheduled to be shipped to Africa in early 1942.

Possibly of even more consequence than reallocation of tanks that were to have gone to North African was revised disposition of close to 200 brand new Stuka model D dive bombers and Me-109F fighters. This new model of Stuka offered some improvements over current older models, especially in bomb load. Many of the older Axis Stukas had been lost or damaged during Crusader. It would take some time to get the current Stuka *Gruppen* back up to operating strengths.

Heinz hoped to convince Mussolini and Italian command to move at least one of their two other armored divisions to the Crimea to train with Hans' group. The idea was to pair German and Italian units. Besides training, these Crimea troops would be collecting and repairing Russian

T-34 and KV tanks from southern Russia. Von Manstein was in no position to refuse any help, especially tanks.

Moving new Stukas to the Crimea would allow them to rebuild in an area more dominated by Luftwaffe fighters and actually somewhat easier to keep supplied. Heinz also suggested that some of the available Italian Stuka pilots be moved to the Crimea, for the same reasons. These bomber units would get experience in attacking naval, ground and fortified targets in the Crimea. In an emergency situation, longer-range versions of these planes could be transferred back to the Mediterranean theater via Greece and Crete.

Sorting out the Crusader battlefield equipment, building fortifications, and flying out a whole Italian infantry Corps were only some of the tasks facing Heinz. Thanks to captured equipment, Tobruk siege artillery and Italian equipment from the departing divisions, they could pick and choose what was needed for the remaining forces.

Wilhelm considered their stock of captured British 25-pounder guns very important. Just as the British used them for both artillery and anti-tank use, so would Axis troops.

(4) Johann Theodor "Hans" von Ravenstein (Hans) – Highly decorated, capable two war veteran and 21st Panzer Division commander. He was a devout Christian and had been an outspoken critic of the Nazi regime since the early 1930s when they had first come to power. He was captured during the African desert "Crusader" battle on 28 Nov 1941 and had the distinction of being the first German General captured in World War II.

Italian Traitor?

Heinz realized that holding Africa was not just about men and equipment. He felt he needed additional backup and conformation for the intelligence information American Colonel Felders in Egypt had just started providing them. They had Italian code breakers and German signal troops to thank for this excellent source of detailed British tank strengths provided almost daily by the good Colonel's reports back to Washington.

In the future, if there was one, they needed to gain the upper hand in the intelligence arena. Was there a spy in the Italian camp? They needed to sort out why the British seemed to know in advance what their moves would be. A first step would be to tighten up security procedures in all forms of information flow.

Colonel Felder's third decoded report was hand delivered to Heinz by *Oberleutnant* Alfred Seebohm, commander of 621st Radio Intercept Company.

"Well Herr *Oberleutnant* you felt compelled to hand deliver our new source of information personally?

"*Ya, Herr Gerneraloberst*, as you know Rommel was always concerned about a possible intelligence leak. However unbelievable, I believe I may have discovered the leak source."

"By all means go on Seebohm."

"Our Italian friends questioned me about Colonel Felder's reference to British Eighth Army Headquarters learning of Rommel's death on the 25th of November. I of course blew it off and said that our good Colonel had obviously gotten his dates mixed up. Surely he meant the 26th.

For heaven sake Herr Generaloberst, not even Rommel's family knew he was dead before the 26th. I knew I had to report this information immediately. My men have secretly checked every piece of Italian radio traffic on the dates in question. Rommel already had us monitoring this traffic for potential leaks. I can confirm that the only way this information left Africa was on the Luftwaffe's Enigma Machine. Can it be possible?"

Many thoughts went through Heinz's mind, not the least of which was the complete surprise of the British when they had attacked Tobruk. From then on the battle had mostly gone the Axis way. He had been uncomfortable letting the Italians in on the attack considering the circumstances, but he needed their help. But he had transmitted no information to Berlin about his intended attack. So in this respect what Seebohm was implying made sense.

"Seebohm, guard this information with your life. Cross-check all your information again and be prepared to show your data to my personal staff tomorrow. If this is true we can not let the English know that we know, so we will keep to our regular schedules, but we will review the information sent."

Wilheim's Miracle Weapon

One problem facing Wilheim with reusing captured enemy equipment was finding a continuing source of ammunition. For 25-pounder British artillery pieces, a solution for future ammunition supply was suggested by this gun's similarity in caliber to German 88-mm guns. The British 25-pounder's caliber was 87.6 mm. Increasing the bore to 88mm amounted to little more than increasing the wear on the barrel.

Firing the shorter German 88-mm shells, which weighted only 22-pounds; captured 25-pounders could then theoretically out-range their British counter-parts. Additionally, these slightly modified guns were still able to fire the standard British rounds, including armor piercing (anti-tank), with only a minimal loss in efficiency and accuracy.

This resulting gun/ammunition combination was so versatile that it was even suggested that they be tried in a limited anti-aircraft role similar to Italian 76.2-mm anti-aircraft guns that were sometimes mounted on trucks.

With their 360-degree firing platform and using the 88-mm anti-aircraft round, they even offered some additional protection against low to medium ceiling flying aircraft. Ability to fire German 88-mm anti-aircraft rounds also allowed skillful artillerymen to employ the anti-aircraft airburst effect against ground targets. Properly timed airbursts had a devastating effect on troops in the open as well as on any soft target without overhead protection. Used in defensive mode, attacking troops could be effectively shelled with little damage to the defenders wire and mine obstacles.

This relative simple conversion worked so well that is was decided that it should be expanded to include captured British 25-pounders in France. The British expeditionary force that had evacuated Dunkirk had left behind some 700 older version 25-pounders; many more than were available in Africa. To date, not a great deal of effort had been made to reuse these artillery pieces.

That was before huge German losses in Russia. Newly manufactured German artillery was desperately needed to replace these losses. Extreme logistical problems in Russia meant that standardization was of paramount concern. Therefore, Russian theater units should get first choice on standard German arms. Access to different types of ammunition available and being developed for German 88 mm guns would continue to offer increased versatility for captured 25-pounders in Africa and France.

British deficiency in medium artillery had not gone unnoticed by

Wilhelm. Adding these modified 25-pounders to existing German and Italian heavy artillery and German 88-mm/Italian-90mm AA (anti-aircraft) guns; the Axis should hold a clear advantage in artillery range.

Following this logic, British troops could be hammered by Axis artillery before the British could get within range. One hard earned lesson in wide open desert warfare was the utmost importance of a weapon's range. When it came to artillery, Italian and German divisions were to be positioned similarly. More heavy artillery was moved closer to the front making it difficult for British to gain an artillery advantage.

It was thought that some accuracy might be lost by converting British 25-pounders to fire 88-mm shells. So Wilhelm had numerous tests conducted to try and quantify this decreased accuracy. British 25-pounders were known to be somewhat inaccurate at maximum range, so it was hoped that this inaccuracy would not increase substantially with the proposed modification.

As testing data was analyzed, Wilhelm and his team were amazed by the results. Their modified gun not only successfully outranged an unmodified 25-pounder, but proved more accurate at extreme ranges. This was an astounding discovery and would prove to be a very nasty shock for Commonwealth troops.

Now with artillery verses artillery duels or counter-battery fire, it would be British artillery that would be at a disadvantage. With these results in hand and the number of modified 25-pounders rising under Wilhelm's careful guidance, Heinz felt justified in shipping all his standard 105-mm Germany artillery to Russia.

CHAPTER 17

Mussolini

On December 20th Heinz boarded a plane to Italy to tour manufacturing facilities and to receive Italy's Gold Medal. Subsequent to awarding of his medal, he had arranged a briefing with the Italian Dictator Mussolini or *Duce* to present his thoughts on conduct of the war in Africa.

In the middle of his presentation, Mussolini interrupted him by way of their translator.

"Field Marshal Guderian, do you have any positive comments about our armaments?"

"Some of your manufacturing firms are resourceful, but even these require more guidance. All production levels need to be increased. I took special interest in your new fighter planes. Your Semoventies (assault guns), proposed new designs and anti-aircraft (AA) guns also showed promise. I realize that neither the Italian nor German people were prepared for the type of war that this is becoming, *Duce*.

I must stress our immediate need of more heavy anti-aircraft guns and above all, long-range fighter aircraft. These anti-aircraft guns are most useful against tanks as well. We have an adequate supply of artillery, but to provide for an adequate defense more ammunition will be required. One failed attempt will not stop Churchill."

Heinz paused to try and judge the expression on Mussolini's face along with the translator, two cabinet ministers and the three generals present. This was not coming out right, it was new political ground for him, but he must try and get Mussolini's cooperation. Deciding on a different approach, he continued.

"I mean no disrespect. I have been told I have a sharp tongue, we Germans are working very hard on upgrades, especially our anti-tank capability. As allies, heavy Russian and British tanks presently present a special problem to us that must be addressed as soon as possible. There is a great need for better anti-tank guns and tank upgrades.

However, perhaps an even more pressing need is a much improved and more rigorous training regiment. Of course the training needs to be comprehensive but it must also be associated with actual conditions and paraphernalia of combat."

"General Guderian, we have heard reports from our troops in Russia regarding the superior Russian tanks. As we speak we are designing a special Semoventi that will mount our 90-mm gun. These will be built and sent to Russia by April. In addition we are modifying over 300 light tanks into smaller Semoventies mounting 47-mm guns that could be shipped to Africa, to Russia or used for our proposed attack on Malta. We also have designs currently for other new tanks and even more Semoventies."

"*Duce*, I am glad you mentioned Russian tanks. I have made an agreement with Hitler, with your permission, to bring some of these Russian tanks to Africa. Your troops in Russia are very correct to ask for a heavy mobile anti-tank weapon to combat these tanks, but I was given to understand that there is a great demand for your excellent 90-mm gun.

The first need is for anti-aircraft use, the second for the Navy, and the third for a new truck mounted weapon. Nothing would please me more than to have these new 90-mm Semoventies in Africa, but I could not in good conscious take them away from troops in Russia. However, I told the designers that based upon my knowledge of mud and snow conditions in Russia, such a heavy vehicle would not have sufficient mobility."

"So what should we ask is your alternate proposal?"

"Instead, using this design, I would propose we convert some damaged Italian M13 tanks in Africa to mount 102-mm guns that were used so successfully by Italian troops against British Matildas. We may even be able to mount a German gun, our ten-centimeter, on this vehicle, if it can be perfected in time. Who knows, if these vehicles prove successful then production could be greatly increased.

Also, we may be able to work out a trade for heavy mobile anti-tank guns that we Germans could supply much quicker to Italian troops in Russia. Then these 90-mm AA guns could be shipped directly to Africa in exchange."

"For the sake of the Italian people, General Guderian, we must hold on to Cyrenaica at all costs, so I will approve all these activities. We also must take Malta to stop the bombing of our cities and secure our Mediterranean influence. Whatever men and equipment can be spared from these efforts could be used in Russia, but we will need a steady source of fuel to do all of this.

We could add at least Littorio Armored Division to Italian troops we are sending to Russia, if you feel this division will not be needed in Africa. This Russian oil Hitler wants must of course factor into all our strategy, so perhaps we can help you Germans."

"*Duce*, any and all help would be appreciated to defeat Communism, I am quite sure. Until we put Malta out of commission, I cannot see drowning any more of our troops in the Mediterranean. German tanks, equipment and soldiers once intended for Africa are already on their way to the Crimea. Foot soldiers in Africa are really a liability; they require us to constrain our movements in order to protect them from annihilation by British motorized units.

They were necessary when we were trying to contain Tobruk, but now they present a resource burden along with Commonwealth POWs. As has been discussed, those units without motor transport can be moved to other areas."

Heinz quickly brought his presentation to a conclusion, but he entertained several more questions from Mussolini as well as the other attendees. Finally Mussolini again thanked him for his service to Italy and bade him farewell.

PART VI

RUSSIA

Chapter 18

Von Ravenstein

Major General Johann Theodor "Hans" von Ravenstein was a Prussian's Prussian. An excellent battlefield commander and fearless leader, he had been highly decorated in both this war and the last. Although of Junker (noble) birth, his family was anything but wealthy and his achievements were a result of his hard work and good fortune.

Unlike some of his contemporaries he owned nothing to the Nazi regime for he was and had been for many years an ardent anti-Nazi. His boyhood dream had been to become a Lutheran Pastor, but his family could not afford the necessary education. Nevertheless, moral tenants of Christianity were deeply engrained in his soul and he understood his footsteps to be guided by divine providence.

Believing God had had a hand in directing him back to the life of a soldier he intended to use these proven talents to God's glory. Therefore when Heinz informed him that he was being transferred to Russia he quietly accepted his fate and determined to prayerfully make the most of whatever situation he was placed in.

Heinz knew Hans' character and took almost an hour out of his busy schedule to meet with him to discuss his new mission in Crimea, Russia. At one point Heinz asked Hans if he had any reservations about being transferred to Russia.

"Heinz, I have heard about Hitler's "Commissar Order" (all Soviet Commissars were to be executed upon capture) and rumors of maltreatment of Russian POWs and civilians. I would appreciate your opinion on these matters?"

"Hans, I can not speak for all German officers and soldiers. My commander, General von Bock, chose not to pass on this 'Commissar Order' to us and I believe that he was not the only commander who made this decision. Regarding treatment of Russian POWs after my troops released them to the proper authorities, I can not speak to, but I must fear the worse. Hans, I will back you up in any action you may take that you feel is necessary to preserve your soldiers' honor and discipline.

Perhaps the safer way to avoid such conflicts is to initially spell out to your command what conduct you consider dishonorable and let it be known that you will not tolerate it. Don't wait until the conflict arises, for mark my word, it will."

Von Manstein

At first Hans was a little unsure of himself as to how to handle his new position in Crimea, Russia with several of Heinz's mandates, initiatives and warnings still echoing in his ears. Basically, Hans was to be Heinz's point man for a massive redistribution and reorganization of Axis forces between the Mediterranean and Russia.

German Crimea forces were commanded by Erich von Manstein. Von Manstein was developing an unparalleled reputation as both a brilliant military tactician and excellent field commander. Another Prussian and like Hans of noble birth his outward public actions strictly followed Prussian officer etiquette. Privately he made his true feeling known to only a very select group of friends. In whose company he would occasionally have his dog demonstrate the trick "Nazi salute" he had taught him.

He had been given command of Eleventh Army consisting of three Corps after the demise of its commander but had done nothing to change the conduct of its troops which pretty much followed Hitler's radical policies to the letter.

Phase one of Heinz's plan involved movement of three divisions and some aviation assets. Fifth Mountain Division was to relocate from Crete to the Crimea by air transport. Twenty first Panzer Division was to be rebuilt in the Crimea using a core of experienced troops from Africa. In exchange, von Manstein was to release his 22nd Air Landing Division to Heniz to participate in the invasion of Malta.

Von Manstein certainly did not welcome the idea of giving up his 22nd Air Landing Division. Twenty Second's fighting spirit could always be counted on. This division was Eleventh Army's spearhead and was one of the finest divisions in the whole German Army. Regardless, von Manstein could use tanks and he was in desperate need of more of any type of support. However, he figured by the time he received this promised assistance Sevastopol would be captured and Eleventh Army would have to carry on with one less division.

Amazingly, five Italian Savoia torpedo planes and crews arrived in the Crimea two days after their discussed projected troop swaps. These bombers had enjoyed successful careers in the Mediterranean employed in an anti-shipping role. They were to help free up von Manstein's twin engine Luftwaffe bombers, which were not performing well in this role.

Moreover, Fifth Mountain Division's engineer battalion showed up a week before von Manstein's main Sevastopol attack was scheduled to start. These mountaineers arrived by air to be replaced in the interim on Crete by select Italian troops.

##

Von Manstein chose to place Hans' new Panzer Division in the eastern part of the Crimea, which was more suitable tank terrain. Hans was ordered to work closely with Eleventh Army's XLII Corps and two Romanian mountain Brigades to defend the eastern Crimea while the bulk of von Manstein's troops reduced the fortress of Sevastopol. However, a deteriorating Russian transportation system and Eleventh Army's base needs limited Hans' accumulation of men and equipment.

Von Manstein worried about giving Sevastopol's defenders more time to reinforce their troops and improve their defenses. Also, Eleventh Army's thin ranks were being thinned further by combat and rampant disease. Consequently, he began his attack on Sevastopol while Heinz's additional troops were still arriving from Africa and the Mediterranean.

Von Manstein had made Hans aware that once Sevastopol was taken Hitler was eager to move further east into the oil rich Caucasus region. However, intelligence Hans gleaned about renewed Russian activity, following the collapse of Hitler's Russian invasion, did not give him a good feeling about their future prospects.

##

So far, Hans' troops that had made it to the Crimea certainly constituted a motley crew, for they were composed of a mixture of *Panzertroopen*, Italian Air landing troops, and miscellaneous specialist personnel. Strange equipment combinations began to appear. For instance, the newest model of Stuka bomber lined up beside 3-engine Italian supply and torpedo planes on the same airfield.

The eastern Crimea was still quiet so Hans prayed they might be given more time to properly rebuild 21st PD and train on their new equipment which was slowly being accumulated. Hans was determined that his troops should learn any unique tactical Russian Front lessons that his knowledgeable *panzertroopen* could provide as well as never forgetting their unique African fighting skills. Valuable fighting and survival skills would help keep all of them alive in this most unforgiving of environments.

Thankfully, Heinz had loaned him some of his key staff officers to aid in accomplishing his numerous responsibilities. Hans could delegate many of his tasks to what amounted to a Corps level staff composed of some of the best talent the German Army had to offer.

Moreover, major offensive action by his rebuilt division supposedly would not occur for some time. It would require time to capture Sevastopol which would be followed by more time to rest and rebuild Eleventh Army.

Radical Change in Plans

In late December Hans was summoned away from the rail-yard where he was collecting, inspecting and distributing new tanks and personnel. He was ordered to report immediately to von Manstein. Upon entering Eleventh Army's crowded war room Hans was immediately addressed by von Manstein.

"General von Ravenstein thank you for your quick response; a problem has just developed"

"What is the nature of this problem Herr General?"

"Hans, the Soviet Navy is on the move. We just received word from XLII Corps that Russians have landed invasion forces in the eastern Crimea near the city of Kerch. As you are aware, our Eleventh Army is heavily engaged at the moment in trying to take Sevastopol. I realize you are just now putting your division together, but it looks like XLII Corps may need immediate assistance from your *panzertroopen*. Moreover, as you can see on the table map here...."

Von Manstein let the rolled up gloves in his right hand fall on the section of map he was referring to.

"We are just about to committed Fifth Mountain troops to expand our northern penetration of Sevastopol. I was hoping this action would bring some relief to our troops trying to break through Sevastopol's eastern defenses; little has been accomplished there.

Consequently my Army is already heavily committed and besides relocating an infantry division would require too much time. We must depend on you and your *Panzertroopen* to do what you can to help out in the current crisis. We need you to buy us some time. I have already informed General Graf Hans Sponeck, commander of XLII Army Corps that you are on your way."

"Herr General von Manstein, to provide the quickest response possible I will not assemble the whole group. I will take only my most experienced troops and form the rest as a reserve."

"Plan on consulting with me prior to making a significant decision that may involve heavy risk to your force, Heinz would never forgive either of us if we used your armored troops improperly. I will add to your battle group my motorized regiment of Romanian infantry; this should provide you with a fairly potent mobile force. You will henceforth become Eleventh Army's mobile reserve."

Many thoughts went through Han's mind as he left Eleventh Army headquarters. Armored cars already in the eastern Crimea would be the first units he would send to the reported landing sites. This could be a rather nasty shock for the Russians, who probably did not know any German armored forces were currently in the Crimea.

###

After assisting XLII Corps troops in destroying the majority of Soviet troops that had landed in the eastern Crimea, Han's combat group was rushed four days later to Feodosiya. General Graf Hans Sponeck, the commander of XLII Army Corps, was extremely worried about another Soviet landing at Feodosiya, a critical pinch point separating eastern and western Crimea. With less than a ten mile march these newly landed Soviet troops could cut off and trap von Sponeck's entire XLII Corp in the eastern Crimean.

With roads in the Crimea now completely frozen, German artillery troops made a frightening discovery. Summer horseshoes on the feet of

German draught horses rendered them almost completely useless for repositioning equipment. It was beyond stupidity which could have resulted in German equipment having to be abandoned as was occurring elsewhere in Russia.

Most wheeled vehicles also suffered severe movement limitations on these frozen roads. Only 21st PD tanks and tracked vehicles could move freely under these conditions and even then they were not as mobile as their Russian counterparts. Additionally all-wheeled drive armored cars and half tracked vehicles retained some degree of mobility.

With substantial Luftwaffe assistance, Hans' combat group was able to effectively isolate the Feodosiya landings and save XLII Corps from being cut off in the eastern Crimea. His division, however, did not possess the strength necessary to root out and completely destroy these Soviet troops which were now present in greater than division strength.

##

By halting XXX Corps' eastern attack on Sevastopol and redirecting an additional regiment that had been in the process of leaving the Crimea, von Manstein was able to free up one and a half infantry divisions to send to Hans' aid at Feodosiya. As these XXX Corps' troops were moving to form a ring around Feodosiya, von Manstein received another urgent request from von Sponeck. With the extreme temperatures, the Kerch straits had frozen over and massive numbers of Russians were trying to cross over this frozen bridge. Von Manstein again ordered von Sponeck to hold and told him that soon much of Hans' division would be headed back to his assistance.

January 8th, 1942

What had been billed to Hans as a period of reorganization and training in eastern front tactics had turned into an intense operational pace and a deadly daily survival game responding to one Soviet threat after another. Hans even had to request emergency issues of ammunition be flown in for his tank guns.

It had been tricky, but with Luftwaffe assistance 21st PD personnel had successfully destroyed many Soviet tanks. Most Soviet tank damage was due to skillful use of the division's anti-tank guns, especially converted Russian field guns and German 88s.

However, Russian tanks and troops just kept coming. With the Kerch straits frozen over, Russian troops poured into the Crimea. Reconnaissance flights indicated massive amounts of Soviet troops and equipment assembled across the straits. This was a major operation designed by Stalin to halt the Sevastopol siege and then destroy von Manstein's Army. When the straights of Kerch had frozen over, Soviets didn't even need their naval vessels to insert more troops into the Crimea.

Indeed, Stalin had even more massive Soviet offensives underway all along the Russian front to rid Russia of these hated invaders. It was not enough to count the number of Soviet divisions involved, for Stalin was prepared to commit several whole Armies to his winter offensives. One of Stalin's most important stated goals with these efforts was relief of Sevastopol and total destruction of Axis forces in the Crimea.

Hans suggested to von Manstein that more Luftwaffe planes needed to be pulled from Eleventh Army's siege efforts to counter what was obviously a major Russian offensive. Most of Eleventh Army's supporting rocket artillery batteries had already been pulled from the siege and moved to the eastern Crimea.

At Kerch, Russians were taking terrible losses as Hans' tanks skillfully sliced into them time and time again. Han's division so far had not sustained significant losses, but they could not be everywhere at once. More and more stable Russian Crimean pockets of resistance based around strong anti-tank defenses were being formed.

They were able to contain these attacks, but what of Soviet masses waiting for the next freezing of the straits. Von Manstein had committed his last fresh infantry division, Fifth Mountain, to the siege and felt real progress was being made.

Apparently, Sevastopol's supply situation was deteriorating as some reduction in the volume of artillery fire from the fortress was noted. However, Hans knew their time in the eastern Crimea was running out. More infantry reinforcements were needed if they were to survive. In the middle of this intense operational action Hans was about to come face to face with hard evidence of horrors committed behind the German lines by Himmler's SS.

Kerch Tank Ditch Incident

Hans' 21st PD Headquarters at Kerch

A young staff Lieutenant opened the door to the small but comfortable, except for the heavy smell of Russian tobacco, peasant hut housing 21st PD Headquarters' orderly room. This let in a flood of cold air and random snow flakes into the once sealed room and everyone in the hut turned toward the Lieutenant as he quickly closed the door.

"General von Ravenstein we have discovered that a large section of the city's anti-tank ditch has been compromised."

"What do you mean compromised, Lieutenant?"

"Bodies sir, the anti-ditch is half full of literally thousands of frozen bodies, Russian civilians by the looks of it, men, women, and children. I have never seen anything like it. All the bodies are frozen solid, we can do nothing. Soviet tanks will be able to roll right through; it will be useless to stop any assault."

The room was suddenly deathly quiet as everyone looked first at the Lieutenant and then at Hans. Every German in the room knew or could guess exactly who was responsible. Many knew of Hans' outspoken anti-Nazi history. What would he do?

"We have no choice; move your troops forward into the ditch for protection and to reestablish the line. I bet they have *Einsatzgruppen* D to thank for their macabre new residence. My guess is that they didn't have time to clean up their mess before they were called away to the west. Let's hope this doesn't undermine our whole defensive effort."

Without arousing suspension, Hans thus exposed *Einsatzgruppen* D's handy work in a slip up that soon became public knowledge throughout Eleventh Army. To make matters worse, LVII Corps would not be able to hold on to Kerch (Hans would use the compromised anti-tank ditch as his excuse to retreat). Afterward, advancing Soviets would get access to this anti-tank ditch containing over 7,000 Jewish bodies plus others deemed unfit to live by *Einsatzgruppen* D.

Hans knew he could do nothing for these dead civilians except to shed as much light on their demise as possible. Was there a way to save others before they too were killed?

One of Heinz's policies that Hans was empowered to implement was to select Russian equipment transported to Africa. This just might offer a cover to save some. However, he would need the help of like minded people to be able to pull such an effort off. He would now be on the lookout for such people.

###

Von Manstein's Eleventh Army reserves were now fully committed. As it turned out, previously promised additional tanks and planes could now not be spared, they were simply too desperately needed elsewhere. Axis forces in the Crimea were on their own. Now the iron will of von Manstein and Prussian military ethos took over, as troop units were packed for a final push toward Servernia Bay and expansion of the incursion corridor.

Sevastopol was far from defeated, but some of the heights overlooking the northern side of the bay were now in German hands and the critical Fort Stalin was in the process of being taken. Under observation by German guns, re-supply of the Sevastopol garrison would be more difficult.

Von Manstein now sought to consolidate his gains inside the Fortress so that even more troops could be freed up for the eastern Crimea. He did not want to lose the ground that had cost so many lives in the north. With the eastern advance on Sevastopol halted the Soviets were able to concentrate their defensive efforts in the north.

###

Hans' tanks and troops had kept any gains made by Russians that had landed at the Feodosiya beachhead to a minimum, putting General Sponeck's mind at ease. Von Manstein began immediate planning to eliminate this beachhead. General Sponeck was fortunate that the Kerch straights remained frozen for only three days, but here yet again Russians were able to establish a beachhead.

Eleventh Army was holding on by its fingernails, helped in no small part by Fifth Mountain division sent by Heinz and tanks and other equipment that had originally been allocated to his North African Campaign.

However, weakened by losses and continuous fighting, they were about to face their biggest challenge yet. Stalin had decreed that Sevastopol would be saved. Once the Kerch straights froze again, the better part of three Russian Armies would devote their lives to fulfilling that promise.

Von Manstein was indeed grateful for assistance that Heinz had made possible. These troops, tanks and additional planes had been indispensable. Also, Heinz had sent von Manstein various specialized personnel and engineering equipment that had proved useful during the Tobruk siege. Some of this equipment would now be used to thwart counterattacks Russians were launching from Sevastopol.

Von Manstein hated to halt his assault on Sevastopol; however, he could no longer ignore the threat of large forces massing in the eastern Crimea. He knew he would have to use additional German troops and equipment to block further enemy gains in the Crimea and so could no longer continue his attack on the Fortress.

In the eastern Crimea, armored troops would now be used as mobile reserve to hold tenuous defensive lines. Just when it looked as if Eleventh Army troops might be gaining the upper hand, significant Luftwaffe assets had to be withdrawn. This was necessary to counter breakthroughs from another major Soviet offensive further north. Stalin was applying pressure along hundreds of miles of front in an all out effort to wipe out the hated German invader.

January 10, 1942 - Crimea

Twenty First Panzer Division along with Eleventh Army troops aided by softening/melting ice across Kerch straits were once again able to halt the Soviet advance. However, Soviets troops now had a firm toe hold, despite heavy losses. Manstein knew that the greatest of the dangers was the Feodosiya beachhead. One and a half German infantry divisions joined Von Ravenstein's battle group and launched an attack on the 10th of January. After three days they successfully eliminated this beachhead.

It was now time to refocus on the Kerch problem which was becoming unmanageable as more and more Soviets established themselves in the Crimea. Von Manstein began to receive some requested German replacements and a few additional Romanian troops. Hans had received additional tanks and more experienced crews to man them had also found their way into the Crimea; many as a consequence of heavy winter tank losses that Germans continued to suffer.

However, the biggest effect was that Sevastopol garrison's full attention could now be focused solely on the northern German penetration. For their part, Germans had managed to widen this northern penetration and thus form a defensible corridor about three miles wide at the narrowest point. German troops were subjected to fierce counterattacks, but they held on. Fifth Mountain and 132nd Infantry Division's losses inside the penetration continued to rise, but Russian causalities were appalling.

Flexible use of Hans' tanks had allowed some of Eleventh Army's assault guns to remain inside Sevastopol and protect their penetration corridor by quickly counterattacking any Soviet gains. Now their biggest worry was the huge guns of fort Maxim Gorki, which had caused many casualties and made supply efforts difficult. Periodic Russian Naval gunfire, including fire from a Battleship, was also troublesome as Stalin committed the entire Soviet Black sea fleet to saving Sevastopol.

Fifth Mountain's westward attacks had taken it almost to the Black Sea coast having captured the important command center (Bastion I) for Maxim Gorki, but they could make no more progress in penetrating closer to the main fortress. Walls of this massive fortress were in places twelve feet thick and on top of this three-story structure sat two Battleship turrets, each mounting two 12" guns. These guns enjoyed tremendous fields of fire. At times, Fifth Mountain troops were able to clear the Russians from the surrounding areas, but then they would be driven off by artillery fire.

Soviet troops knew what was at stake and were determined to hold out. Even German engineers had nothing that offered a solution to the massive structure. Normal Luftwaffe bombs had no effect at all and Russians had moved anti-aircraft guns into position around the ring of forts making air attack difficult.

Finally both sides were spent and settled into an uneasy peace broken only by the unsettling sounds of big guns firing. It would be difficult to take the rest of Sevastopol until this fort could be conquered. On the other hand, divisional artillery had found suitable firing locations and was making life difficult in the Port of Sevastopol.

CHAPTER 19

Fortress of Malta and Black Sea Waters

Heinz knew that the challenge of taking the British held island of Malta would require major commitments from both Italy and Germany. Heinz had managed to convince Mussolini and Kesselring to order large scale planning to begin, but a review of projected requirements meant that even with intense preparation several months of effort would be required.

Equipment and supplies must be assembled and men must be trained. Shortage of fuel might be the real showstopper. Italians were projecting what Grand Admiral Raeder considered excessive amounts, this at a time when German petroleum reserves were being drained dry by Russia.

It would take time to sort out all of this and prepare Malta for invasion. Some Russian oil would solve the Axis's problem, but could they get it? According to Hitler, Russians were still in a position to threaten Axis Romanian oil from their bases in the Crimea and Sevastopol.

Any additional fuel crisis would quickly spell the end of everything. Without fuel, the British would simply take over the whole Mediterranean, including Italy. So before Hitler would release the resources to capture Malta he demanded the entire Crimea under German control.

Employing some of his forces in Russia until Mediterranean shipping could be made safer seemed logical and could help with the nightmare Russian Winter campaign that was beginning. Hitler and Hadler had readily agreed with his decision to send the first companies of tanks with some personnel from 21st Panzer Division to Russia. By this time, Hans had over a hundred gun-armed (Panzer III and Panzer IV) tanks with his division.

Heinz saw no reason to create new Panzer Divisions when the existing Panzer Divisions in Russia were experiencing severe shortages of tanks and he told Hitler so. Germany's heavy losses on the Eastern Front could not be quickly made good by existing production levels. However, Heinz did intend to eventually create a new light division in the Crimea with equipment and replacements accumulated over the next few months. This division would be named 90th light division.

##

Grand Admiral Erich Raeder was very encouraged to hear about possible expansion of the alternate shipping route across the Black Sea. Nevertheless, he was concerned that Goring's Luftwaffe would fail to achieve their stated anti-shipping goals. Goring refused to release control of "his" planes and continued to make stupid decisions in regards to matters that really should be handled by Raeder's *Kriegsmarine*.

Raeder had been impressed with Italian success with small naval units, so he began to talk with Italians about providing help and he was willing to trade. Indeed, since the attack on Moscow was stopped this was the only chance remaining for Axis success this winter.

Soviets Walk on Ice

Even with gradually increasing assistance of Eleventh Army's supporting infantry, it still became necessary to move the main Crimea defensive line further west. Regardless of losses, thousands of Russians crossed the straits. It was worse by night, when Axis forces were less effective at targeting them.

To top it all off, due to another massive Soviet attack, an extreme crisis developed to the north around the city of Karkov. In an effort to stop this Soviet advance Luftwaffe units and even an additional promised tank battalion had to be diverted to aid troops around Karkov.

At last, Germans in the Crimea realized they must fall back or be outflanked. Von Manstein then had LIV Corps' 22nd Division secretly airlifted from Sevastopol to the eastern Crimea to form a new defensive line.

But von Manstein still hoped to deny the Russians additional landing fields on the Crimea and at least keep Kerch in artillery range. On the German's left flank Russians bulged the line until the Axis were forced to man an old defensive line that cut the Kerch peninsula in half from North to South.

Here the thin lines of infantry would have a chance of holding, while the mobile forces held a line that ran roughly west to east, attempting to keep Kerch within artillery range as long as possible.

Their offensive capability had decreased due to their losses, but the Russians were still attacking. Stalin's Navy was trying desperately to both keep Sevastopol supplied and support their Kerch offensive, but their losses were quickly mounting too.

Slowly Hans was acquiring all the elements of a full-fledged Panzer Division. With programmed rotations from Africa, the experience level of these troops was increasing as well. Although von Manstein had to pull a good portion of his infantry away from the attack on Sevastopol, they still held on to gains realized in the northern part of the fortress and to a limited extent in the east as well. Despite various Russian landings, Manstein had managed to keep the bulk of his LIV Corps inside the old Sevastopol outer most defense ring.

Because of constant need for the Luftwaffe in other parts of the Crimea and the weakened state of LIV Corps, forward progress had been nonexistent. They were, however, able to bring the port facilities of Sevastopol under exacting artillery attack. This prevented the Soviets from being able to fully use the port facilities to their maximum advantage to supply and reinforce their troops in the Fortress.

More than anything else, this also prevented Soviets from being able to exert the level of offensive power necessary to drive LIV Corps back out of the Fortress. Hitler also demanded that Sevastopol's airfields be kept under constant artillery fire to prevent repeat raids on the important Romanian oil facilities. In order to bring to bare more effective artillery fire on all these required targets, LIV Corps troops really needed to take the fort of Maxim Gorki.

It was easy for hard pressed German soldiers to tell when reinforcements and supplies had successfully made it into Sevastopol. Usually, artillery would start aggressive shelling the morning after a successful supply run. This relationship was not lost on those on the receiving end of these attacks. Every effort was made to disrupt the nightly shipments. When Germans were successful in stopping such shipments, a sort of stalemate came into being, with neither side having sufficient power to destroy the other.

###

Of the three sea landings Soviets had attempted in the Crimea, two had been destroyed. The third landing twice had the advantage of a solid ice bridge formed across the Kerch Straights. Dispersion of available air and mobile Axis forces fighting the other landings along with strong Russian naval support also worked in favor of the Soviets.

Despite fearful losses the Soviets had established and expanded their Kerch beachhead. Here again, von Manstein did not currently possess forces necessary to destroy this large beachhead, which was being steadily reinforced.

These were dark times indeed when Soviets seemed to be gaining the upper hand all along the very long Russian front. A lack of supplies, adequate clothing and the worst winter in 100 years also took its toll on Germany's soldiers and their allies.

This winter battle of 1941/1942 would even scar Hitler and convince him to transform himself from Dictator to Warlord. He would use these difficult times to purge more generals who did not conform to his way of thinking and thus in his own mind make his power absolute. Conversely, Stalin was doing the opposite and putting more power into the hands of Soviet Generals and other qualified officers that he was having released from concentration camps in Siberia.

Stalin's freeing of qualified officers was of course limited to those still left alive after his brutal purges. These freed officers would now be role model loyal communists, but understandably reluctant to take independent action that might result in a return to Siberia or worse.

CHAPTER 20

Fulfilling Guderian's Dream

Wilheim Begins Reorganization

Although, only one of the original German Panzer Divisions was to remain in Africa, it was to be supported by two new light divisions. One light division was named Africa Light Division. The other was given the name of Fifth Light Division, which was the original name of the very first German division moved to Africa. Each light division contained two motorized Infantry Regiments (somewhat under strength due to losses).

Some Corps units and elements of departing 21st PD would provide a basis for Signal, Reconnaissance, and Engineering Battalions for these divisions. Captured tanks were used to constitute tank battalions for these light divisions which would later become motorized divisions.

Most Corps and Army level special purpose units were all to remain. These units were needed to handle all the issues posed by the large quantity and variety of captured material. Axis forces were able to form especially strong reconnaissance battalions using some of the large number of British and in some cases, Italian armored cars that were available. Wilheim took a special interest in these reconnaissance battalions which past experience proved could have a significant impact of desert style fighting.

Heinz intended on reducing his overall troop strength by over one half. Combat power and mobility of the remaining German and Italian troops was to be increased to compensate for the greater number of British troops. Above all, except for certain specific fortress troops, no "leg" infantry divisions were to be left in Africa.

Wilhelm Bach or "Papa" Bach as he was often called meant to leverage every possible troop and weapons system available to him. His intent was to leave no stone unturned to maximize the defensive and offensive capability of Italian and German troops. Reforming mismatched equipment left in the desert into a potent mobile army would require some original thinking, skilled labor and lots of hard work.

Wilhelm's efforts could not be conducted in a vacuum; decisions made in Africa affected other areas. There was great anxiety and an urgent need in the Axis camp to address problems resulting from Russian tanks as quickly as possible, so enhanced anti-tank capability was on everyone's mind.

Heniz was sympathetic to providing assistance for the Russian struggle, but he was also making special demands for troops and equipment required for an invasion of Malta. Wilhelm suggested some swap deals.

Items that perhaps were less effective or in excess in Africa might be swapped for items urgently needed for invasion of Malta. The same logic would be applied to specialized troop skills. Both theaters were plagued by logistical problems of monumental proportions.

For the time being in Africa, actions were focused on holding on to Tobruk and frontier areas. Heinz also intended on making his open desert flank secure. He began consulting Italian and German desert experts. Various expeditions and raids were planned to challenge British control of the Sahara. Special units, tactics and equipment were tested for desert suitability. Italian and German desert specialists were employed to locate oasis and suitable alternate desert airfields. Moreover, Heinz allowed his *Brandenbergers* a free hand in keeping the British off balance.

Local Arabs were more disposed to Germans than they were to Italians. Most German former Foreign Legion members were formed into units to work with existing Axis Oasis Companies in newly formed Africa light division. They would eventually form a brigade sized combat group to hold the desert flank and work with *Brandenbergers* throughout Africa.

Once airways were made reasonably safe for transports, the next job was to make it very dangerous for any Royal Navy surface vessel. Just as he was trying to keep his ground and Luftwaffe forces at minimum levels, Heinz did not want large naval units creating supply needs that would be difficult to fill.

He suggested to Kesselring that German bombers and Italian torpedo planes operate mainly from Crete, Greece, Rhodes and other Italian islands. Operating from these bases they would be responsible for air interdiction of supply convoys from Alexandra to Malta. Ridding the Mediterranean of troublesome British submarines would be more difficult.

###

Although Axis intentions were mainly focused on Malta and Alexandria; Gibraltar was really the greater problem. Even if Malta could be successfully blockaded from the East, it could just as easily be supplied from

Gibraltar. From Gibraltar with support from Malta, the British could threaten many parts of the western Mediterranean.

These three great British bases were mutually supportive and perfectly positioned to control the Mediterranean. Capturing Tobruk made British communications with Malta more difficult, but the British seemed to be willing to make any sacrifice to keep Malta operational.

Unfortunately for Malta, starvation of the Garrison seemed to be the best current option for the Axis. It would take time for plans to be refined and forces to be assembled for possible invasion of Malta. This was true even though an invasion of Malta was an operation that had been under consideration for some time.

Heinz was still not sure where they should strike after Malta. Getting the Italian and German high commands to agree on targets would be a problem. An even worse problem would be getting commitments in resources to make attacks successful. Hitler's fear of "over the water" attacks was well known. He once made the statement that:

"I am a Lion on land, but a lamb over the water."

A lot of essential resources needed for invasion would have to be created or borrowed from another Theater. It would take time to assemble, train and arm paratroopers and other personnel needed.

Concentrating on Transport Planes

Without robbing nearly every air transport plane Germans possessed, transports were simply not available. These slow, obsolete planes were performing what Hitler considered indispensable functions on the Russian front and could not be spared. The need for transport planes was so great that even bombers were being converted to transport duty.

Next, Heinz turned to Italians. He suggested that some of their older bombers could be converted and used for transport duty or possibly glider tug duty. However, the industrial capability of Italy was impacted by their almost total lack of raw materials.

Therefore, wrecked planes on the desert battlefield and the still unscavenged wrecks of JU-52s from the great Crete invasion were to be collected by Italian soldiers and used for building additional transport aircraft. With Kesselring's help, agreement was obtained to stop production of all older Italian fighters. Italian radial engines thus saved would be used to increase transport aircraft production.

All Italian fighter aviation industry was to concentrate on producing newer Macchi and Reggiane fighters. Any resulting shortfall of front line fighters or fighter engines was to be made up by Germans. Italians had noted a decrease in the bombing attacks on their ports and cities after arrival of German fighters on Sicily so there was more willingness on their part to pursue these changes.

Conference with Hitler – February 3, 1942

So that was the end of that, Hitler liked some aspects of the plan, but raids were all he would agree to after Malta fell. Even with recent British naval losses Hitler was still concerned with the British Fleet and their response to major activities of any kind. He again mentioned his overall fuel situation concern to Heinz. He would not even agree to immediately removing all German paratroopers from Russia and for the time being 22nd Air Landing Division was to remain under von Manstein's control.

These valuable troops had already suffered heavy losses, but there simply were no reinforcements to take their place. Besides, Hitler felt Italians should carry the main load when it came to capturing Malta. After all didn't the Italians claim to have a parachute division and a recently raised air landing division?

"Let them train in the line with our troops; that should get them fit. I am sure von Manstein could use their help in capturing Sevastopol. We are short replacement troops on the whole Eastern Front, besides I have already discussed increasing the Italian commitment in Russia with Mussolini."

Heinz and paratrooper General Student were flabbergasted by these pronouncements from Hitler. This was clearly an impossible suggestion. A compromise was reached to obtain a few paratroopers in critical skills, but under no circumstances would any members of 22nd Air Landing division be released until after the capture of Sevastopol. Von Manstein was not in a position to release a single soldier. Conquest of Sevastopol and then the Caucasus must take precedence over every other endeavor.

Anxious to show that Italy could make a real contribution, Mussolini sent some of his best torpedo and Stuka pilots to the Crimea. Thus, Giuseppe found himself headed to Germany. There they were to be given a crash course on the newest model of Stuka and formed into a new unit.

Nearly 100 of the latest model Stuka, as well as additional new Messerschmitt-109 F's had been allocated to replace African losses and regain control of the skies from the RAF. There was no room, few pilots, or fuel for the extra Stukas in the Mediterranean and these additional planes could greatly help with sealing off Sevastopol from naval reinforcement.

CHAPTER 21

Admiral Lutizo

With Malta urgently requiring supplies, the British were the first to try and break the Mediterranean gridlock. With the first decent break in weather, they combined a task force coming from Gibraltar to deliver more fighters with a convoy from Alexandria. The Gibraltar task force was completely successful, after flying off fighters at extreme range to Malta they returned safely to Gibraltar or "The Rock" as was its common nickname.

The convoy from Alexandria contained four merchant ships and was escorted by cruisers and destroyers. However, this convoy was less successful, two merchant ships were sunk and the rest damaged so badly they had to return to Alexandria. However, wily British Admiral Cunningham had hedged his bets.

Independently, the fast tanker *Berconshire* sailed ahead of the main Alexandria convoy and arrived in Malta without being observed by the Axis. Also, the fast cruiser-minelayer *Abdiel* made it safely without incident.

Well protected by anti-aircraft (AA) guns and extremely fast, the *Abdiel* quickly unloaded her cargo and was on her way again. *Berconshire* was hampered by the poor state of fuel offloading facilities, which had not been completely repaired from earlier bombing damage.

German bombers went after her with a vengeance. Malta gunners, with their freshly delivered ammunition made it a costly battle. Not only was *Berconshire* left sinking and burning, but also Malta's fueling facilities suffered additional damage.

Assessing all the facts, Cunningham decided to temporally dismantle Force K (British surface naval forces at Malta). The remaining vessels of Force K would return to Alexandria and be used to help fight the next convoy back to Malta with enough fuel to hopefully reestablish Force K as a viable threat to Axis convoys.

The Axis were bumping a limit of what could be achieved with air supply alone to Africa. A couple of emergency runs by isolated merchant ships, fast Italian cruisers and even a few Italian subs supplied some needs, but it was past time to assemble a convoy. Italian scientists had managed to assemble a few crude detectors able to pick up British radar signals. Moreover, two radar sets they had coerced out of the Germans were to be mounted into the newest Italian Battleships.

The most dangerous time of passage to Africa was now thought to be during hours of darkness. Therefore, the middle part of the journey was to take place during daylight hours when the convoy would cross the heart of the Mediterranean. There had to be a compromise between escort strength verses a need to keep the date of the convoy secret.

After all, British battleships were currently out of commission, so there was not a need to involve any ships larger than a heavy cruiser in the convoy. However, Ultra intercepts of Axis signal traffic kept the British aware of the approximate time of the convoy.

Admiral Cunningham thought this was a perfect opportunity. Force K would join with his cruisers and destroyers to annihilate another convoy along with their escort. As always, they would use radar to give them a range of detection advantage. The battle area would even be within range of supporting airfields, a perfect set up and patent Cunningham trap.

The more British planners thought about it, the larger the operation became. A new crop of fighters that the last transport from Gibraltar had delivered to Malta had not lasted long under guns of Sicily's fighters and bombers. New ways to deliver larger numbers of fighters were being discussed with Americans and English Spitfire fighters were even being considered. However, these operations were still in the planning phases, but larger supply efforts from the east could quickly be made ready.

The British plan was to destroy the Axis convoy and at the same time screen and escort additional supply ships to Malta. By addition of what remained of Force K to available Alexandria ships, the British could assemble a fairly substantial cruiser and destroyer task force. An RAF element containing bombers and long-range fighters was considered adequate for the foreseen engagement.

Italian actions conformed exactly to what the British expected. The convoy left protection of Crete shortly before dawn. According to plan, the Axis convoy would attempt to make the entire crossing during daylight hours. However, with the slow moving merchant ships, this would not be possible. Knowing the importance of the convoy, Italians assigned escort command to one of the more able naval commanders, Admiral Lutizo. Cruiser, destroyer and torpedo boat commanders had also been hand picked for their past successful experiences.

Springing the Trap

First, Force K left Malta and steamed straight for North Africa, its departure was noted and their progress was reported by shadowing aircraft. They were followed two hours later by cruisers and destroyers of the eastern Mediterranean fleet. Finally, five merchant vessels and a tanker left Alexandria for Malta.

Admiral Lutizo was kept informed of all these moves. His first concern was British submarines on the outbound voyage. He knew there would be at least two to contend with and probably more on the return trip. He was fortunate to have a torpedo boat fitted with German sonar to provide some protection from British submarines.

As they got closer to Africa danger of British aircraft would increase substantially and he knew darkness would not provide total protection. Lutizo suspected that British aircraft also had radar, but even Germans seemed skeptical of this. His one hope was that they could reach the limits of detection from the Tobruk radar installation before the British attacked.

Except for absence of battleships, a major naval engagement with significant ramifications was developing. The original Axis plan had called for splitting merchant vessels and tankers between African ports of Tobruk and Benghazi. Off loading capability of Benghazi was not substantial and reduced even further by repeated bombing raids. However, Tobruk capability was even worse and might even be called primitive in spite of efforts to repair previous damage. Moreover, Tobruk's harbor was still littered with shipwrecks of all matter of description, presenting a hazard in itself.

Warned that Cunningham was trying to cut him off from two directions, Lutizo made a decision later in the day to take the entire convoy into Tobruk. So far the decision to make a daylight crossing had proved the correct one, only one British submarine had been encountered and torpedoes it fired had missed. Had they had more time this submarine could have been tracked down and possibly destroyed. Instead, the convoy reported its location and continued to stream toward their destination.

Their special air cover had kept all but one British plane away from the merchant vessels. This lone plane carried bombs and not torpedoes; it successfully hit what would turn out to be the most important vessel in the entire convoy. Fortunately, this bomb damage did not affect the vessel's speed. Had it done so, it would have amounted to a death sentence for the crew.

The naval battle was about to enter its next most critical stage. For the British, night was their ally. Both sides had accurate information as to the other's location before the sun went down. The British plan was still very much alive and flexible enough to take into account a complete or partial shift of the convoy to Benghazi. The wildcard at this juncture was Tobruk's radar installation and if it could be kept running and properly interpreted during this critical time. It provided enough information for Admiral Lutizo's ships to avoid contact and safely enter Tobruk harbor. At last they had crossed this dangerous sea, but now the British had them bottled up.

But on the other hand, waters around Tobruk were not entirely safe for British cruisers and destroyers either. One British destroyer was torpedoed shortly after midnight by an Italian submarine, but Cunningham's ships were compelled to stay. At the very least they would draw attention from merchant ships headed for Malta and disrupt unloading of desperately needed Axis supplies.

Unloading of merchant ships began that very night. The first vessel to be unloaded would be the merchant ship that had been struck by a bomb earlier. Part of the cargo of this vessel was captured stocks of 94-mm British AA shells left behind at Dunkirk.

Wilheim had talked his way into procuring these stocks as well as placing more emphasis on conversion of these guns to fire Italian 102-mm rounds. Most of these guns had survived Axis assault on Tobruk and others had also been captured on the battlefield. They were now an important part of the Tobruk air and sea defenses along with other Italian and British guns. As an emergency measure due to the arrival of the much needed convoy, an entire German flak Battalion had also been ordered into Tobruk.

Tobruk was about to undergo yet another siege in its' long history of being fought over by both sides. Once again this coastal fortress became the pivotal point in the struggle for control of the central Mediterranean. Slim forces left to both sides would be ordered to race to the "sound of the guns." Presently Italian supply services were struggling to unload critical cargo at the totally inadequate Tobruk docks.

One bright spot was a special German ship that had been designed to transport locomotives to remote parts of the world, the *Ankara*. This ship had its' own, on board cranes and had brought in the first shipment of a few Russian tanks along with additional captured Matildas from France. Using this ship's cranes, these tanks could be directly off loaded and did not pose a drain on the limited Tobruk dock space. In fact, after all of its' cargo had been off loaded; it aided off loading of one of the other ships into smaller boats.

It took the British time to realize the entire convoy had disappeared into Tobruk. Their radar had picked up the last of the escort, but then had lost ships with interference from surrounding landmasses. Now, they would have to bombard these ships inside Tobruk harbor. To do this they would need the RAF to drop "Christmas Trees" (parachute flares) to identify the exact location of the harbor and ships. However, with each of these steps valuable time had been lost.

British ships thus spent a lot of time milling about close to the coast waiting on the RAF. They did not appreciate that their location was being pinpointed by the Tobruk radar installation and that the Axis intended to do a little illumination of their own.

The RAF finally arrived and began dropping what illumination flares they had on the harbor. This forced the Axis to also try and light up the British ships with flares of their own. It was a pretty inefficient way to direct fire from both sides. However, Axis planes, subs, motor torpedo boats and shore batteries could now also take a more active part in the conflict. This started making the area very hot for the British ships, forcing them to move away from Tobruk and sending some of them back to Alexandria with damage.

The Stakes are Upped

Clearly the situation had escalated beyond control and in some respects it represented the desperation British felt. Every available British ship and plane in the eastern Mediterranean was committed. By morning the gravity of the situation had begun to sink in to Italian high command. They requested immediate German aid.

If the British succeeded, Malta would be successfully supplied and North Africa successfully isolated and another entire Italian cruiser group destroyed. The situation called for desperate measures. Radar or no radar, Italian battleships must leave port. As it turned out installation of radar on the *Littro* could be completed in two days, but absent necessary testing and training it would be virtually useless. Still, two days would not really affect the Tobruk convoy, offloading the merchant vessel would take that long.

However, in two days time, supply ships would have reached Malta and broken the blockade. While preparations continued to sally a true Italian battle fleet, a fast cruiser task force was ordered to sea in 12 hours to intercept the supply ships bound for Malta.

All aircraft, German or Italian were now under control of Field Marshall Kesselring. He was quick to appreciate the gravity of the situation as well. Over 2000 Italian and German warplanes were under his command, but they were scattered all over the Mediterranean. Little had changed in overall aircraft distribution of either side in Africa since Crusader, except for addition of three Groups of Italian Macchi 202 fighters and one of Reggiane 2001 fighters.

These more modern fighters had not appeared in force since Crusader and had been limited to mainly group actions and smaller concentrations. Nearly all older types of Italian fighters were still present with many in process of being converted into fighter-bombers. Now was the time to break out emergency fuel reserves and put all these aircraft to work defending Tobruk and attacking Cunningham's cruisers and destroyers.

In the midst of all this was still the core of German fighter defense - the two Groups of JG 27. One pilot who was already well known was going to cause the British some especially painful losses over the course of the next few days. The name of this pilot was Hans-Joachim Marseille. During course of the ensuing battle, he would be able to shoot down an incredible total of 19 British planes. Added to his previous victories he would become eligible for the Knight's cross and be well on the way to establishing an impressive reputation.

For German and Italian fighter pilots it was an ideal situation. They were close to home airfields and for once they were given all the fuel and ammunition they could use since fresh supplies were now sitting in Tobruk harbor. Their one charge was to prevent any damage to the precious merchant ships. With their weaker armament Italian fighters were not as successful as German 109s in bringing down British planes; nevertheless, British Hurricanes and American built Tomahawks were at a significant disadvantage.

Even thought Reggiane 2001 fighters were not as fast as Macchi 202 fighters, they were more maneuverable and had greater endurance over the battlefield. In these types of situations, 2001 fighters once again showed their superiority. However, neither side displayed a very organized effort. Therefore, "friendly fire" incidents were again problematic.

Even lowly Italian biplanes (CR 42s) were inserted into battle. Now regulated to ground support, they had bombs that could be used to annoy British cruisers and destroyers. Even though Giuseppe Cenni had left for Russia, both Italian Stuka and CR 42 pilots remembered his exploits.

German pilots generally looked upon Italian skip-bombing techniques as unorthodox and ineffective. However, it was Italian pilots that caused most damage to British ships. For the British had concentrated their AA efforts on the highflying Stukas and torpedo carrying Savoia bombers and had more or less ignored low-level fighter attacks.

The British task force also had to deal with Italian heavy cruisers, whose 8-inch guns greatly outranged their cruiser 6-inch guns. However, they really did not have a lot to fear from the Italian 8-inch guns. These uniquely designed guns had been spaced too close together and this affected their accuracy; it was a design flaw that would never be fully corrected. Still the volume and determination of this shelling left its impression on British sailors and contributed to Cunningham's decision to withdraw.

Axis naval forces were free to declare a major victory and they did. The heavy cruiser escort force even attempted to chase British ships back to Alexandria. However, the heavy cruiser *Trento* got torpedoed while doing this. Damage was significant enough that making it back to Italy was out of the question; therefore, *Trento* had to limp back to Tobruk. There she would remain until temporary repairs could be completed. This was just the chance the RAF wanted to try and even the odds for the losses that they had just incurred.

To add insult to injury, most Italian supply ships were reloaded with Commonwealth prisoners of war from the Crusader battle. Italians then reminded the British of their mutually agreed to prisoner exchange agreement. They then notified the British of the merchant ship's new cargo and that the new destination of these ships was the British port of Alexandria. There they were to be off loaded and refilled with Italian prisoners of war.

Thought up by the cunning Admiral Lutizo, the British had no alternative but to allow safe passage of these vessels. There ensued a mad rush to round up as many Italian prisoners of war as they could lay their hands on. Not only would Heinz have fewer mouths to feed (a great concern of his) in North Africa, but all the Italian merchant vessels would be assured safe passage back to Italy as part of the British/Italian prisoner swap agreement. Very soon there would be many happy Italians when these prisoners were reunited with their family and friends.

CHAPTER 22

Under the Guns of Maxim Gorki

When von Manstein had been informed of major Soviet landings at Feodosiya, he knew he would be forced to make some hard decisions. He was just about to commit the bulk of Fifth Mountain Division to breaking through to Severnaya Bay. Instead he ordered Fifth Mountain to strike northwest toward the town of Mekensia to join up with Eleventh Army's 24th ID. This heavily wooded and mountainous terrain was ideal operating territory for mountain troops.

After two days Fifth and 24th Divisions closed the two mile gap that existed between them and in the process sealed a pocket containing several thousand Soviet soldiers. This operation secured the left flank of Eleventh Army's LIV Corps and allowed for a considerable shorting of the German siege ring around Sevastopol.

This same maneuver was next attempted on the right flank by Eleventh Army's 22nd and 132nd Divisions in an attempt to drive due west to the Black Sea. They got as far as the heavily defended control bastion for the fort of Maxim Gorki but could not completely close this pocket before they came to the end of their strength.

With one last effort LIV Corps attacked and took the commanding hill topped by Fort Stalin. In their efforts they were greatly aided by certain specialized weapons, Engineer and signal equipment that had been intended for use in North Africa. Despite severe losses LIV Corps had secured an observation point which enabled Eleventh Army's artillery to effectively shell the port facilities of Sevastopol.

At this point, von Manstein was forced to abandon the assault on Sevastopol and go on the defensive; thus ended the last still active German offensive action on the Russian front. Unfortunately, Eleventh Army's divisions still found themselves in a difficult position. Whenever their smoke screens cleared Soviet artillery and naval vessels, whose homeport they were trying to destroy, pounded them. In addition to this, guns of fort Maxim Gorki could still observe and shell their rear areas.

Unconquered, this concrete battleship threatened all gains that had been won at such a great cost. Mounting four 12-inch guns in two battleship turrets, overall measuring some 900 by 120 feet, and with concrete walls in some places over 12 feet thick; Germans had no answer to this imposing three-story monster. They were even thankful for the terrible weather that often obscured Soviet artillery observation and allowed them to receive supplies and improve their defensive positions.

However, LIV Corps troops did possess important positions that were in defilade to the huge guns of Maxim Gorki, but that was as far as they had gotten. Gradually they brought in more artillery to begin to systematically destroy the excellent harbor facilities vital to maintaining the Soviet Black Sea Fleet. Soviets had been successful in continuing to use these facilities to build replacement submarines, but this accurate German shelling put an end to this activity.

Consequently von Manstein persuaded Hitler to release special armored piercing rocket bombs from the Luftwaffe on an emergency basis. Normal aircraft bombs previously had absolutely no effect on the thick concrete walls of Maxim Gorki.

In the event this failed, he even convinced Hitler to release highly secretive concrete piercing 21-cm shells. Only a few individuals knew the existence of these special shells and their ability to penetrate earth and concrete fortifications was almost unbelievable. Hitler was so worried that this technology would fall into the hands of his enemies that he had forbade their use without his express permission. These shells were loaded onto a special train and began to make their way toward the east.

Very soon after this train arrived, Ju 88 bombers carrying the rocket-propelled bombs attacked Maxim Gorki. Before any real damage was done, they ran out of their limited supply of bombs. Maxim Gorki had a few pox marks on the exterior and some internal damage had been done, but the turret guns were still in action. A planned follow up infantry assault was called off.

To add insult to injury, the Soviets began to repair the damage and even use some of the holes as added defensive positions. More than 1,000 defenders of Maxim Gorki took enormous pride in the fact that the invaders could not defeat their fort. But unfortunately their turret gun barrels were worn out and needed to be changed. If fact their sister fortress in the south, Maxim Gorki II not only needed to change their worn barrels, but had also experienced an explosion in one of their turrets.

##

At last, suitable 21-cm guns positions were completed, carefully concealed, and located where neither guns of Maxim Gorki or direct naval gunfire could reach them. Exhausted LIV Corps troops who had endured so much were discouraged and did not think much of this latest attempt to damage this unsinkable land Battleship. At the very least, much larger guns were needed; some began to believe that there was not a gun made that could penetrate the thick walls.

They did; however, become more curious when they were forbidden to go near the guns and von Manstein with his staff showed up. They were also given a warning order to prepare for yet another assault on the Fortress that had gained almost mystic proportions to both sides.

The first few shells fired by the 21-cm guns appeared to have no effect at all, making only small, almost unnoticeable holes in the imposing northeast wall. Then all hell broke lose, first the guns of Maxim Gorki opened fire searching for this latest attempt to silence their fury. They were soon followed by some naval guns and other Sevastopol artillery. The 21 cm guns continued to fire. After about twenty total rounds had been fired by the German guns, the nearest 12-inch Maxim Gorki turret fell silent. Now a selected Regiment of Fifth Mountain with engineering support began their attack.

Engineers scurried up the concrete face and quickly filled some of the holes created by the special 21-cm shells with explosive charges. On closer examination, one could see that the 21-cm shells had actually created extensive cracking in the massive concrete wall. After charges these engineers had set were detonated, there was again deep disappointment. The charges had produced more cracking and had widened many holes, but there was still no clear way to enter the fortress. Russian resistance on the exterior of the Maxim Gorki was mounting as they clashed with German assault troops.

The contained effect of explosions from the 21 cm shells had caused extensive casualities to the Fortress defenders and narrowly missed one magazine powder room as the special shells continued to penetrate interior walls. Structural damage, smoke, debris and secondary explosions impeded movement to the threatened sector. Some Russians who were trying to defend against this latest attack were killed outright when German Engineers detonated their charges adding to the smoke and confusion inside the Fortress.

Once again von Manstein's 21 cm guns opened up, concentrating on expanding the most likely opening into the Fortress. This worked. Then Engineers began their dangerous work, this time they were able to plant most of their explosives inside the Fortress. This second explosion caught the attention of every Russian inside Maxim Gorki, as the explosion shook the Fortress and the hot explosive gases looked for a way of escape. The resulting flying concrete even injured some Germans and Soviet command temporarily lost communication with the Fortress. Power was cut to the western turret. Yet, for a while Soviets did not comprehend how badly Maxim Gorki had been damaged.

Maxim Gorki I continued to inflict causalities on Germans as the remaining dazed survivors fought for every room. Flamethrowers, grenades, smoke and choking dust created unbearable conditions for both attacker and defender. The battle hung in balance.

However, Soviet command insisted that a working Maxim Gorki must not fall into German hands. Hardened Commissars were ordered to destroy the main magazine if it looked as if Germans were going to get the upper hand. Attack was followed by counter attack. Finally, Germans gained control of the upper floor and thus access to the Fortress 12-inch guns.

With the tide turning in the Germans favor, the order was given to blow up Maxim Gorki. Destroying themselves and all those still engaged in fighting Germans in the process, Commissars carried out their orders. The ground shook for miles around as the main magazine erupted. The hole in the east wall was turned into a giant cannon as the contents of the interior of the fortress was turned into debris and blown for hundreds of yards. Much of the explosion force followed this path as the superheated gases spewed out. Climbing thousands of feet into the sky was a massive smoke plume originating from the opening widened further by the internal explosion.

Those not killed immediately by the explosion died from smoke inhalation, as smoke pored from the hole in the east wall and even the 12-inch gun turrets on top of the fort. Not one person inside the structure survived the explosion. Soviet command was satisfied that the guns of Maxim Gorki would never fire again.

This senseless act was compared by von Manstein to mass killing of wounded Germans discovered at Feodosiya in January. There German wounded had first been thrown out of the hospital into the snow and then had water poured on them, a truly grotesque site when discovered after Feodosiya was recaptured.

This tit for tat was beginning to characterize the war in the east with Stalin and Hitler vying for who could be the more barbarous. Who started first did not really matter now.

In the end, German troops were able to seek protected refuge in and behind the very structure that had caused the death of scores of their comrades. Soviet commanders assumed that Maxim Gorki was destroyed beyond repair.

Hitler was on edge and concerned more about potential loss of his technology than troop losses. He was finally relieved when von Manstein informed him that Maxim Gorki was in German hands and no Soviets had escaped. His confidence in von Manstein grew a notch, but he still demanded all traces of the wonder weapon's use be covered up.

Von Manstein used the newly captured concrete mammoth to great advantage. Additional artillery was emplaced behind the fortress and began to take total command of Severnaia Bay and the interior of Sevastopol. The location for Maxim Gorki had been well chosen by Soviet Engineers. From the top of the fortress few things in all of Sevastopol could escape observation. Counter battery fire began to exact revenge on Soviet artillery sites that had killed so many.

PART VII

THE TIDE TURNS

CHAPTER 23

Convoy Challenge

This time Churchill decreed nothing would be left to chance. Two convoys would leave simultaneously from Alexandria and Gibraltar. Scratching together every ship they could, both convoys were very substantial. Starting from Alexandria there would be eleven merchant ships and tankers. Added to this impressive convoy would be eight merchant ships and one tanker coming from Gibraltar.

Escort was equally impressive, from Alexandria – six cruisers, 24 destroyers and escort vessels. From Gibraltar – two battleships, 3 carriers (one American carrying Spitfire fighters for Malta) plus more cruisers and destroyers. This constituted the bulk of the Commonwealth Mediterranean Fleet, augmented by vessels from Britain's Home Fleet and even some American vessels. Two fast minelayer cruisers traveled independently. Several British Mediterranean submarines were pre-positioned to support this major operation.

Selected Axis airfields were to be attacked by raiding parties; some raiding parties would travel through the desert and some would be dropped near targeted airfields by submarine. All Axis airfields were to be continuously heavily bombed during course of the operation. An entire reinforced British armored division with supporting infantry would make a diversionary attack, coordinated with widespread artillery pounding of all Axis lines.

With a bombing campaign on Malta in full swing, Germans and Italians suspected some sort of major supply effort, so the operation did not catch them completely by surprise. However, the sheer size and scope did come as a shock.

German radar installations had been completed and installed on Italy's two modern Battleships, *Littorio* and *Vittorio Venneto*. The Italian battlefleet, at Admiral Raeder's suggestion, had been divided into two main attack groups for just such an action. Plans were in place to leave port within hours of notification.

Their western attack group consisted of *Littorio* and several destroyers and torpedo boats. The eastern attack group contained destroyers, torpedo boats, cruisers and *Vittorio Venneto*. If necessary, either group could be reinforced by Italy's three older battleships and more cruisers. Italy's eastern attack group could also add additional cruisers and destroyers, if deemed necessary. This battlefleet disposition was also to approximate the composition envisioned for actual invasion of Malta.

##

Spies and reconnaissance provide warning of the two impending convoys to the Axis. Warning orders are issued, submarines and motor torpedo boats began moving into selected avenues of approach. Air raids on Malta were halted and some aircraft began preparations to fly to Sardinia. An invasion of French territory or Italian North Africa could not be ruled out. Everyone knew that the British were unpredictable. Eastern and western Italian fleets prepared to sail at a moments notice.

Reconnaissance confirmation of an almost empty Gibraltar harbor and a large Alexandria convoy already on the move was not long in coming. Tobruk radar picked up a large number of enemy bombers approaching. Every fighter that could fly was ordered airborne. North African fighter forces now consisted of almost four full Groups of Macchi 202 fighters and they had been learning some tricks from their Axis partners. These Italian fighters had a higher rate of climb than German Messerschmitt 109F fighters and were expected to be the first to try and break up bomber formations.

The last torpedo

The very successful British submarine *Urge* was assigned to keep watch on the main Italian Naval base. During the night, a group of ships could be made out in the distance leaving base. It was a submariner's dream; in the middle of a large number of escorts was one of Italy's newest battleships. *Urge's* captain submerged his vessel and tried to maneuver for a textbook shot, but they were not in the right position. Besides this Italian escort group knew what they were doing and getting a better firing position was not possible.

However, the target was too important to let it slip by; they fired all four bow torpedoes at this battleship. With maximum range and a wide spread there still might be a chance of hitting the battleship. They waited, but did not hear anything, a bitter disappointment.

"Let's surface and report sortie of a battleship."

"Should I order the bow tubes reloaded, Captain"

"Yes, but there is no rush, we will probably never see an opportunity like that again."

Italian Naval Staff Officers had agonized over information that was continuing to come in from several sources. There was just no way that a major naval Operation from both ends of the Mediterranean was not taking place.

However, fuel was being carefully stockpiled for the invasion of Malta and ordering sailing of the remainder of the fleet would consume a great deal of the precious commodity. At last, in the west, remaining Italian vessels were released, but it was too late for the two groups to sail together.

A new concentration of vessels was sighted some fifteen minutes after *Urge* had completed her transmission concerning sortie of the Italian battleship and its escort. It looked as if their group of Italian ships were now headed back to port. *Urge* did a crash dive and submerged just in time to avoid detection.

When they came back to periscope depth its Captain got his second major shock of the night. There were now three different Italian Battleships making their way out of the naval base. This time they were in a better firing position, but their bow tubes where still not reloaded. Making a radical 180-degree turn *Urge* aligned her stern tubes, fired two torpedoes and crash dived to maximum depth.

After the calculated torpedo run time, *Urge*'s crew heard one muffled explosion, but their sonar also picked up sounds of multiply surface ships headed in their direction.

Unequal Battles

For the convoy that left Alexandria it seemed that nothing had gone right for the British. On the other hand, the convoy from Gibraltar left just the opposite impression, for almost nothing went the Axis way.

In the eastern Mediterranean RAF attacks and British raiding parties were largely ineffective in destroying Axis airfields. The Axis were acutely aware how tempting a target their airfields were and effectively protected them with warning radar, guards, fighter aircraft and AA guns. Bombers sent to destroy these Axis airfields were instead decimated and this time it was as if they had been brushed aside and thrown back to Egypt.

Conversely, Axis air attacks on British ships were more concentrated, coordinated, aggressive and deadly. Again, even obsolete CR 42 bi-wing fighters were to be sent after the ships, as some of them had been modified to carry a single 250 kg German or 160 kg Italian bomb. Using their skip-bombing technique (the "Cenni-bounce"), this time they proved highly effective against lightly armored naval targets.

Warships also proved vulnerable to this type of attack; especially while escorting slower merchant ships and performing anti-submarine sweeps. Axis planes made good use of numerous airfields along the North African coast, including Tobruk, to reduce their transit time to and from convoy attacks. Over the course of one day and into that night, British losses became crippling. Over one half of the merchant ships were sunk or damaged.

Additionally, losses were not limited to just merchant ships. One cruiser and two destroyers had been sunk and others damaged in the melee. Some damaged destroyers had to return to Alexandria, others became occupied collecting survivors and the convoy became more spread out. Because of danger posed by even bi-plane fighters, none of the Axis planes could be ignored. Once again British AA ammunition levels became a concern early in the struggle.

##

Out in the desert, a barrage from more than 300 British artillery pieces blindly fired on Axis lines had produced no response, but the location of these guns had been plotted for future reference. Following the barrage, inexperienced First Armored division charged ahead confident of causing some damage and then returning to their lines. Most tanks taking part in this attack were Crusaders and Stuarts.

Wilhelm's mobile defense offered token resistance to slow the advance until the tanks had outpaced most of their artillery support and their infantry were still in carriers and trucks. Axis troops then opened a weathering artillery fire from mostly light mobile Italian guns, many mounted on trucks. For under Wilhelm's tutorage, many different weapons had been mounted on captured British and American vehicles.

First Armored was then attacked by fighters and fighter-bombers. Finally the door was slammed shut and First Armored was trapped. German and Italian tanks backed up by mobile artillery closed the escape route back to the British lines. It began almost as quickly as it started. In less than two days First Armored Division had been wiped out. An accompanying Infantry division also suffered heavily.

More than 150 British tanks were either destroyed or captured. Over 8,000 Commonwealth soldiers were killed, wounded or captured. Once again the Allies were on the wrong side of the intelligence exchange, as the Axis had been forewarned of the attack. Crippling of a whole armored division was a difficult pill to swallow on top of other recent failures. Obviously the reduced Axis forces were still capable of stopping an attack of this size with their mobile forces.

##

With confidence in their overwhelming strength, the Gibraltar convoy proceeded east with few incidents. There were some submarine and motor torpedo boat attacks, but damage was light. At the appointed time dozens of Spitfire fighters were launched from British carrier *Argus* and the American carrier, *Wasp*. With their job finished, these two carriers and their escort headed back toward Gibraltar as the supply convoy continued on toward Malta.

More losses came from Axis aircraft, but convoy AA and fighter support kept losses manageable. Neither were they panic stricken by the thought of an Italian battleship headed their way, which they had already been warned about. *Nelson's* nine 16-in guns added to *Malaya's* eight 15-in were more than a match for an Italian battleship's nine 15-in guns. This convoy was going to make it.

Italian ships seeking to control a daylight battle lost precious time getting into position, their lack of efficiency by not engaging in naval exercises definitely showed. Just prior to opening fire, the British naval commander was surprised to learn of a second Italian fleet composed of an additional two battleships with escorts heading in their direction.

The British Commanding Admiral did not panic; they handled their ships well and roughly handled the Italians. Battleships from both sides scored hits on each other, but it was the Italians that were driven back.

Littorio received two hits, one serious and several near misses; she retreated and with her went the rest of the Italian fleet. *Littorio* had managed to hit the *Nelson* twice, but one of her shells had failed to explode. Both British Battleships had ignored the two older Italian Battleships. They did not fear the old 12-in guns of these ships with their limited range and sent only a few destroyers to handle this latest distraction. They had ample time to deal with this second threat.

However, the British were unaware that when these older battleships had been modernized their guns had been altered. These alterations increased both their shell weight and range. Their firing at extreme ranges shocked the commander of *Nelson* although his ship really had little to fear from these altered guns either.

The older battleship *Malaya* did have something to fear from these Italians guns. Here again the British were lucky, the Italian modifications to the older 12-in guns had been obtained somewhat at the expense of accuracy.

During the quick exchange of gunfire, *Malaya* was only hit by two Italian shells. However, one penetrated to her lower decks before exploding causing fires and many casualties. This shell also caused damage to the bottom of the hull of the old ship which at first no one suspected since the explosion occurred deep within the ship.

Almost as quick as it started, this second battleship exchange was over. The two older Italian Battleships escaped without damage from their slower counterparts whose concern was protection of the convoy and speeding *Littorio* on her way. The convoy continued on as if nothing had happened, despite being damaged both British battleships kept station. They had taken everything the Axis had to dish out and it looked as if the relief of Malta was now a certainty.

Out of the Night

Admiral Lutizo's bridge staff was intently starring at the German made radar screen of *Vittorio Venneto*. These Italians were still unsure about depending upon this device, but then the British convoy was due to reach them in daylight hours, still they were in a very exposed position.

Being able to keep tabs on vessels around them did make them feel more comfortable and their German radar had passed every test. *Vittorio Venneto* and her escorts formed a sort of patrol line as they hoped to block the way to Malta for a Commonwealth western bound convoy from Alexandria.

##

Radar on the fast British minelayer, which was the size of a cruiser, making for Malta picked up the Italian patrol line first. They slowed and turned away to the north from the suspect contact at high speed. No sooner had they done this than another contact appeared.

"Is the whole bloody Italian navy out tonight? We will have to try and pass between them," voiced the minelayer's Captain.

###

"Are we sure it is not one of ours", questioned Admiral Lutizo?

"Absolutely, Admiral and from the looks of it this ship is making better than 35 knots, look at this radical course alteration. We must act quickly."

"I still will not open fire until I confirm its identity." Admiral Lutizo responded. "Order a torpedo boat closer, we will both turn on our searchlights and identify this vessel. Intercept course, all ahead full, sound general quarters and prepare to fire on the unknown vessel."

Seeing both vessels alter course toward him, the Captain of the minelayer turned supply vessel decided to make a run for it. Not only did this action attract attention of *Vittorio Venneto*, but also the rest of the Italian fleet. Lutizo's fleet also contained a cruiser that was as fast as this minelayer; Lutizo ordered this cruiser to block the escape of the suspect ship. Seeing the searchlights and hearing the guns of the *Vittorio Venneto* brought many ships to the scene of the action.

Held in powerful searchlights before she could get away, the minelayer's fate was sealed. She did send an open dispatch before the sinking vessel struck her colors. The dispatch contained the following information: location, "being attacked by many vessels including at least one battleship, severe damage, sinking fast, abandoning ship."

This message was studied carefully and viewed with dismay by the westward bound convoy. How could this happen at night, something was greatly amiss. Were these powerful vessels headed for them at this very moment?

With losses the convoy had already endured, it was possible they could be completely wiped out by this latest threat. With their complete destruction, what would the overall naval defenses guarding the Middle East have to fall back on? Reinforcements would take time. The convoy reversed course, but this would not save them from another day of brutal air attacks.

##

The Italian Navy had lost a battle and perhaps much more. Enough British merchant ships had been saved to assure Malta's continued survival. Two Italian Battleships had been damaged, one the pride of the fleet, without so much as slowing the convoy down. Many Spitfire fighters had been successfully delivered to Malta in plenty of time to make Malta harbor safe for the merchant vessels headed her way. The bad news went on and on, including apparent waste of important fuel reserves for no real purpose. Any plans for conquering Malta may have to be delayed - so much for the great victory to recover Italian naval prestige. All this effort and lives wasted and the British again in control.

##

Back in the eastern Mediterranean, Admiral Lutizo had waited patiently even after given definitive news the western bound convoy had turned around and was headed back to Alexandria. He did not trust the clever British. He needn't have worried, by the time the convoy made it safely past North African airfields they were down to their last AA ammunition. Over 25 percent of the vessels that left Alexandria had been sunk; most of the rest had damage of one sort or another. To a man, the Navy felt the RAF had let them down. Admiral Vian had never found himself in this position before. To make matters worse as they neared Alexandria the weather began to deteriorate.

Italian high command was reluctant to send the results of the battle that had occurred in the western Mediterranean to Admiral Lutizo. They were right, a fiery individual, he had some choice words for the handling of the main fleet.

"Four battleships and most of the fleet and they could not close the deal – Mother of our Lord this is disgraceful. How can any Italian sailor hold his head up again? Plot me a direct course to Malta, destroyers in the van - cruisers behind us. Set speed to 18 knots, maximum submarine sweep. Let's see if we can get some more use out of this radar", as he rested his left hand on a table and looked over the shoulder of the bridge radar technician.

"Sir, have we been ordered to intercept the other convoy?"

"No, we have been ordered home, there is a severe weather forecast alert and a faint heart if you ask me, but we are going to make a slight detour. Pull our recent mining charts for Malta. There may still be time to save the situation."

Second Fliegerkorps reacted swiftly to knowledge new Spitfires had made it to Malta. It was now up to them alone to destroy the merchant ships, which would soon be arriving at Malta; before they had a chance do that they must first destroy these Spitfires. All remaining planes of JG 53 were ordered into the air, followed by bombers. Nothing must be held back. Every last fighter on that island needed to be destroyed and quickly.

By the time the weather began to deteriorate, they had almost accomplished their goal.

"What a break this lucky convoy has had. With this weather they can sit safely in Malta's protected harbors and unload their cargos while we are grounded." A despondent Luftwaffe bomber pilot stated.

As the weather began to get worse, Lutizo's ships increased speed. Then in a move that could result in his court marshal, Admiral Lutizo sent his cruisers and destroyers racing for the nearest safe Italian protected harbor and continued alone in *Vittorio Venneto*. Lutizo knew the Mediterranean and knew his huge battleship had nothing to fear from predicted gale force winds headed their way.

The eastern bound British convoy had done the same; they sent their faster escort vessels ahead to Malta. It looked like they were just going to make it to Malta's protected harbor and their minesweepers would also make sure Malta's minefields were safely cleared.

###

There was not even time for proper identification; Lutizo knew these ships had to be the British convoy. They went in with all guns blazing hardly able to see in the worsening weather, but their radar held up. In 18 minutes it was all over, one main gun salvo for each merchant ship was all it took. Every radar blip was accounted for despite worsening weather. What ships that were not destroyed outright, Mother Nature would take care of. The lucky convoy's luck had just run out. There would be no survivors from the merchant vessels.

"Helmsman, take us home, economical cruising speed. Gentlemen - now that is how the British would handle the situation. Remember, the rest of you were just following the crazy Admiral's orders."

In spite of the terrible weather, Admiral Lutizo slept more soundly than he had in quite some time. In his dreams, he could not yet see the faces of British sailors he had just killed but faces of Italian sailors that haunted him were strangely dim.

Supreme Italian Naval Headquarters – Discussion among Senior Staff Officers

"Regardless of the consequences of Lutizo's actions, direct disobedience of orders can not go unpunished."

"Agreed, what was Lutizo thinking? Taking our last undamaged modern Battleship unescorted to Malta in Gale Force winds."

"Yes, a brave man, but one that I would never trust with one of our major warships again", as the conversation rotated around the meeting table

"We must be careful in how we deal with the good Admiral, he has Mussolini's ear."

"Believe it or not, Admiral Raeder has requested we provide a small naval contingency in addition to certain air force units for their siege of Sevastopol; perhaps we have just found the right man to command such a force. Doesn't Mussolini want us to put our best foot forward on any aid we send Germans in Russia? Would you gentlemen not agree?"

"If Lutizo is going to waste our last oil, let him go to Russia to secure more for Italy. Is it not an important mission?"

"Agreed, a perfect fit, (this statement drew nods from all but one of the meeting's participates) I am sure our good Admiral will enjoy as always being under German command."

"Gentlemen, I am afraid our controversial Admiral will never sit in the command chair of a battleship again. The order confirming his transfer will be written tonight", as the presiding senior Admiral closed the emergency meeting.

##

Lutizo was not the only causality of the battle fought against the British convoy bound for Malta from Gibraltar. Two battleships damaged and out of action and a third placed in harms way by an imprudent Admiral. The entire effort was deemed another national embarrassment and a waste of precious fuel. The Italian Navy criticized the Italian Air Force and the Air force criticized the Navy.

Their overall effort convinced many that if a slow convoy could not be stopped, neither could a British response to a direct attack on Malta. Above all the Air Force component of Sardinia defenses must be substantially increased. The vaunted torpedo arm of the Air Force was especially faulted; there was ample blame to go around.

No detailed accounts of the battle were permitted in the newspapers, but a victory was claimed. There was a frenzied effort to repair damage to the two battleships, the invasion of Malta could not occur until this happened. Efforts were also redoubled to hasten commissioning of the newest Battleship, *Roma*.

Aftermath of the battle was so bad; Italians actually approved major changes. All agreed that cooperation between the Navy and Air Force needed the most work. Capital ships needed to operate under a protective air umbrella; however, that umbrella needed to be greatly expanded so convoys could be attacked at a greater distance from Sardinia.

Stationing more torpedo planes and bombers on Sardinia with the needed range was not a problem, but solving the issue of long range fighters was going to be very difficult, if not impossible. The Italian navy really needed carriers, but they currently had none. Again, these problems must be resolved before the invasion of Malta. They would find some help in of all places France in an overlooked French fighter.

Italian naval command failed to realize the significance of losses the British had experienced during the combined convoy attempt. By comparison, the British losses in the east had been minor.

The torpedoed old aircraft carrier *Eagle* sank before it made it back to Gibraltar. Even the crew of *Nelson* was gravely concerned as the ship made its way back to Gibraltar in rough weather with an unexploded Italian 15" shell still buried deep within the vessel's hull.

##

As an integral part of this "do or die" Malta relief convoy the old British Battleship *Malaya* faithfully fulfilled her duty. When attacked by

Italian Battleship *Littorio*; *Malaya* together with Battleship *Nelson* damaged and drove off the more powerful ship.

Unfortunately, two older Italian Battleships used this diversion to strike *Malaya*. As a result *Malaya* was hit by two shells from their recently modified 12.6 inch guns, one of which penetrated to her lower decks before exploding and blowing a hole in *Malaya's* bottom.

On their return trip to Gibraltar flooding as a result of this hit gradually increased beyond the capability of *Malaya's* pumps to handle. Nevertheless, with less than 150 miles to go it looked like she just might make it; but then they were overtaken by a developing Mediterranean storm. This storm produced darkened skies, wind and high seas that began to break over the ship's deck.

Continued flooding from battle damage to the battleship *Malaya's* hull combined with the storm caused her to founder 100 miles from Gibraltar harbor. Loss of life was very high; many rescued seamen from the *Malaya* and *Eagle* were washed overboard in rough seas. The only fortunate circumstance for the British was that they were able to successfully hide the losses of both major warships for some time.

CHAPTER 24

Skip-Bombing in Russia

The railway system in western Russia was slowly beginning to function again after the severe winter weather and this brought much needed supplies and replacements into the Crimea. However, rail transportation in Russia still left much to be desired and Russian roads were worse.

Even with the winter ice problem, a much better source of supply would have been the Black Sea. On the other hand, threat of Russian submarines, surface ships and even planes made this sea route very dangerous. Aiding hard-pressed Luftwaffe forces already in the Crimea, new D model Stukas began to concentrate more and more on efforts against the Russian Navy.

In the past, there had never seemed to be enough time to properly train Italian Stuka pilots. Now under watchful eyes of their Luftwaffe counter-parts their skills began to improve. One Italian pilot, Giuseppe Cenni, did not require much instruction. Indeed, it was Giuseppe who was soon teaching German pilots.

Recently Giuseppe scored one very notable success on a medium sized merchant vessel that was trying to enter Sevastopol bay by night. This achievement was duly noted and Giuseppe technique began to gain some notoriety among German and Romanian pilots. Other aircraft, including twin-engine bombers, soon tried Giuseppe technique. This greatly enhanced effectiveness of the few Axis aircraft devoted to stopping flow of supplies into Sevastopol.

To date, the few German bombers carrying torpedoes had not been effective. German bomber pilots had not been properly trained in this type of warfare. Even when German torpedoes successful hit a target, they did not always detonate. This gave rise to even greater frustration with the lack of results from German bombers whose mission it was to cut off Sevastopol's supply line.

Subsequent experimentation on bomb types led to trial use of Giuseppe's "skip bombing" with modified depth charges in a similar role. This allowed larger bomb loads used at closer ranges, without fear of damage to aircraft dropping the weapon. Although there was a shortage of depth changes, patrol planes need carry only one type of ordinance equally effective against ships and submarines.

With critical need for more effective anti-naval aviation in the Crimea, a Group of Italian torpedo bombers was added to the Italian contingent. These Italian torpedo planes were well tried three engine Savoia bombers.

These Savoia bombers had been responsible for many successes in the Mediterranean and unlike their German counterparts Italian torpedoes worked well. They were also more rugged and carried better defensive armament than their German counterparts. Additionally, the hand picked Group sent to the Crimea contained some of Italy's better pilots. They would turn in a very respectful performance.

Mussolini was not to be outdone by aid Germans had sent to the Mediterranean. He hungered for any chance to increase Italian territory; therefore, even more Italian assistance would be forthcoming. Mussolini began to make quite a show in Italian papers of Italians helping their "struggling" partner in Russia, despite the fact that the Mediterranean was flush with German military equipment.

Hitler had previously been lukewarm about Italian divisions in Russia. However, with crippling winter manpower and equipment losses, he could ill refuse any offered assistance. He was even pressuring other Axis partner countries like Romania and Hungary to also send more divisions.

With more effective anti-shipping efforts in place, interference with German supplies crossing the Black Sea began to decline. Implications of this were not lost on Grand Admiral Raeder, Hitler and even Hadler. Even a small increase in supplies to Russia would be of immense benefit.

On many levels and for many reasons total ground transport capability in Russia was an utter disaster. There was even a desire that the Black Sea route be opened straight to the Mediterranean. However, Russian and British submarines were still a concern. To completely eliminate this threat, the whole Russian Black Sea coast must be conquered and then British submarine patrols halted.

A sortie of Sevastopol's garrison troops currently under siege could not be ruled out. Hence, not all German infantry investing Sevastopol could be freed up to hold the Western Crimean line. Also, von Manstein eventually wanted to put 22nd Infantry Division into Reserve and give this unit time to rebuild in preparation for its part in an invasion of Malta.

Von Manstein was patiently awaiting arrival of promised 22nd Panzer Division to provide extra resources to call upon. He had also requested additional Romanian divisions. In fact, he left no stone unturned trying to obtain additional resources. He needed and could make use of any troops, artillery, tanks, and planes as the Russians were making an all out effort to rid the Crimea of Axis troops.

A similar situation existed along the entire Russian front, as Stalin continued to mount offenses. Every tank, plane, gun and soldier was indispensable so resources shifted from Europe or Africa might mean the difference between defeat or victory in Russia.

Great interest was shown in examining defenses used by the Russians in the part of Sevastopol that was in German hands. Patterns, designs and weapons of the Russian defense were studied to reveal weaknesses. This allowed development of detailed plans of attack to include weapon selection and tactics, especially for those fortifications that were under direct observation. Fortifications already under Axis control were used for training, when time permitted. Examination of the huge fortress, Maxim Gorki I, was especially revealing.

This difficult fort had finally been captured in late February. A certain Italian Admiral on an observation tour of Odessa and Sevastopol showed especially strong interest and requested permission to study reuse of the fort's massive guns in firing on the remaining garrison. These 12-in guns could be trained on naval targets as well as some of the other defenses within Sevastopol.

Russians had not been able to completely destroy these guns before Germans had captured the fortress which contained them. Even if only one of the four large guns could be made to work, it would greatly aid the siege. Their 12-in caliber was common and a supply of ammunition would not be a problem.

February 14, 1942 – Sevastopol Valentine's Day Gift

Sergeant Wagner could not believe his eyes; out of nowhere a battleship and other naval vessels were entering Severnaia Bay. He called up artillery support to fire on the Bay. This was part of a fresh Russian effort to fanatically defend Sevastopol. Warships brought supplies in right under the noses of the Germans. These ships soon became the Luftwaffe's prime targets.

Thanks in part to Italian efforts, unarmed supply ships had already given up trying to run this gauntlet, so now Russians were using warships to deliver troops and supplies. Destruction of Sevastopol dock facilities made this unloading difficult and meant a great deal more time would have to be spent under guns and bombs of Axis Forces.

A call went out to focus artillery fire on these warships, if not to destroy them, to at least damage supplies they had brought. In response, these Russian Warships began to pound the German held positions, together with Sevastopol Garrison artillery. After it was over, of three Russian Warships that had entered Severnaia Bay, only the cruiser and battleship were leaving. The third warship, a destroyer had been sunk.

Strangely, this battleship had fired only for a short time. Siege forces were not aware that this battleship's main guns had been worn out during previous support visits. Running low on ammunition, the cruiser, together with the battleship left after unloading their replacement troops and only part of the supplies they had brought.

Both ships had taken numerous artillery hits and near misses from the Luftwaffe's planes. However, both ships were able to leave under almost full power. A real opportunity had been lost to destroy these two capital ships. Losses among unloaded replacement troops and those that had come to assist in unloading were substantial. German losses were also significant and von Manstein decided a better response was needed the next time these two uninvited guests showed up.

##

Giuseppe was frustrated by his lack of success which was no better than the performance of the other Italian pilots during the recent excursion of Soviet warships into Severnia Bay (Sevastopol's harbor inlet). However, German pilots had achieved even less during their disorganized response.

The immediate result of shelling by warships and the after effects of off loaded supplies and reinforcements was another very tough Fort Stalin battle. German troops held on by their fingernails. Generally, narrow Severnia Bay, covered by extensive Soviet AA fire was not the best place for Cenni to use his skip bombing techniques.

Besides, they had no suitable bombs for sinking a ship of that size. For some time, Giuseppe had heard tales of the famous German Stuka pilot, Rudel. Rudel had bombed and sank a battleship and a cruiser last year in the battle for Leningrad. Knowledge of exacting details of Rudel's exploits and techniques were almost required credentials for any real "Stuka pilot", because sinking a large Capital ship was a secret dream of every bomber pilot.

Exploits of Italian "MAS" human torpedoes and their sinking of two British battleships in Alexandria harbor, by now common knowledge, was a source of great pride to all Italians. Loss of British warships, especially three battleships, had changed naval balance in the Eastern Mediterranean. Italian aircrews wondered among themselves, could they duplicate these great Italian achievements here in the Black sea?

Giuseppe invited himself to the Luftwaffe planning meeting to devise a fitting reception for the next time Soviet heavy warships showed up. Special armor piercing bombs had been ordered from Germany and then actually arrived fairly quickly. Giuseppe made sure he was allocated one and that it could be quickly fitted to his bird at a moments notice.

Chapter 25

A Life for a Life

February 20, 1942 – Return Engagement

This time escorting an entire convoy, the Russian battleship returned to deliver reinforcements, supplies and to kill Germans. Catching this slower convoy early, Giuseppe did what he did best and put a bomb into the side of a large merchant vessel. This merchant vessel immediately began to take on water and lose speed. After Giuseppe returned to the airbase, his ground crew struggled to quickly load the special armored piercing German bomb.

By the time he returned to Severnia bay, German Stukas were already queuing up to take turns high above the battleship and her charges. As Cenni struggled to gain height a powerful explosion suddenly threw his plane violently to the right. His rear gunner, a wonderful and trusting comrade, was killed outright by this explosion.

His Stuka's controls were sluggish and his plane began to lose altitude. Quickly he jettisoned the Stuka's heavy bomb, but the plane was still diving. He was headed straight for the mountains at the southeastern corner of Sevastopol. More Soviet flak began to find his range, his engine was hit, but his Stuka continued to fly. He was able to clear the mountains, but he was headed out to sea and still losing altitude.

He regained a small amount of control and was able to turn the plane back toward land. Making a quick assessment, the cockpit glass had suffered such severe damage that it could not be opened. He realized too late that he was actually still making good speed.

In fact, the plane would soon be over Soviet controlled Crimea. Giuseppe had heard enough stories about the fate of Stuka pilots captured by Soviets that he must act quickly lest he not survive this adventure. Cutting his engine off, his Stuka now began to lose altitude very quickly, but his airspeed was still too high. He nearly lost consciousness when the plane impacted on the frozen ground.

Giuseppe's luck was still not holding out as the wrecked plane caught fire upon impact. He began to wonder if perhaps it wouldn't have been better crashing on the Soviet side of the main battle line, at least maybe death would have been quicker.

Suddenly, many soldiers, Italian soldiers, surrounded his plane. At first they struggled to remove the cockpit cover, but they too couldn't get it open. They then began to frantically shovel snow on the plane. Would the plane explode before they put the fire out? Thankfully, they were able to extinguish the flames and pry out Giuseppe and the body of his rear gunner.

"Well if it isn't my old Tobruk friend."

Giuseppe turned to his right to see who was addressing him. He put the voice and face together instantly in spite of heavy winter garb.

"Gian, I did not know your unit had been moved to the Crimea. You and your men saved me from a fiery death, so now we are even. How did you get here."

"Giuseppe, my dear friend, I am now officially with Littorio division, but really I have spent most of my time collecting and repairing Soviet equipment in an attempt to stun the British in Africa. By the way I have even managed to collect a few aircraft weapons that may interest you. I am very sorry about your comrade, but come take a look at my tank, while we try and find a way to get you and your gunner back to your unit."

###

"OK Gian, I give up, what is so unique about your tank, it does seem to look a little different. Yes, you added a muzzle break."

"We have exchanged our Italian 47-mm gun mounting for a modified Russian tank 45-mm gun mounting."

"So Gian what does this do for you?"

"Giuseppe, this Russian gun is longer and provides more velocity and hitting power than our Breda 47-mm after my conversion."

"Gian, what is the bottom line here?"

"I got the idea to modify the Russian gun when we tried to convert some British 2- pounders to fire our 47-mm ammunition. The Breda conversion would not work on this Russian gun either, but a conversion to the Czech 47-mm works just fine after some struggles. This gun's performance is quite good, especially using German ammunition. Giuseppe, there are hundreds of these Russian guns lying around.

I am telling everyone that will listen what an opportunity this is. I had to make a lot of modifications, but finally worked out all the "bugs." My dream is to someday give the British a nasty surprise, but I wouldn't mind trying it on these Russians either. But hop on the tank and let me take you to see one of our prizes." …..

"Wow, what a tank." Cenni was certainly impressed, especially when the giant tank was viewed beside its Italian counter part.

"If this doesn't shock the British, then nothing will Gian."

"Agreed, it was really a German generals' idea, but the British will never know. See our Italian markings. Come with me, I will show you another Russian item the Germans don't care much about that may be of more interest to you. We are collecting a lot of weapons from various battlefields." …

"This is an unusual looking plane Gian."

"Truly, according to the Germans, very crudely made and it is powered by a diesel engine, doubly useless to the Germans. However, look at the under-wing rockets."

"Yes, these could be useful, but analogous to your interests I am more interested in these wing mounted guns. These are 20 mm cannon; our Air Force is desperate for a decent fighter gun. I have been on the receiving end of these Russian 20mm cannon, like you Gian, I am warming to the idea that certain Russian guns have a lot of potential.

Germans will not furnish us many of their 20mm cannons for our fighters because of their own internal needs, but you know our country has a history of copying weapons. For the time being I would like to strip these two guns and take them back with me, I will also take back a couple of the rockets. I wonder if this 20 mm cartridge is similar to the ammunition used in some of our flak guns? I can see how digging through this captured material could be very rewarding. Can your teams locate any more ammunition?"

"Giuseppe, there is a lot of resentment in our Army about the number and quality of weapons our government provides. I will see that both get back to Africa when the rest of the Russian equipment gets shipped, you get the word to your fighter buddies in Africa to make the necessary connections.

I am still going to try and find a use for these rockets; they have a hollow charge anti-armor warhead and should not be left on the battlefield to simply rust. Let's grab some of the Russian 20-mm rounds and compare them to our own. You can take both with you to see if anything can be done. Now, back to camp, I think we might be able to rustle up some wine to warm you up and maybe a proper Italian meal in the process. What say you?"

###

"I very much appreciate the hospitality, Gian, but especially saving my life. So what are you doing in Russia, why did you leave your unit in Africa."

"Well Giuseppe, apparently I made an impression on the Germans and so here I am, speaking passable German has its disadvantages. I did not complain too much, except for scrounging Russian equipment I would rather be grinding British under my tank treads. Besides there are a couple of girls in Africa I left hanging, a cute colonist and a Luftwaffe Nurse."

"Well, no Italian colonists here for sure, but we do have a Luftwaffe hospital near us and I have seen some German nurses there. So Gian, you don't care too much for our beloved British Tommies?"

"You don't want to get me started. My only brother lies somewhere at the bottom of the Mediterranean, just one of the Italian victims of several one sided British Naval victories. The honor of our brave sailors, soldiers and indeed the whole nation has been effortlessly destroyed by one British victory after another. Italian cities are bombed, thousands of our soldiers sitting in POW camps, not to mention our captured territory they had taken.

I agreed to come to this God forsaken place to find and then bring back Russian tanks like I showed you. I believe, with just a few of these tanks, we can make life unpleasant for British Tommies. Tell me; won't you be glad to get back sinking their ships? By the way Giuseppe, I never asked, do you have any brothers fighting in the war?"

"I tell you Gian flat out I don't like the fact we are in this War. I fear our fellow countrymen don't realize what will happen to us if we lose. Raiding Arabs may just be one of our problems, but your colonist girl friend and her family will certainly not fare too well. The British may portray us as incompetent, but they portray our ally as evil. With what little I have seen and heard since coming to this brutal land, they may be right. Germans seem nice and polite in Africa; here it is a fight to the death. If Germany does not exterminate Soviets, then Soviets will exterminate them.

I fly with a new urgency, just as Germans do. When I get back, I will try and sink that battleship again. Some of our naval comrades in small boats and submarines are in the process of trying to stop the Russian fleet. It's a little one sided wouldn't you agree, a few small boats against a battleship, cruisers and destroyers. By the way, to answer your question before I started my tirade I have no brothers or sisters."

This was not true; Giuseppe could not bear thinking about his half brother and sister. After he had tracked them down, they had written each other a letter only once in over twenty years. He had their photo together with his nephews in his drawer at home. After exchanging pictures, they never wrote back.

They had not asked about their father, their grandparents or even tried to visit their graves. His father had left a good impression on all who had known him. Eventually dying from wounds he had received during the Great War, he had been buried a hero. Life had been hard for Giuseppe and his mother without him.

What Giuseppe would never understand was this totally callous attitude toward their father. They seemed and looked perfectly normal. Was it the result of poison spread by his father's first wife, lack of character on their part or a combination there of? Regardless of the reason, on many levels, he felt their conduct morally objectionable. Even brutal incidents he had witnessed on the battlefield had made more sense to him than their behavior.

##

For days afterward, Gian thought about what Giuseppe had said. He had after all grown accustomed to his new command and what Giuseppe had said made sense. He had to admit, despite his hatred for all things British; he knew that they would be a more generous conqueror than these brutal Communists.

Living in a world controlled by Germans was really not all that appealing, but living in a world controlled by Communists was inconceivable. In this regard Italy had brought some good to Russia. For wherever Italy's soldiers had gone they had encouraged the reemergence of religion; maybe after all this was their destiny.

A Battleship's Fate

The Russian battleship *Parizhskayaya Kommuna* withstood all attacks and even though some artillery hits were registered on the superstructure, the battleship was still completely functional. She had rendered excellent service in the supply role and also in past gun support to the Sevastopol defenders. This great ship had been a major player in defending the Black Sea region in World War I and was well on her way in accomplishing even greater feats in the Great Patriot War.

Responsible for causing the Axis pain in many facets for the struggle for Sevastopol, once again she was headed out of Sevastopol back to her homeport. That's where Italian torpedo planes caught her. *Parizhskayaya Kommuna* had not completely reached open water when she took a torpedo hit. This torpedo caused her to lose speed and take on water. The Captain of *Parizhskayaya Kommuna* knew his ship was doomed if he continued the return trip home in their current condition. Instead he decided to return to the relative safety and superior dock facilities of Sevastopol harbor.

All was going well, despite the torpedo hit, for *Parizhskayaya Kommuna* as she reentered the port channel. The captain felt he could easily reach his normal shallow berth. If flooding could not be controlled, the worst that would happen is she would settle to the bottom. If that happened, *Parizhskayaya Kommuna*'s main deck would still be above water. Repairs would take sometime, but the ship would be saved.

In the meantime, the battleship would render some fire support to the besieged fortress. Then the worst possible scenario happened. Just as *Parizhskayaya Kommuna* cleared the harbor entrance she struck a mine. To avoid completely blocking the harbor channel entrance, immediate action had to be taken. Turning as quickly as the now almost unresponsive vessel would allow she cleared the main entrance and settled to the bottom by her bows.

After sustaining two major hits, the Captain was still somewhat pleased with himself that he had saved the old ship and kept the harbor entrance open. Then in horror he realized what had happened. Resting in her current position *Parizhskayaya Kommuna's* guns were in almost complete defilade to the fortress perimeter. So, in this position, the battleship's guns were practically useless. Inspection revealed the combination hits had rendered the Battleship's superstructure unstable.

Any attempts to fire the main guns in her current condition would cause worse flooding and cracking to occur from external damage to her hull. Cold Black Sea water had compounded damage to the World War I era battleship. An important part of the Soviet fleet that controlled the Black Sea was now unusable. Thankfully, the ships pumps and watertight compartments were keeping further internal damage to a minimum. Still, before it was all over the Captain and most of his crew would find themselves with a rifle in their hands.

However, *Parizhskayaya Kommuna's* contribution to the defense of Sevastopol was not at an end. Her ammunition and much of her fuel was off loaded and several of her smaller guns were stripped for use in general defense. Much thought was devoted on how to repair or move her.

After removing nearly everything of value, salvage work began on the ship's internal equipment. The idea was to repair as many watertight compartments as possible, refloat the ship and then move her into dry dock where the rest of the damage could be repaired. It was time consuming work, the water was cold and time was running out. So far any attempts to reposition the wreck threatened to produce additional hull damage.

Prior to inflicting major damage on *Parizhskayaya Kommuna*, Italian Savoia bombers had enjoyed a successful reputation in the Mediterranean. Now, they had provided a very meaningful contribution to the intense struggle for Sevastopol and control of the Black Sea. This assistance was not lost on Germans who began to pay a little more attention to potential power of the aerial torpedo and mastery of this potent weapon Italians had demonstrated. First the British, then Japanese and now Italians had demonstrated to the world that the balance of sea power could be shifted when this weapon was used effectively.

PART VIII

WORKING BEHIND THE SCENES

CHAPTER 26

Desperate Men – Special Weapons

All winter long desperate Germans held on by their fingernails. There were a few notable large battles, but hundreds of smaller desperate struggles were more the norm as the strength of both sides ebbed lower and lower.

Russians were also conducting some sieges of their own. In the north, two pockets of German resistance were completely surrounded. One large pocket was at Demyansk and a smaller one at Kholm. These surrounded pockets did not serve a great purpose except to expose men to the elements and death, but Hitler refused to give them permission to retreat. To illustrate deplorable conditions of these pockets 3500 men at Kholm had not a single anti-tank gun of any type. Their only defense against tanks was snow walls and bundles of hand grenades wired together.

Fortunately, special weapons were finally flown into the pockets to give them some chance against hordes of Soviets. Among these weapons were small squeeze bore anti-tank guns. These had been released from stocks intended for Africa at Guderian's request. Also a new faster firing machine gun (MG-42) made its appearance. With these new machine guns German Infantry now had a real defense against mass charges of Soviet troops.

Several German soldiers owed their lives to these special weapons and brave air crews that flew in the face of massive Soviet resistance to bring them to the defenders of Kholm and Demyansk. All survivors would never forget the experience, but from a practical point of view, many valuable transport planes and crews were lost in these efforts.

Back to Ground Zero – The Folly of Trying to Talk Sense to Hitler

Heinz traveled again to Germany in early 1942 to personally present his updated plans for prosecution of war in the Mediterranean Theater and to stress weapons programs he was pushing. He felt confident that nearly very detail had been worked out. Some historic paratrooper problems would be handled with innovative solutions.

It was projected that only a few new paratrooper automatic rifles would be available for the invasion of Malta since they were just now coming off factory assembly lines. As an alternative, paratroopers were to be given a larger percentage of machineguns. There were also special gilder transports and numerous specialized armored vehicles in the works, many being constructed in France.

However, it would not be an easy sell; Hitler had stated that the time for surprise paratrooper attacks had passed. Fuel was short and confidence in the Italian Navy's ability to go head to head with the British Navy was not high. Germany was faced with an uphill struggle for the Russian summer campaign and resources for additional operations would need to be kept to a minimum.

General Student, head of Germany's Paratrooper Arm, traveled with Guderian to meet with Hitler. Student opened their presentation with the specific status of the units detailed for the invasion. Both Guderian and Student acknowledged there were still significant risks.

They were still short of paratroopers and German transport planes were tied up in Hitler's relief operations. Due to heavy losses in Russia, only two battle thinned regiments of trained German paras plus a Battalion of Engineers had been raised.

Italians contributed an additional division, but this division was really about the size of a German Regiment. This shortfall was to be covered by 22nd Air Landing division plus a new Italian air landing Division. Hitler listened to all the plans and proposals, but he seemed more interested in discussing the details of specific items of equipment.

"Field Marshal Guderian is it not true that you have been able to solve most of your supply issues for the reduced German and Italian forces now present in North Africa? Is it also not true that our Luftwaffe now controls skies and seas over and around Tobruk and Crete? Also, I am told that we can not possibly meet these Italian fuel requirements for the proposed operation."

"Yes mein Fuhrer, Italians have done all they can to economize on fuel. However, we must have the entire Italian Battle Fleet available with fuel to maneuver if we are to succeed. Italian Battleships will need to complete destruction of Malta's anti-aircraft defenses to minimize losses to our paratroopers and transport planes.

There are contingency requirements that can simply not be left unfulfilled in case of a major British counter attack. However, in absence of a major naval battle, some stocks will remain for future use. Also, with elimination of Malta, we should be able to substantially reduce overall future 1942 fuel demands."

"I will consider your proposals General Guderian, but as I said I will first meet with Kesselring and Raeder in two weeks to discuss our overall strategy before I will give my final approval. Continue to make your invasion preparations, however, first things first.

If I do not get the oil of the Caucasus, then I must terminate this War. You are to be commended on your conduct against the British. Due to the stable situation in the Mediterranean, Italians have agreed to provide quite a number of divisions for our summer offensive in Russia. Nevertheless, your desert forces will be reinforced in sufficient strength to allow you to conduct a diversionary attack to tie down the British and protect our southern flank. This diversionary attack should be your primary focus and in any event must successfully take place before the attack on Malta begins."

"Mein Fuhrer, we cannot expect the Allies to allow us to remain in North Africa indefinitely. They grow stronger every day with American planes and tanks; soon it may prove impossible to remove them from the Mediterranean or stop them from doing the same to us. We know from last year how quickly Malta can regain strength. It simply must be taken.

All these expected resources have been carefully coordinated with planned events in Russia. As you know, we have done much to minimize our demands so that German soldiers in Russia do not suffer because of us. Look at the men and equipment that are now in Russian that were supposed to have gone to Africa and in some cases even transferred directly from the Mediterranean to Russia."

"English divisions grow fat off of American aid—just like the Russians. Our U-boats need to put a stop to that"

"Unless we at least take Malta soon, I am not sure we can hold the Mediterranean long term, mein Fuhrer, regardless of the strength of our ground forces. Even if we hold the eastern Mediterranean, holding Malta and Gibraltar gives the British the flexibility to attack anywhere in the western Mediterranean.

In the mean time, we will require special ground reinforcements for a limited attack on the British, but it will be conducted as you wish in conjunction with our attack on Malta. What is needed is your assistance in procuring more Russian tanks and other specialized weapons."

"We will eventually send you the rocket units you have requested or should I say traded your artillery for? Your siege artillery will remain in Africa and will even be increased as you requested. Great plans are in the works and sometime in the future we may be able to provide you with some new incredible heavy German tanks that are being designed. These new tanks are far superior to anything the British and even Russians have.

Regardless, your plans should assure that none of the current territory we hold is lost. I would think you would agree that Italians can ill afford any more embarrassing defeats. They are still very pleased with our conquest of Tobruk. As I mentioned, they are making a substantial manpower and material commitment to our up coming Russian summer offensive, up to and possibly including two of their armored divisions," Hitler replied.

"All the more reason, mein Fuhrer, to let us continue to fortify Italians with Russian tanks."

"Very well, you have my permission to accelerate the Italian recovery efforts in Russia. However, your Italians are showing up all over the place and I hear that they are interfering with certain necessary occupation state operations. Himmler has expressed concern. So warn these Italians to restrict their activities to gathering Soviet war materials and strictly observe off-limit areas."

Heinz spent more than 45 minutes going over various technical and armament issues with Hitler. Some arguments he won, some he did not. Heinz, Student and the other service attendees then left Hitler. Heinz did not know if he had been able to get through to Hitler or not, but he felt compelled to make an effort. If things did not change, he foresaw more disasters.

In his own mind he began to question Hitler's concern over the involvement of so many Italians in Russia. This simply did not make sense. What could be more important than having the Italians help in recovering valuable war material? What exactly were Himmler's thugs up to that was as important as winning the war?

As far as he was concerned whatever Himmler's thugs were engaged in could not be as important as saving German lives. Could these isolated incidents comprise some more sinister master plan that Hitler obviously has knowledge of? Guderian simply determined to conveniently forget this part of the conversation with Hitler. All current Italian efforts would continue with a warning to avoid built up areas, if possible.

Chapter 27

Lost Engine Found

While he was in Berlin, Guderian intended to make several stops. One was to his friend Eduard Milch who was the Luftwaffe Chief of Staff. Heinz made an appointment and dropped by the well appointed office one afternoon.

"Well my old friend, how are things going, how is the family?"

"My family is well and yours? However, dawn to dusk and more I have a desk and phone overflowing with war problems Heinz, they plague us all."

"My family, too are fine, but you are right, war problems are what is on our minds these days. Tell me Eduard, what do you think of our new Armaments Minister, the Fuhrer's architect?"

"His appointment won't affect the Luftwaffe much. We have Goring to defend our interests, for what it's worth. However, I understand he plans to economize on tungsten and some other rare metals and raw materials in short supply. I am told he intends to limit its use to machine tools. This could have a big effect on production of certain classes of weapon systems for the Army, Heinz but I suppose you already knew this."

"Yes, there could be disastrous results for tank and anti-tank guns at this worst of all times. Perhaps I will visit him, Eduard. I need to try and accelerate some tank and assault gun conversions, anyway. Maybe I will have to add him to my "list" of favorite people to try and talk sense to. By the way, speaking of weapons production there is a matter I would like to discuss with you."

"Why, Heinz is there something I can do for our soldiers on the ground?"

"Yes, you see I have had to get involved in Luftwaffe business to survive in the Mediterranean. Given my past vested interest in tank engines I have made some rather shocking observations concerning new Italian fighter aircraft. With Kesselring's assistance, we are trying to change the Italian aircraft production priorities to focus on production of transport aircraft for invasion of Malta. To increase production of transport aircraft we have talked Italians into halting most of their older obsolete fighter production.

They will instead build only new fighters based mostly on using either German or their production copy of German engines. Their older fighters are completely at the mercy of the British and American planes in Africa. They are too slow and are too weakly armed. It has been decided to try and make use of these out of date fighters in ground support and anti-ship roles. Eduard, there is even some thought of sending more of them to Russia where they seem to have enjoyed some level of success."

"Heinz, now you really do have my interest. We are desperately short transport aircraft and experienced pilots. If you convinced Italians to do this, it could turn out to be a great benefit to our overall war effort. Even now, as you know, a few of their transport aircraft are providing very valuable service on the eastern front. So about these new fighters, Italians fashion themselves quite good aircraft designers, as I recall?"

"Yes, when married to our German engines the results have brought us success against the British planes. I hate to think what would have happened if we had not had the influx of these new planes in the latter stages of our struggle for Tobruk. I was so grateful that I went specifically to tour Italian aviation factories, Eduard."

"With performance surpassing our Messerschmitts with the same engine, I understand. Actually, I have never cared much for Willie Messerschmitt or his planes and lately it is getting much worse. It is coming to light that his new twin engine fighter, Messerschmitt 210, is a total failure, a national disgrace. Orders were placed ahead of time; there are literally hundreds of airframes in various stages of fabrication. I fear many of our countrymen will die on the ground and in the air because of this failure. It is so bad; we will have to restart production of Messerschmitt 110 fighters, which are terribly out of date.

Time is something none of us have with Hitler demanding that Russia be finished off this summer. Along with our other setbacks and current demands the Luftwaffe is almost as hard pressed as our Army. We are back to focusing on maximizing single engine fighter production. However, both Messerschmitt 109 and even the excellent new Focke-Wulf 190 fighters have their limitations. Our older successful designs are all becoming obsolete and their future does not look bright. Heinz, many of our new designs are just not going to work out."

"By the way Eduard, I don't want to add to your burdens, but I told Kesselring that we need some of your new Focke-Wulf 190 fighters in Africa. Also, I had occasion to aid in location of a new DB 605 engine that the Italian firm of Reggiane had ordered. At their request, I had a high priority search instigated to locate this engine in December of 1941.

In fact, I found the whole logistical system from Germany to Italy was in shambles when I arrived in Africa and in much need of better management. This engine was located on a remote railroad siding in northern Italy. A little later this engine was installed in one of Reggiane's newly designed airframes."

"Well Heinz that does explain some of our problems trying to satisfy Rommel (making a slight facial grimace) but to address your other issue a Focke-Wulf tropical version is not available yet. I will look into it."

"Also Eduard, I would like to show you some Luftwaffe witnessed test results. Italians are quite excited, but despite their best efforts production of this plane will be very slow. I though it was best to come to you and not try and pass something on to Goring directly, but I really think Italians have something here that could have significant impact."

"Of course", Eduard replied as he reached across the desk to take the folder from Heinz, opening the small booklet and flipping to the second page.

"If these results are typical, this aircraft could have a bright future. I would have imagined it faster than the Messerschmitt 109, but to achieve this high a ceiling is quite an unexpected surprise. This could be the high altitude interceptor we desperately need, if we can address production concerns. I can tell you it is a real pleasure to see a new aircraft exceed expectations for a change."

"Yes Eduard, it is possible this aircraft could be as powerfully armed as our Focke-Wulf with the new wing design and look at the projected range given the on board fuel capacity. That is the reason I took special note of the Reggiane firm, it seems all their aircraft have been designed for longer range. Although, I understand there may be some design problems with the wing fuel tanks. As you can see, this range not only exceeds our current single engine fighters, but also your Messerschmitt 110s.

If Reggiane could extend the range even further, this plane could provide extended fighter coverage over most of the Mediterranean. Between you and me, I am still greatly concerned about the British going after French North Africa. If fighter protection could be provided, we might be able to talk Italians into more Mediterranean adventures with their surface fleet, provided we can get the fuel. Add to this the fact that the French would never tolerate Italian troops on their soil and you can see the position we could find ourselves in."

"Well, I see your reasoning Heinz. The failed Messerschmitt 210 was supposed to be the truly long range destroyer fighter we have always needed, a jack of all trades. However, this Italian plane can actually fly without killing the pilot and might be brought up to full production quickly, with a little help. Heinz, I will see Reggiane gets some more DB 605 engines, advanced propellers, 20mm cannon and more Luftwaffe assistance to continue testing. Who knows, maybe we can fix this wing of theirs - add more fuel or strengthen it to carry more weight?

I will personally visit Reggiane and the other Italian manufacturers. Perhaps we can improve their manufacturing efficiency; I know they claim to be short raw materials. Besides, Goring is already chiding me for asking for such a large increase in fighter production. I think he does not realize what we are going to be faced with."

"I can tell you we will put them to good use against the British and American planes. I am concerned that the British will be reinforced with such large numbers of planes, that we will not have sufficient airfields or planes to challenge them. Coupled with our overall fuel situation, the future does not look bright. Every tank, plane and ship must be worth the fuel it consumes.

I really hate to ask, but since the Messerschmitt 210 is not flying why not let the Italians have a few more 601 engines and some of the 20-mm cannon at least until the bugs are worked out? Of course Eduard, Hitler will have to approve. He seems to monitor war production carefully."

"Heinz, I will assign some staff officers and do what I can. Also your request for some Focke-Wulf 190 fighters shouldn't be too hard to fulfill a little later this year. I foresee a time when we will not be able to pull the fighter units out of combat quickly enough to convert over to all the new planes coming out of our factories."

"Eduard, I appreciate your help in this regard. I have critical issues regarding the direction of Army armament production priorities which I must focus on. Convincing those in power to adopt these ideas is the primary reason for my trip."

"Actually, it is I that should thank you; some of your proposals may substantially benefit the Luftwaffe. Good luck with Speer, I count him as a friend. I believe you will at least find him intelligent. I know you do not quietly suffer the stupid."

"Eduard, on another subject, just between you and me, any idea what Himmler's thugs are up to in Russia? I have been hearing rumors and Hitler seemed determined to keep it quiet."

"Not sure I really want to know, I have always found it best to stay as far away from Himmler as I can. Heinz, you know I have some Jewish blood in my family. Besides, the SS does not really bother with the Luftwaffe, thankfully. As long as I continue to provide a useful function, they may keep me around. As you are now learning, being a Field Marshall still carries some weight, even with Hitler.

I can only tell you on top of everything else I am told we are facing a severe food shortfall; I would not want to be a member of any group out of favor with our leadership at a time like this. I am sure Hitler will do everything he can to make sure no German citizen that the party has a need for will starve. I leave the logical conclusion of that statement to your imagination."

##

Heniz was determined to see this new armaments minister, if Speer would agree to it. Many things were in a state of flux and no doubt Hitler would provide his own directions, which could produce the same disastrous consequences as his interferences with the Army.

There was no doubt that Speer had Hitler's confidence, but he would probably also do exactly what Hitler told him too. The last thing needed in the Ministry of Armaments at this terrible time was another "boot licking cutthroat Nazi." The meeting with Speer tomorrow could be as fruitless or as frustrating as recent encounters with Hitler these days, but he had to give it a try.

Chapter 28

Some Help for the Infantry

The next day Heinz made his way to Speer's office. To his surprise, Speer's secretary ushered Heinz into see him as soon as he arrived. He did not even have time to sit down.

"Field Marshall Heinz, your reputation precedes you. It is indeed an honor. You are not only a legend on the battlefield, but from what I am just finding out in the armaments world at well. What may I do for you?"

"Herr Minister Speer, first congratulations on your appointment. I asked for this personal meeting so we could discuss the path forward for our field armaments.

"That is indeed a broad topic, but I must tell you I feel we must work very hard to achieve increases in arms production that the Fuhrer requires. Previous methods and organization must be changed if we are to meet these new ambitious targets. I assume there may be some specific items that concerned you?"

"Minister, then let me get right to the point. I have heard rumors that our stocks of certain metals and materials may limit the production of certain weapons."

"That is correct Field Marshall. Unfortunately, as a country and economy now on a full war footing we face shortages in a number of areas. Decisions have already been forced on us. I would imagine you are concerned about the future production of tanks. However, I can assure you we will try and significantly increase tank production based upon projections as the Fuhrer has directed.

Not only will production of current models be increasing, but also many resources are at work designing newer improved models. I must admit it is hard to determine the really important issues and where we should focus, but I assume that is why you have come to see me. I am told you had a lot to do with the design of our current generation of tanks and our newest anti-tank gun. Am I right?"

"Herr Minister, you are very perceptive, if I may be frank. I am seeking your help for urgent matters. I have with me a document which outlines areas for immediate improvement where I feel we will experience our greatest short falls in 1942.

This does not address the new generation of equipment currently under development, but only pressing needs for a Russian summer offensive and our intended attack on Malta. I would like to summarize the reasons why I have made these recommendations. I have just reviewed them in a broad context with the Fuhrer: but material shortages may impact these plans."

"Of course, I value your opinion and vast experience Herr Field Marshal and so does the Fuhrer, I would assume? This may not be the last conversation we have on this subject since I know you intend to continue to try and influence material production in your conversations with the Fuhrer. Perhaps we can arrive at a compromise, I am not knowledgeable when it comes to armaments, but I have a pretty good idea what the Fuhrer will approve (meaning what he could talk Hitler into allowing)."

"Certainly Herr Minister, first as you know we face a serious crisis on the entire Eastern Front in facing superior Soviet tanks. Various crash programs are underway to restore the German soldier's confidence in his weapons. With few exceptions, heavier Russian tanks are responsible for death and defeat whenever they make their appearance in significant numbers. I requested a heavy anti-tank gun be developed when we first encountered these tanks."

From here on Heinz spent the next 20 minutes summarizing the history of tank and anti-tank development and manufacturing by Germany itself, her allies and her enemies.

"Well said Herr Field Marshall, I will study your recommendations. Your timing is good to implement some of these ideas. I am sympathetic and will do what I can for the existing and proposed tank upgrades. I will try to procure additional guns and upgrades for your tanks.

This may require a special contract, I know just the firm, if the Fuhrer will approve. However, I must tell you we face a severe shortage of tungsten and other strategic metals of which we can do nothing about. We require first use of these metals for our machine tools to make the weapons we are discussing.

As for your Russian tanks, particularly T-34s, our material concerns prevent us from duplicating the aluminum diesel engine. We are currently able to provide limited rebuilds and some parts, but that will be it. The Fuhrer is also very concerned about the tank killing ability of our guns. He desires the largest guns and strongest armor possible. As you probably are aware he has begun to concern himself greatly with new tank designs."

"Herr Minister, the capability of all our current and future tank guns is and can be quickly enhanced by the use of tungsten carbide ammunition. Is it possible to access alternative metals for these applications or to phase in your changes? Also, our current recovery efforts could be modified to recover some of the previously fired tungsten shells. We are already doing this in Africa and Russia and we can do still more.

Barring this, I am afraid we will need new tank and anti-tank guns that do not rely on tungsten. Squeeze bore guns are somewhat limited, especially when providing a high explosive shell of sufficient power. Since it is the Panzer III that must hold the line until production of the Panzer IV and the new models are able to supply our Panzer Divisions with sufficient tanks. At this time any type of tank on the Eastern front is put to use regardless of its effectiveness."

"Herr Field Marshall, I know, at present, most of the still limited production of the PAK 40 is going to the tank destroyer you requested on the Panzer II chassis. With much of the production of the long 50-mm gun currently going to the Panzer III; that leaves nothing for the infantry except older converted French 75s. So everything you are suggesting would be a step in the right direction."

"Herr Minister, I am appreciative of your support. However, I fear that without a more effective gun, the life of our Panzer III will be very short lived. The Panzer IV may become our main tank, by default, because it can handle the extra gun and ammunition weight. I fear that any gun larger than our new Panzer IV gun would increase vehicle size to a level that produces limitations. New designs present new problems; I would be especially concerned about the tank's engine and drive train.

While this problem may be solved by conversion to an assault gun, a tank without a turret is limited in what it can achieve in an offensive role. However, I must admit in the desert an assault gun armed with the available long Russian guns would enjoy significant technical advantages, turret or no turret. In the defensive mode we find ourselves in, this weapon could take advantage of the challenges of fighting in open desert. Are there no other technical alternatives that are being considered? These decisions will ultimately affect lives and maybe even the fate of our nation."

Speer and Heinz discussed many other issues in a frank and open manner, including the best way to defend infantry against enemy tanks. Guderian did not know that Speer would be as good as his word. He assimilated information very quickly and was Heinz's equal, in quickness of mind. Being careful not to reveal his source, he was able to accumulate information that confirmed what he had been told by Heinz.

He thus modified on his own certain programs that escaped Hilter's direct attention. He began to be concerned about what Heinz had said about Panzer III tanks and their immediate future. How could a more effective gun be mounted? What were the options? At any rate, there was a significant manufacturing commitment to long 50-mm guns, with no alternative, it would not be possible to stop manufacturer of tungsten based anti-tank ammunition. In fact, careful examination would show that tungsten based ammunition was still being produced for other obsolete anti-tank guns.

After Heinz left, Speer had others check his weapons production proposals covered in the folder he had left. Some had minor comments, but overall they agreed it was a well-conceived and comprehensive plan. Some changes were necessary to review with Hitler, but Speer was now well armed with data that confirmed what action needed to be taken. Speer also knew how to persuade Hitler to follow his recommendations and lots of data was one of the keys.

PART IX

SECRETS AND SETBACKS

CHAPTER 29

Alkett Saves the Day

Before Heinz left Germany to return to Africa, he received an urgent message to meet with Wilheim Bach at the main Alkett production facility. Heinz assumed there were difficulties and he hoped he had not presented plans that were unworkable under current conditions to Speer. After meeting Bach and being introduced to a couple of Alkett engineers and the main director, they moved to a secure conference room within the facility.

"Herr Field Marshall, I have been learning a great deal about guns and tank design since I told you our best defense in Africa was a mobile one. These gentlemen have been most helpful and the director even received a phone call from Speer after your meeting. Unless Hitler objects, your plans will be implemented and besides we still have some flexibility with regard to special designs for the invasion of Malta."

"So what is so urgent that I must journey here personally?"

"I believe we have come up with a new tank design that will meet with your approval and go a long way in solving our current problem with these heavy Russian and English tanks. We have tried to think of everything, but we know the real test will come from you. Therefore, allow us to review our proposal and design drawing for this new tank with you Herr Field Marshall."

"Of course, you can begin."

One of the Alkett engineers stood up and spoke while the director and the other engineers gave him their attention.

"This new tank must meet an almost impossible set of conflicting conditions and must do it immediately. Allow me to brag a minute Herr Field Marshall; I believe you have come to the right place. First, the best basic German tank design is also the most prolific, the Panzer III. If we use this vehicle as the basis for our design and plan for downward compatibility of improvements we solve many of the Army's design considerations.

Our principle concern is weight. Even with new wider tracks and improved torsion bars we are still limited. The Panzer III, as you know is capable of carrying more overall armor than the Panzer IV as has already been done in Africa. With face-hardening and a new technique called space armor, many believe we can render this tank frontal immune to Russian field guns. All this is planned and soon production can begin.

Now it all comes down to the gun. When the Fuhrer got so upset that his instructions had not been followed and that a short 50-mm gun had been placed into the Panzer III instead of the long 50-mm, it was our firm that designed the mounting in one month. However, production of the upgraded Panzer III is now limited by production of the long 50-mm gun itself.

As you know, your release of long 50-mm anti-tank guns that had been intended for Rommel has allowed increased production of these tanks. However, these guns have been removed from their anti-tank carriages and really taken away from the Infantry in desperate need of any kind of protection from the Russian tank onslaught. We are aware more than others of the desperate conditions on the eastern front and are trying every way we can to increase production.

We understand that the long 50-mm gun gives our troops a fighting chance whether mounted in a tank or on an anti-tank carriage. However, it is barely acceptable today and soon will probably be totally unacceptable. Did I mention the gun's HE capability? We are being told that even the 75-mm gun is currently lacking in destructive ability. Am I correct to this point?"

"I disagree with nothing stated so far, so what is your proposal?"

"You would agree Herr Field Marshall that most of our problems would be solved by mounting the new long 75-mm gun in the Panzer III? This cannot be done, as you are aware without a great deal of difficulty and is predicted to be a total failure. Even if all other technical issues could be resolved, we will not even be able to produce them fast enough to meet even the demands of Panzer IV tanks.

What else then? We have looked at all other options, including all current and planned future German guns. All require unwanted compromises and material shortfalls kill the rest. That's when we began taking a second look at your 65-mm Italian gun. Here is the preliminary design to mount it in the Panzer III, almost a perfect match."

"Yes we have been all through this; it was all I could do to convince the Italians to mount a few in their Semoventies or in their new proposed medium tank. Only a few prototypes can be made with their limited machinery and we are actually taking away from the production of another important gun that is very much in demand, argued Guderian."

At this point, the second Alkett engineer stood up and rolled out another set of drawings on the conference table.

"Herr Field Marshall we are in the process of acquiring some of the Italian machinery that was used during the Great War to manufacture the original 65 mm artillery piece and ammunition. We can use this equipment to manufacture our own 65 mm guns and ammunition to German standards. This 65 mm gun will use the same shell casing and block of our current 50 mm gun. Only the barrel will be different. If all goes well we will have the first guns ready in two weeks, with a successful tank mounting a week after that."

All looked to Heinz to see what he would say. He was looking intently at the proposed ammunition load and gun specifications for the new proposed tank.

"Well it just might work. It would be better if the barrel was longer, but this is a start and retrofitting could be done in the field. This may be one of the most important weapons programs Alkett has yet come up with. Uses of this gun potentially go far beyond even Panzer IIIs. Looks like I will need to swallow my pride and pay a return visit to Speer before I head back to Africa."

"No need", the Alkett director now spoke up.
"Speer says you owe him one, this is now his idea. It will simply be a part of his new armaments streamlining efforts. All that was needed was your approval for your new *Malta* tank and of course you must provide tanks to work on. We are already working on modifications to short 50-mm gun mounting. How soon can you get us a new Panzer III? Moreover, Speer sends word that he may be able to find an alternative for tungsten that may meet your needs."

CHAPTER 30

The God Haters

During his trip to Germany and France to check on certain manufacture and weapons facilities Wilhelm Bach made a detour to pay Heinz a visit at his home. Heinz and his wife warmly welcomed him at their door. Then the two of them retired to Heinz's study.

"Wilhelm it is good to see you, please plan on dining with us tonight. In addition to checking on your progress, I know I promised you a continuation of our conversation, but the time never seemed quite right. As you well know every minute is precious in trying to correct our technical deficiencies.

I believe many of our troops in Russia owe their lives to our combined efforts on their behalf. By minimizing our needs in Africa we allow more resources to be devoted to defeating the Soviets. Even when we appear to be holding our own in Russia the conflict disturbs me greatly. I know for a fact that there are horrors upon horrors taking place in Russia both in the front lines and behind them. I knew combat and hardship in the First World War, but this seems different, a kind of unworldly madness. Only my hardness as a soldier and knowledge of what I must do to try and save our country seals me against the evil I sense."

"Herr Field Marshall, thank you for the dinner invitation. I believe it is as you sense, I too have heard rumors. So much death and destruction with no end in sight consuming the whole world it seems. It is altogether different from our struggle in Africa between Christian nations."

"Yet Wilhelm we must be strong for the sake of our soldiers. My two sons are among them. How can I as a Prussian Field Marshall even think about not doing my duty? However, I can assure you and I will not engage in any cowardly action or any action that would wrongfully harm any of our troops, no matter who orders it.

I have spent my whole life trying to perfect a type of warfare that would quickly decide battles with less loss of life. So in light of all this, let me ask the obvious question left over from our last conversation, would you classify our current political leadership as *God Haters*."

"Naturally Herr Field Marshall, classically so, but then again I would classify a great many in our modern world as *God Haters*. Did you or I start this war, could we have prevented it?"

"That's how you see it Wilhelm?"

"Yes, Herr Field Marshall, there have always been *God Haters* present, but recent events have given them more power to spread their vile ideas. They have come up with what they consider logical alternatives to a created world. We too could spend many hours going over how these *God Haters* create their own truths in order to fulfill their selfish desires and control the lives of others. In time if we leave them in control they will rewrite history and retell the story of this war as far as their lies will take them. The truth may disappear in time.

They give themselves fancy names like *Socialist* or *Communists*. For heaven's sake Stalin and Hitler signed a pact together, are they so different? They both lay claim to the moral high ground, but would create a God for us that duplicates their flaws? The French Revolution started with such intentions; then developed into an epidemic that consumed Europe before it was destroyed. Is Hitler not doing the same thing and wouldn't Stalin if given the opportunity?"

"Interesting Wilhelm; so according to your theory this maelstrom will consume us?"

"Yes, I fear regardless of the outcome of this War, all of Europe is doomed, perhaps even western civilization as we know it, unless we can somehow prevent it. I believe we are all put here for a purpose with unique talents. Your talents, Heinz have been a foundation upon which perhaps some of the greatest military victories in history have been won.

Germany is once again a great nation, but what does the world see when they look to Germany, just someone to fear? Do we really want persecution of Jews and execution of Russian political officers without trial to be what we are remembered for?"

"So then Wilhelm; in your mind, who is worse Hitler or Stalin?"

"Stalin - of course. Never has there been such evil walking the face of the Earth and Lenin deserves the same place in Hell, God forgive me. Moreover, their God is the scientific subterfuge of Darwin. At the heart of it all is the softhearted Englishman that has caused untold misery. His theories were Communism's perfect creed to help spread their evil, bring to a halt perhaps the free and natural progression of Christian society in Europe. It was an almost perfect lie that also underpins Hitler's radical racial agenda.

The fate and future of Europe will be decided in Russia. And in the Mediterranean we may decide the fate of our ancient enemy, Islam or even a possible future Jewish state. Whose side will Germany be on? With the advent of Martin Luther I believe Germany brought the world a blessing. Now with Hitler and his race war we have brought an evil mentality of colonial discord to the whole continent."

"Well Wilhelm, I asked for this, any other conspiracies you need to share with me?"

"Heinz, I believe that is sufficient for one night. So when do we destroy these British, do we have an exact date for the invasion of Malta? Already the American influence is becoming greater and greater. Over the long term does anyone really think we can gain the upper hand over the industrial might of the British, the Russians and the Americans?

We must strike and destroy them, conquer Malta and then build an even greater defense. But this will simply guarantee that the initiative will pass to them. Sooner or later one of their Generals or Admirals will strike us where we least expect it. Do you deny this?"

"Wilhelm, you have an uncanny ability to predict a dismal, but probably correct outcome. We will strike first to produce a localized quick victory and gain better defensive positions. Then we must build sufficient reserves to counter their next move, but as you say the next moves will be on their terms. I must confess to you and you alone that I don't think my health will hold out to see this thing through."

"Then I will pray for us all, because I do not believe anyone else has the talents to keep pulling off these stunning victories necessary to keep the wolf away from our door. If we are defeated, God help us. No one came to Germany's aid after World War I and I believe it will be worse this time."

Wilhelm also had two other meetings before he caught a plane back to Africa. One of his meetings was with his nephew who was home on leave and occurred on a railroad platform with both men in uniform. For the second meeting he removed his uniform which was very recognizable with all his specific First and Second World War decorations. He even changed walking canes before exiting his back door to walk four blocks to a fairly remote small local hotel.

There he met two other officers, also in civilian garb. Wilhelm sat down at the table and ordered a beer. After exchanging a quite greeting, the taller of the two men spoke first.

"Well Wilhelm, what can you tell us about Hitler's newest Field Marshall? Where does he stand?"

"He has not turned me in yet which I suppose is a good sign. He believes the resistance is all talk and that no one has really put forth a viable plan for removing Hitler. He is of course right. Heinz was not pleased with Hitler's dismissal of officers following our setbacks in Russia. I believe he thinks he would have been included if he had not been sent to Africa.

There is more. He told me a high connected military officer informed him that there is a significant food shortfall especially in the occupied territories. He implied that Hitler and his cronies will undoubtedly use this as an excuse to rid themselves of their enemies. We may already be too late to save any of them. If it is true, then this is very depressing news. "

"Yes, depressing news all around. Despite eastern front losses, it looks like Hitler is still managing to come out on top in public opinion with all the blame falling on the officers he dismissed. Not sure Hadler has really been an asset to our enterprise with his on again – off again attitude toward Hitler", bespoke the taller man.

"Past successes worked in Hitler's favor, now it seems failures work in his favor as well. He will probably be successful in hiding these starvation deaths as well. Is there any chance of stopping this madness", chimed in the shorter of the two.

"I shall continue to work on Heinz and anyone else that will listen, but I do not expect much change in the status quo? Von Ravenstein, who is a good man, was transferred to Russia late last year. I am sure he will have his fill of Hitler before all of this is over. Perhaps another resistance voice in Russia. Let us all pray the fire does not consume everything. God speed to all." Wilheim finished his beer and rose to leave.

CHAPTER 31

Worn Down

Heinz had scarcely been back in the desert two weeks when his prediction came through. It was early evening; together with some of his staff they had journeyed to a remote location deep in the Saharan desert. There in a tent they had planned on spending the entire day reviewing enemy activity, training and logistical issues with selected commanders.

Mid morning a horrific sandstorm quickly developed nearly blowing the meeting tent away and causing everyone to scramble for whatever cover they could find. After spending an incredibly uncomfortable three hours, the meeting began again and never really got back on track. Completely exhausted, Heinz excused himself and with a heated discussion still going on sat down by himself on the other side of the tent.

Suddenly in a tent full of people the entire tent began spinning. Heinz, knowing he had a heart condition, feared the worse. Having lost his equilibrium, he had to be helped to stand and immediately sat back down again. He was taken to the closest field hospital. There, carefully monitored and medicated, he spent the most restful night of sheep he had in a long time. He was awakened a couple of times to check vial signs, but did not wake up on his own. Finally, a doctor woke him after he had slept a full 21 hours. He immediately had another episode of the room spinning and loss of equilibrium. He then slept an additional nine more hours.

This time he awoke on his own, but was a different man. Oddly enough, he was hungry and he ate rather well, he then asked if any real coffee was available. Some was provided, but this and the food did almost nothing to effect his energy level. He could do no work; concentration was impossible. After only two hours of being awake, he was totally and completely exhausted. Assistance had to be provided for even a trip to relieve himself, which took forever. Again, he slept, this time for 19 hours.

When he awoke this time, he did not even try to work. He was hungry among all things and more than anything he just wanted to return home and rest. His third period of lengthy sleep was interrupted by another room spinning episode. His staff and the local medical personnel were frantic. What was wrong? What could be done?

At last a senior physician was brought from Africa Korps headquarters that had been in Africa for over a year. This doctor examined Guderian and read over his medical records. Then, during Guderian's next waking period, he spoke to him.

"Herr General Field Marshall Guderian you are suffering from what we have chosen to call "Desert Colic." I believe that your condition has been brought about as a result of your total physical and mental exhaustion and our desert environment. In your invalid condition you can no longer serve. When viewed with your existing heart condition and general poor overall health, I am recommending you be returned to Germany and be placed in a hospital near your home town as soon as possible."

"Assuming I decide to follow your recommendations, how soon can I return to duty?"

"I do not know. We do not have enough data to determine when or if ever you can return to duty. I am struggling with the quacks in Berlin who will not even acknowledge the existence of a new or unrecognized illness, much less suggest suitable medication. I do not believe the condition is fatal by itself, but in your case I urge extreme caution.

The desert is hard on all of us, but most cases as severe as yours that I have examined have been restricted to older soldiers under extreme duress. I saw it completely debilitate one Sergeant Major. His commanding officer claimed that this man was the toughest most dedicated soldier he had served with. I believe rest helps, but no one has recovered well enough in Africa to return to full duty. As soon as I write up your diagnosis, I will recommend immediate evacuation."

"What you say is hard, but I have never felt so weak in my entire life. It is not right for a soldier to have such a condition and it occurs when our nation needs us the most. I would have rather been shot and then I would know where I stood."

"I will pray for you and our nation that you recover soon Herr Field Marshall."

Farewell to Africa

As his evacuation plane lifted into the night sky, Heinz caught his last look at Africa. He wondered if he would ever see this strange country again. He would try and stay on active duty, but he knew his health would never be the same again. Heinz had not told the doctor that he had difficulty remembering the names of anyone he had met since he had been stricken. Was this his flight to obscurity; how would he be able to function? It had always been an uphill battle to convince others of the correctness of his ideas. Now his credibility would always be in question.

Had the course of history been altered or had he merely helped to postpone another inevitable catastrophic defeat of his nation. Many things were still left undone, but there was nothing more he could do. He felt that he had let everyone down. Perhaps Wilheim was right, maybe Germany was not meant to be saved.

PART X

EPILOGUE

Heinz Guderian's Fate
and the Legacy of Operation Crusader

After recovering much of his health in the Fall of 1942, Heniz was anxious to commence a tour to see how his *panzertruppen* were faring with their enemies and the new weapons they were being given. The first segment of the tour would involve the important Eastern Front. Hitler was especially anxious to hear how the new Tiger tanks had performed during the battle for Leningrad. He had heard some reports, but he was anxious to get Heinz's take on their effectiveness. Heinz had convinced him to hold off on some of his incessant meddling in tank technology. However, some damage had already been done.

The southern front was next; Heinz knew that they were in the midst of a fearsome battle and that the whole front was receiving priority on everything from equipment and manpower reinforcement to replacements. This was where Hitler thought the final decisive battle of the eastern front was being fought. His favorite General, Paulus was in command of embattled Sixth Army trying to take the final ruins of Stalingrad.

Heinz had planned on only spending a couple of days in the south. Unfortunately, the conditions he encountered forced him to alter his plans and spend an extra day visiting different commanders and seeing the situation himself. Even this was not enough time to take in all the problems he came in contact with.

Heinz was appalled by the way logistical and combat operations were being conducted on a wide scale. He had lectured other commanders and everyone he had come in contact with about the importance of quickly repairing damaged tanks or returning them to Germany to be rebuilt. But here in Paulus' area of responsibility he found the worst offenders. After three days, he met privately with Paulus and some of his staff to discuss his preliminary findings.

"I must confess General Paulus that I am shocked by the condition of the repair and supply facilities for the mechanized units in Sixth Army's area of operations. I am also very concerned about the current disposition of these forces and their potential vulnerability. If the mobile forces are not put on a more sound footing, it could jeopardize this whole front. They should be withdrawn from the Stalingrad street fighting at once.

The closest parallel I can draw on is your <u>own</u> assessment of Rommel's continued assaults on Tobruk in 1941. There you clearly delineated in your reports the logistical problems posed with his African operations. Are you not concerned that you are repeating the mistakes he made in Africa with perhaps even worse consequences?"

"Herr Field Marshall, I am merely following my orders from the Fuhrer himself. According to him the Soviets are on their last leg. Hasn't he always been right before?"

"My dear fellow, it is you and your men that will suffer the consequences if disaster strikes. Winter is the Russian's time; make no mistake if I can see these flaws so can the Soviets. Never underestimate your enemy. Remember the battlefield axiom that it is almost impossible to recover from an initial incorrect deposition of your forces.

I must submit my report as I see it. I will do all I can to help, but it is up to you and your staff to quickly correct this situation. Your fuel situation alone should demand immediate emergency shipments or instant force redistribution."

Afterwards Paulus reflected on Heinz's words and ordered some changes. These actions by Sixth Army's commander resulted in some adjusts, but nothing substantial. However, many in Paulus' staff were shocked by Heinz's blunt criticisms. Heinz commanded tremendous respect throughout the Army. News of this confrontation spread throughout the ranks and many began taking matters into their own hands. Some of Paulus' division commanders began conducting mock exercises to test response and warning systems. The end result was a Sixth Army that was slightly more prepared for a Soviet counterattack.

On to Africa

Next, it was more of the same as Heniz took off for North Africa. Redistribution of forces due to the Allied invasion required an assessment and evaluation for possible equipment transfers. After the formalities, the first visit was to Wilheim.

"Well my esteemed friend, you, the Italians and the Africa Korps really dealt the British a blow. I know that it was your hard work and planning that tipped the scales. Moreover, no one can stop talking about the Italian performance. Italian paratroopers have even got Hitler's attention. Again they turned in a sterling performance. I believe even the Italian newspapers did not go on too much. Despite their earlier losses, the military is now popular in Italy again. That is, until this invasion of French African territory placed them in danger again."

"That is a change on our leader's part; I believe he has ignored us ever since Rommel was killed. Nevertheless, God be praised, because you had as much to do with a victory as anyone. You inspired us, trained us and provided the tools to make this fight. If the Italians would admit it they owe you too. The desert did not defeat you, you defeated the desert. It is certainly good to see you being yourself again."

"I can tell you how good it feels to be up and about again, even with the great weight of responsibilities that face us. Not sure how much help you will get now. There is the whole British Empire plus the Americans to fight in the west now. You must hold here while we try to organize something to the west before the Mediterranean comes crashing down around our ears.

As you know one of your German divisions has already left as well as much of your Luftwaffe support. The hard times we have faced may only be the beginning. I will try and help with what I can, but large quantities of weapons and men will not be possible at least not until early in 1943. Wilheim, do you have anything else up your sleeve that could give us an edge; you know we tend to think along similar lines?"

"Come take a ride with me in my Volkswagen, Herr Field Marshal. It is a short drive; let's do some inspecting."

##

"Heinz, you are familiar with most of the equipment changes and modifications that both our troops and the Italians worked so hard to complete. Of course the standout was the modifications to the British 25-pounder artillery pieces. I still don't think the British have picked up on this yet.

The bulk of these guns were some of the first weapons we sent west. So now we will have our work cut out for us to collect and modify what was left behind during the latest battle. You know about most of the other modifications, I am sure you must deal with them every day. I must brag that our armored cars played a significant role in our victory. Only German armored cars were sent west, in this regard we need some help. The British have introduced new models and improvements.

Now this is what I wanted to show you (as Wilhelm's Volkswagen slid to a stop). This is the latest American tank, by all accounts a very good design. Of special note to you is the very large turret ring, greater than any tank we have yet encountered, even in Russia.

Except for the gun and the speed, I believe this tank is superior to even the T-34. Their side armor is more vulnerable (as Wilhelm and Heinz began walking around the tank), like the American Grant tank. Still this is an outstanding tank and one that apparently can be easily mass produced.

So we have enough of these new tanks that the British call *Shermans* to be able to consider mounting a decent gun with a three man turret. I was thinking about the PAK 41 that worked so well in our armored cars. Also, the turret is big enough to perhaps fit a PAK 40 or modified Russian long 76.2. The work will be challenging, but I think our people can do it. What is your recommendation, Heinz?"

"The PAK 41 is probably a good choice. Except no more are being made due to the shortage of *Wolfram* and as you say those PAK 41s that are available should be installed in your larger German armored cars. Also, I do not believe there are even drawings showing how it might be mounted in a tank. I have another gun for you."

"Heinz, I thought you might have something up your sleeve. After all you are now Inspector General of all *Panzertroopen* are you not?

"Rank does occasionally have its privileges Wilhelm. This gun was manufactured to fit our new medium tank that has failed so far to make it to production. At least a couple of hundred of these guns with tank mountings that could not be made to work in a new style of turret are available. I can tell you the whole painful story later, you would not believe Berlin politics, in spite of the fact that there are lives on the line.

Actually, you have given me an idea that will get us out of a bind. The adaptation of this gun to the American tank will be given the highest priority. With the problems we are having in fielding a new medium tank it will be some time before they can make a real contribution on the battlefield. However, if we can quickly get these guns installed in your American tanks it will help develop our training and tactics. If I can supply the guns, can you get enough of these tanks running to form a battalion and make this effort worthwhile?"

"Heinz, it may be possible. Moreover, if we can get the machine work done, we may be able to mount the Sherman's turret on to the American Lee chassis if this is as important as you say. Many of the Shermans were knocked out by hits in the side armor by our smaller tank and anti-tank guns. The turrets may still be good in many of these vehicles. Unfortunately, once hit these tanks like the Lees have a tendency to catch on fire."

"Now Wilheim, what else have you discovered on the battlefield?"

"It is not just me, Heinz. Honestly, you inspired us all, even the Italians to examine all the possibilities in tactics and equipment. Many of the rank and file soldiers try to come up with more ways to better use what we have and what has fallen into our hands. When you fell ill, it actually strengthened everyone's resolve. Sometimes I get overwhelmed with all the suggestions that are made, but I try to examine as many as possible for feasibility.

"Wilhelm, no one understands more the importance of this work than you and I expect it to get harder not easier. Therefore, I have obtained permission for you to join my staff. You will remain here, but I want you taking some leave time back home in Germany after you pick your staff.

While you are in Germany you can make arrangements to gets things rolling. By the way this appointment comes with a promotion to Major General; this should impress everyone you have to deal with while making these changes happen, even the Italians. I have already cleared the promotion and the appointment, the paper work will follow."

"I hardly know what to say Heinz."

"Say yes, and get to work. Not that you really have a choice, Herr General."